YOU DON'T MISS A GOOD THING,

UNTIL IT'S GONE

KANIYA AND LUCKY'S STORY

1 | Page

WRITTEN BY: NIKKI NICOLE

Hi, how are you? I'm Nikki Nicole the Pen Goddess. Each time I complete a book I love to write acknowledgements. I love to give a reflection on how I felt about the book. I've been writing for two years now and this is my 15th book. When I first started writing I only had one story I wanted to tell and that was Baby I Play for Keeps. Two years later and I've penned a total of 15 books. I appreciate each one of you for taking this journey with me. I'm forever grateful for you believing in me and giving me your continuous support.

Book 15 is special to me because I'm closing something special. I wanted to give a little insight, about this book. One of the hardest things about writing this book is letting Kaniya go. I'm going to miss Kaniya so much. She gave me life with no parole. Every emotion I felt it. I made sure you're going to feel it too. I can't wait for you to see how much she's grown. I witnessed the growth as I go back in and read my work.

I dedicate this book to my Queens in the Trap. I swear y'all are the best. Y'all go so hard in the paint for me it's insane. Every day we lit. I appreciate y'all more than y'all will ever know. The Trap is going up on a Wednesday. I can't wait for y'all to read it.

It's time for my S/O **Samantha, Tatina, Asha, Shanden (PinkDiva), Padrica, Liza, Aingsley Trecie, Quack, Mauris, Shemekia, Toni, Amisha, Tamika, Valentina, Troy, Pat, Crystal C, Crystal L, Missy, Angela, Shelly, Latoya, Helene, Tiffany, Lamaka, Reneshia, Charmaine, Misty, Toy, Toi, Shelby, Chanta, Jessica, Snowie, Jessica, Blany, Neek, Sommer, Cathy, Karen, Bria, Kelis, Lisa, Tina, Talisha, London, Naquisha, Iris, Nicole, Koi, Haze, Drea, Rickena, Saderia, Chanae, Chenelle, Shanise, Nacresha, Jalisa, Tamika H, Kendra, Meechie, Avis, Lynette, Pamela, Antoinette, Crystal G, Crystal W, Wakesha, Destinee, Daerelle, Ivee, Kimberly, Kia, Yutanzia, Seanise, Chrishae, Demetria, Jennifer, Shatavia, LaTonya, Dimitra, Kellissa, Jawanda, Renea, Tomeika, Viola, Kelsha, Gigi, Dayna, Regina, Barbie, Erica, Shanequa, Dallas, Verona, Ming Lee, Stacey, Catherine**

If I named everybody I will be here all day. Put your name here_____ if I missed you. The list goes on. S/O to every member in my reading group, I love y'all to the moon and back. These ladies right here are a hot mess. I love them to death. They go so hard about these books it doesn't make any sense. Sometimes, I feel like I should run and hide.

If you're looking for us meet us in **Nikki Nicole's Readers Trap** on Facebook, we are live and indirect all day.

S/O to My Pen Bae's **Ash ley, Chyna L, Chiquita, T. Miles,** I love them to the moon and back head over to Amazon and grab a book by them also.

To my new readers I have five complete series, and a standalone available.

Our Love Is the Hoodest 1-2

Cuffed by a Trap God 1-3

Baby I Play for Keeps 1-3

For My Savage, I Will Ride or Die

He's My Savage, I'm His Ridah

Journee & Juelz 1-3

Giselle & Dro

Join my readers group **Nikki Nicole's Readers Trap** on **Facebook**

Follow me on Facebook Nikki Taylor

Follow me on Twitter @WatchNikkiwrite

Like my Facebook Page AuthoressNikkiNicole

Instagram @WatchNikkiwrite

GoodReads @authoressnikkinicole

Visit me on the web authoressnikkinicole.com

email me authoressnikkinicole@gmail.com

Here's a playlist I made for you

https://itunes.apple.com/us/playlist/you-dont-miss-a-good-thing-until-its-gone/pl.u-38oWXL4I1oGzaV

JOIN MY EMAIL CONTACT LIST FOR
EXCLUSIVE SNEAK PEAKS.

http://eepurl.com/czCbKL

Table of Contents

Chapter-1 14

Lucky 14

Chapter-2 25

Cynthia 25

Kaniya 30

Lucky 32

Chapter-3 41

Killian 41

Kaisha 44

Lucky 52

Cynthia 55

Chapter-4 58

Kaniya 58

Gabrielle 76

Chapter-5 79

Kaniya 79

Gabrielle 82

Kaniya 85

Lucky 90

Chapter-6... 94

Raven 94

Tariq... 98

Chapter-7... 100

Yirah 100

Lucky 104

Kaniya 109

Chapter-8... 118

Kaniya 118

Chapter-9... 127

Lucky 127

Kaniya 131

Lucky 133

Kaniya 137

Chapter-10... 144

Killany... 144

Raven 148

Chapter-11... 154

Kaniya... 154

Khalid... 160

Kaniya 167

Khalid... 180

Chapter-12.. 184

Kaniya 184

Chapter-13.. 192

Kaniya 192

Chapter-14.. 208

Lucky 208

Chapter-15.. 212

Cynthia.. 212

Kaniya 216

Kaisha 218

Chapter-16.. 224

Lucky 224

Chapter-17.. 236

Kaniya 236

Tariq... 240

Chapter-18.. 245

Kaniya 245

Khalid.. 250

    Chapter-19... 256

Lucky 256

Kaniya 258

Khali.. 265

Khalid.. 270

    Chapter-20... 274

Yirah 274

Kaniya 278

    Chapter-21... 284

Kaniya 284

    Chapter-22... 300

Lucky 300

Yirah 302

    Chapter-23... 305

Kaniya 305

Khalid.. 317

Kaniya 327

Khalid.. 331

    Chapter-24... 337

Lucky 337

Khalid.. 341

    Chapter-25.. 351

Khalid.. 351

Kaniya 353

    Epilogue 361

Kaniya.. 361

PROLOGUE
ONE YEAR
AGO

Chapter-1

Lucky

> *I see you winding and*
> *grinding up on that pole*
> *I know you see me looking at*
> *you at you and you already know*
> *I want to fuck you, you*
> *already know*
> *I want to fuck you, you*
> *already know*

The sounds of Akon blaring through my speakers. I'm sitting here chilling; my eyes are low as fuck. I got a lot of shit on my mind, and it's hard for me to focus on the beautiful sight in front of me. My wife is putting on a show for me. Ever since I got this stripper pole and stage put in our room, she's been dancing like she works at Onyx. It's like she gets a thrill sliding down the pole. I walked up on her and grabbed her ass cheeks. She looked over her shoulders and smiled at me.

"Aye Red, you got a man? What's it gone cost a nigga for one night of your time?" I asked.

"I'm married; my husband is a very Lucky man and I don't cheat." She sassed. She purred like a sex kitten.

"Oh, he is huh? I still want you, I'm going to take you from your husband."

"He's crazy?" She smiled. I carried her off the stage and laid her down on our bed and placed kisses all over her. I love my wife so much.

"You better let them niggas know you're married. I'm crazy ass nigga and I don't give a fuck, make me act ignorant if you want to Kaniya." I whispered in her ear. "I'm still a young fly nigga. I still got these hoes going wild."

"Lucky you better stop fuckin' playing with me. I'm telling you now. Make me kill a hoe over you. You think this shit is a game, stop playing with me. Line these hoes up, so I can shoot these hoes dead in your face." She argued. I always knew what to say to take her there.

"Calm down baby give me a kiss, ain't nobody weighing up to you but Jamia." I laughed. I would say life's good, but that's too much like right. It's always some extra shit brewing in the background. If it ain't directed it ain't respected. The only thing I want to do is make love to my wife and spoil my kids that's it. My wife was due to give birth to my son Jeremiah in a few months.

I have an issue that keeps stabbing me in my side. My wife told me a few months ago this guy her mom knew by the name of Kodak. He was from Atlanta, but he lives in Florida and he just got out the FEDS. He was claiming that he was my father. I looked at my wife like she was crazy. Who the fuck was this Kodak nigga claiming to be my father? My father was dead. Deuce is the only father that I ever had. He showed me the game and gave it to me. Where the fuck was this nigga when I was growing up? Why is he lying on my mother, claiming I'm his son?

My wife stated when my mom and her mom got into it; at the hospital her mom dropped the bomb, and my mom was shaking, and she didn't say shit else. This topic has come up more than once. To make a long story short. I guess my mother in law is dating him and they're supposed be coming here tomorrow and the nigga wanted to meet me. I don't know how I feel about that.

"What's wrong?" She asked. Kaniya stroked the side of my face and rubbed my back.

"Nothing." I wasn't ready to speak on this situation just yet.

"Oh, so we are keeping secrets now?" She sighed.

"Kill it Kaniya don't do that. I don't know how I feel about meeting this Kodak nigga tomorrow."

"Did you ask your mammy about it?" She asked. I swear I'm sick of the beef between her and my mother. I'm sick of it. I love my wife and I love my mother too.

"Watch your mouth before I put something in it." I argued.

"You can it's not an issue. I like tasting you. Anyway, call your mom and ask her. Since when have you been scared to get anything up off your chest?" She argued and stared me down.

This is one phone call that I didn't want to make, but my wife was pressuring me with her messy ass. She called my momma from her phone and placed it on speaker phone. My mom answered on the first ring.

"Ma, what you are doing?"

"Nothing Jamel, what's up? Where are my grand babies?" She asked.

"Who is this fucking nigga Kodak that's claiming he's my father? You got something that you want to tell me?" I asked. I was tired of beating around the bush.

"Jamel Williams, watch your fucking mouth! I'm not telling you shit over the phone, so your nosy ass wife can tell her mammy my fucking business. You know where I live, you are more than welcomed to come by." My mother argued. I wish my mother wouldn't have said that, she's only adding more fuel to the fire.

"Lucky you better get your mammy; because when my mother confronted her she didn't have shit to say. Now she got base in her voice. Let me call my mother so she can get at her." My wife argued.

"Kaniya watch your mouth, your mother doesn't put no fear in my heart. Kaisha knows about me. I spared you and her." My mother argued. I didn't want to call my mother in front of Kaniya for this reason alone.

"Ma and Kaniya chill out. I just asked you a question. I'll be over there, give me an hour."

"That's fine baby. Please make sure you leave your whore at home. Yirah is over here with my grandson Jamal and I don't have time." My mother laughed and hung up.

"Lucky, your momma got me so fucked up. I will beat her ass and Yirah's. What the fuck is she doing over there? I haven't killed a bitch in a long time, bring me out of retirement. I dare her to try me. They must have forgot how crazy shit gets.

I'm about to make an example out of somebody today for trying me." My wife argued she was putting her clothes on now ready for war. I swear she lives for this. She's waiting for somebody to say the wrong thing to her, so she can pop off.

"Kaniya calm down baby, you pregnant with my son. It's not even worth it. Obviously, she has something to hide, but you are coming with me. You ain't never been a whore. You are my wife and I love you with every fiber in me. I don't give a fuck about none of that shit she is spitting. Grab that Glock though so you can do Yirah if you want too.

I love my wife and I love my mother too. I hate that they're beefing, but shit y'all know my wife is crazy and she ain't backing down. I refused to continue to let my mother disrespect my wife. Kaniya suited all the way up, she threw on some black leggings, her black timberlands and a wife beater.

She grabbed her bulletproof vest and the chopper hanging up in the closet. I don't know why my momma thought it was cool to add fuel to the fire and say that Yirah was over here. My mom liked Yirah more than Kaniya, but I don't give a fuck.

"Kaniya, you don't need all of that stuff." I argued.

"Lucky, if a bitch thinks they can try me and live to laugh and tell about it, they got another thing fucking coming and your mammy ain't excluded." My wife laughed.

"Kaniya chill out. I don't give a fuck who you decide to body, but if you even think about killing my momma you can keep your ass at home and I'm dead serious. I know a few niggas I would like to body, but you begged a nigga not too. He's tried me one too many times but that ain't the issue."

"Whatever Lucky, you always taking up for her. She always disrespecting me and guess what, you don't say shit. She called me a whore did you clear that up? Nope. Guess what, that disrespect shit stops today. Fuck a gun, I can kill a bitch with my bare hands, these motherfuckin' hands is registered to kill a bitch. I'm setting your momma straight. I'll meet you over there because you might not like what the fuck I say and do." My wife explained.

"No, you ain't driving shit. Kaniya don't fucking play with me. We done came along way. We don't do slick shit. We move as one. Fix your face and bring your ass on, all of it." I don't care about her having an attitude. We ride together.

———

Kaniya and I made our way to my mother's house, the whole ride was quiet. No music no nothing. I was deep in my thoughts and she was too. My wife could tell that I was thinking too hard on something. She massaged my hand and started rubbing my legs. I looked at her and she licked her lips.

I knew what that meant and sure enough she reached over and unbuckled my belt and pulled down my shorts and went to work. She knew I loved slow head while I drove. She was sucking my dick real foolish and nigga was about to wreck.

"Gawd damn K, slow down a nigga about to wreck." She ignored me and started licking, sucking, and slurping hard on my shit and playing with my balls. I bust all down her throat. She grabbed a wipe and cleaned me off and got the mouth wash out of the arm rest and gargled her mouth clean.

"Nut does a body good."

"It does, doesn't it." My wife laughed. We finally pulled up to my mother's house. I opened the car door for her and we headed into my mother's house. I used my key and let myself in.

"Mother where you at?" I yelled as I walked through her house looking for her.

"Have a seat, I'll be there in a few." She yelled. I sat on the sofa and Kaniya sat in my lap. Yirah walked out in some little ass shorts and a crop top. She wanted me to see her ass too. I looked at my wife to avoid eye contact with her. She knew what she was doing.

"Lucky, baby, damn I missed you." My ex Yirah stated. She wasn't paying attention at all. She finally looked up and saw my wife.

"Yirah cut that bullshit, don't ever disrespect my wife." I could tell Kaniya was fuming hot she kept trying to get up. I was holding her down. If I let her loose it was a wrap.

"Lucky I told you to leave your whore at home because Yirah was here." My mother yelled.

"Mother watch your fucking mouth. I won't let you disrespect my wife at all. She has never been whore." I argued. I need her to stop saying that. Kaniya is the mother of my children regardless of how she may feel about her.

"Lucky why are you defending this whore?" My mother asked. She was looking at Kaniya instead of me.

"Baby no offense but your mother keeps using the whore word too fucking loosely. Cynthia understand me when I say this. I don't give two FUCKS how you may feel about me, but YOU ain't gone keep disrespecting ME. I may be a WHORE in your eyes, but the fact remains the same.

I got LUCKY all of him and can't ONE BITCH out here change that, not even the BITCH that birthed him. Not even the BITCH that's standing in this room right now eye fucking HIM while I'm here. Yes, BITCH I'm talking to you. When you're dead and gone and he's mourning your loss it's still gone be ME, that FUCKS and SUCKS him to ease his pain. Unlike you I'm real about any everything that I do. The fact that remains the same is Kodak his daddy or not? We didn't come over here to conversate?" My wife explained.

"Chill out Kaniya, don't upset my son." I argued.

"Lucky your wife is very disrespectful. I don't want her here at my house. I don't know what you see in this hoe." My mother argued.

"You tried it, Lucky see's in me what your two-baby daddies didn't see in you," My wife argued. I can already tell this conversation isn't about to go anywhere, with the two of them going back and forth.

Chapter-2

Cynthia

I used to like, no let me change that I use to love Kaniya. She was perfect for Lucky. Everything they have now, I wanted that for the two of them. All bets where off when I figured out that Kaisha was her mother. Kaisha ruined my fuckin' life. When Lucky started cheating on Kaniya I was happy as hell. I wanted Kaniya to feel how I felt when his father left me for her mother. I introduced Yirah to Lucky. We have the same hair stylist. I knew she would be perfect for him. Yes, Kodak was Lucky's father. Kodak's real name was Jamel. At least I gave him that much.

Fuck Kodak, it was supposed to be me and him forever. I had him no matter what. I hustled with him, I was his rider, and I took plenty of chances for him. Everything changed for us when he laid eyes on Kaisha. Kaisha wasn't even from the Westside. She started hanging out with Valerie, my brother Nick's baby momma. Valerie didn't like me. I knew she put Kaisha on him because Nick was cheating on her with one of my best friends. Until this day she still doesn't know April and Nick share a daughter.

She's a few months younger than Nikki. Kodak knew Kaisha was a bitch that he couldn't have because of Killian.

Kaisha was forbidden fruit, but nooo…that nigga just had to try his luck. Kaisha took the bait and that nigga said fuck me. I was keeping his work at my mother's house in case the police kicked in the apartments he hustled out of. It was Kaisha this and Kaisha that but as soon as Killian and she got married she cut that nigga off.

He tried to come back to me, but I was with Deuce and pregnant with his son. He knew I was pregnant, and I taunted him, telling him Lucky wasn't his, but I knew he was. I had to hit that nigga where it hurts, and it was his son. I'm the reason he did 20 years in the FEDS.

"Mother is he my father?" He asked. Lucky already knew the answer to his question. He just wanted me to confirm it.

"Yes, he is." I sighed.

"How could you?" He asked.

"I'm grown, and I don't have to explain shit if I don't want too. He ain't never did shit for you Lucky. He's been gone for twenty years, he ain't never reached out to you.

I see his mother and sister all the time, they ain't never asked about you. His folks don't give two fucks about you." I argued.

"Damn momma I still had the right to know."

"Not now Lucky, I will not explain this shit in front of her. I told you not to bring her." I argued. "I meant what the fuck I said. I'm not talking in front of her period."

"Mother this is my wife." He argued.

"I don't give a fuck who she is. Your wife or your whore, it doesn't matter to me. Your whore's mother is the reason you don't fucking know your daddy. I'm not speaking nice because I don't have shit nice to say." I argued. I was stating facts. Kaisha knew she had a man, but she wanted what was mine too. Kaniya's a whore too, she fell right off Kaisha's tree.

"Lucky I'm ready to leave right now. The only reason I haven't reached over and slapped the SHIT out of your MAMMY is because of you. A BITCH can't talk to me any kind of way without getting these motherfucking hands." His wife argued.

"You can leave WHORE, because you weren't invited to my house. You haven't been welcomed here in a long time. I don't know why in the fuck you thought today would be a good day to come here. As you can see my daughter in law Yirah, she's already here." I argued. Kaniya reached over Lucky and shoved me in my mouth. I stood to my feet in a fighting stance.

"Lucky you better get this bitch before I do." I argued. Lucky ushered Kaniya out of my house. It took everything in me not push him out the way to get at her ass. Yirah would never be disrespectful how Kaniya has been. Kaniya stopped in her tracks and yelled.

"He can catch all this body from this BITCH. I can't wait to get home and fuck him like a porn star and handle all his stress he has built up. It's always me remember that," she sassed. If she only knew, the only reason I haven't rained on her parade is because my son is standing here. She'll get hers though, I'll be here laughing thinking about how cocky she is.

"I hate her momma, so much." Yirah cried. She loves Lucky and he loves her too. She should've spoke up.

"I know baby, it'll be okay. Just be patient. I know Jamal is his. He looks just like him and Jamel. If I were you I would have another test done. I love my son to death, but he should've never allowed her to talk to me any kind of way. She's just like her mother was and still is a whore, but I refuse to allow my son to be happy with her."

"I've done that, and Jamal is his. Here's the paper work."

Kaniya

I can't wait to have Jeremiah. I swear I endure the most shit, when I'm pregnant. I swear to God she's going to feel me. As soon as I drop, I'm running down on her ass. I refuse to argue or go back and forth with anybody. Arguing only pisses me off, laying hands on a bitch is therapeutic for me. I'm not doing it, we can fight and get all the bullshit over and done with. Cynthia doesn't like me because of my mother. What the fuck does that have to do with me? It's childish as fuck if you ask me. My mother better handle this bitch before I do.

Yirah knew better than to open her mouth up. I caught her looking at Lucky a few times. He knew to hold me down. I beat her ass once and I would stomp her fuckin' teeth out. Lucky hopped in the car and pulled off like a maniac. I should've drove myself. I could feel him starring a whole in me. I refuse to look at him. I just want to go home and relax, that's it. I was relaxing at home until she started talking shit over the phone about me.

"Kaniya, I know you feel me looking at you." He said. Lucky turned down the music. He grabbed my hand and kissed it. I turned around to face him. He was angry, and I know it's because of me. His eyes were red, and a vein appeared on the side of his neck. She started with me first.

"I'm sorry Lucky, your mother doesn't like me. You don't ever have to worry about me, going to her house with you again. She called me out of my name numerous of times. She's very disrespectful and I couldn't take it anymore. She was reaching so hard." I explained.

"I know and I'm sorry for that. I want you to be the bigger person Kaniya. I love you and I don't give a fuck how she may feel about you. I love you Kaniya regardless" he stated. Why couldn't she accept I'm the one he loves?

"I love you too Lucky." I was the bigger person. I'm pregnant and I didn't beat her ass. The fuck he thought this was. On my unborn child, I'm gone beat his momma ass after I have Jeremiah. Cynthia has tried me for the last fuckin' time. I don't even want my mother to touch her, I want too. Lucky will be mad at me for a few days, but oh well. Cynthia ain't never had her ass beat before. I couldn't wait to be the one to do it.

Lucky

Yirah - Can we talk Lucky, please?

Yirah - I love you Lucky.

Momma - Lucky I don't feel good, my chest is hurting. I think I'm having a heart attack.

B etween Yirah and my mother I swear I'm going to end up losing it. My phone was on the night stand and Kaniya was asleep. Yirah has been blowing up my phone since I left my mother's house. By the time I made it home, she's called me at least twenty times and sent numerous text messages. I care about Yirah and I do love her, but I'm not in love with her. I love my wife, but she's making it real hard for me. Every time I go to my mother's house she's always there, throwing herself at me. I curve her every time. I'm not trying to take it there with her. I jumped out my bed instantly. I noticed Kaniya started stirring in her sleep, she must have felt me move.

"Lucky, what's wrong?" She asked.

"My mother called and said she's having chest pains. She thinks it maybe a heart attack. I'll have to go over there and see what's up. I'll be back in a few."

"Okay be careful and call me when you make it. I hope she's okay."

"I will, get some rest. I'll be back before you know it." I kissed Kaniya before I left out. I didn't feel like leaving home this time of morning, but it's my mother and I don't want to see anything happen to her.

—

It was a little before 2:00 a.m. before I made it to my mother's house. I keyed in and it was pitch dark. I walked upstairs to my mother's room. She was looking at TV. She glanced and looked up at me. I could see the tears in her eyes. I could tell she was sick and in pain. Kaniya took shit way too far. She was too old to be jumping on my momma. My momma was too old to be fuckin' with her.

"Lucky I'm glad you came. I thought you weren't coming. The ambulance came, and my blood pressure was through the roof. They said it was due to stress. I could've died, it's all Kaniya's fault. You chose her over me, how could you, I'm your mother for God sake," she cried.

"Shh, stop crying momma. I love you and I would never do that. I love you and I love my wife. I don't want my wife and my mother at each other's neck. How do you think I feel momma?"

"I know Lucky, but you deserve better than that. I feel a lot better since you're here. Can you stay here with me until the morning? It'll take some of the stress away," she asked.

"Yeah momma, I'll stay."

"Thank you." I kissed my mother on her forehead. My room was down the hall. I didn't cut the TV on. My mind was in a million places. The little bullshit my mother and Kaniya has going on, it's stressing me the fuck out. I kicked my shoes off and laid back on my bed. I sent Kaniya a text and told her my mom wanted me to stay the night. The beef between my mother and Kaniya has too end immediately. I heard my door open and I knew it wasn't my mother, it was Yirah. I could tell by her silhouette.

"Yirah, don't come in here. I'm not for it." I argued. She thought that shit was funny, but I was dead serious.

"Lucky I just want to talk for a few minutes, that's it." She explained. Yirah dropped her house coat on the floor.

"Put your house coat on Yirah. I'm not trying to take it there with you. If you wanted to talk, talk but put your clothes back on." I argued. Yirah refused to pick her house coat off the floor. She approached the bed and stood in between my legs trying to straddle me and unbuckle my pants. "Don't do that." Yirah grabbed my free hand and placed it on her pussy. She was wet too. She wanted me to finger fuck her, but I couldn't.

"Lucky, I'm in love with you. I can't shake you and I've been real patient. I've been going with your flow for as long as I can remember. I played the background with Kaniya and Melanie. You know I'm not a hoe. The whole time we fucked around I only fucked you. It bothers me why would you deny Jamal as your son to pacify her?

I had my own DNA test ran a few weeks ago and he's 99.999% yours. I wanted to talk to you about that before I hit your wife with these papers" she explained. I knew Yirah was up to some bullshit.

"What the fuck do you want from me Yirah? Kaniya was just here, why didn't you say shit? If he's mine, I'll take care of him." I argued. I knew Jamal was mine. I just didn't want Kaniya to know. It's hard as hell denying your own flesh and blood. I feel like shit, I swear to God I do. Jamal looks just like me, the older he gets.

"I want you Lucky. Jamal and I need you. I didn't create this baby by myself. We made him. He's our love child. You were fuckin' me raw when I begged you to strap up, but you didn't want too. I knew this would happen and it's not fair to him. He can't have his father because of his dad's wife. I always been good to you. Whatever you wanted me to do, I've done it. I'm tired of being quiet. I want her to know. I don't care about you losing whatever the fuck y'all have going on. My son is losing too, and I lost you to her as soon as you found out you fathered Jamia and Jamel. You were through with me and our son," she cried.

"Stop crying Yirah, you know I'll take care of you and my son. You already know that. Whenever you need something, don't I give it you? I need you to be patient with me. I'll tell Kaniya myself, just give me some time. Can you do that for me? I've hurt her enough and I'm not trying to hurt her any more than I already have. Jamal was made during our relationship and I don't want to hurt you anymore than I already have. I'll get you and Jamal a spot, is that cool? $4,000.00 a month, is that cool for you and him?" I asked. I couldn't tell Kaniya that Jamal was mine. I should've done it a long time ago, but I knew she would never take me back if he was.

"It's a start Lucky, but why can't you just tell her? She already knew it was a possibility he may have been yours any ways. Those were your words not mine. Just tell her. Can you just be honest for once? It's not even about me, but Jamal. I'm so tired of coming second hand to her. When she left you and ran off with Tariq, it was me. I was the one who was there for you. After she killed your father and ran off, I was the one holding you down at his funeral. I'm good enough to run to when she's not around, but whenever she comes back in the picture, it's fuck me? It's not fair to me. It's cool though I'll find me a man to treat me and my son like somebody" she cried. Yirah raised up off me while her phone started ringing in her housecoat. She answered it on speakerphone.

"Hello" she cried. Yirah was doing the most. Who the fuck was calling her phone this time of night?

"Damn baby what's wrong? You want me to come through, so I can hold you?" he asked. Yirah got me fucked up, she knew better than to entertain another nigga in my fuckin' presence. I stood up from the bed and grabbed her. She tried to run and reach for the door, but I stopped her. I slammed the door shut and I could tell she was nervous. She should be. I could feel her heart beat.

"Yeah, I'll come through. I have a babysitter" she cooed.

"Stop crying. You can bring him too. I got both of you. I keep telling you that Yirah, give me a chance."

"I know, I'll see you in a few." She stated and smiled. I watched Yirah like a hawk, she wiped her tears quickly. Yirah was feeling this nigga, whoever he was. I wrapped my hands around her neck forcing her to look at me.

"Let me go Lucky," she cried. Yirah knew she fucked up. That nigga said way too much.

"I'm asking the fucking questions not you. Who the fuck was that? Don't have my son around any niggas period. Do you fuckin' understand me? Are you giving my pussy away Yirah? Have you fucked that nigga? Why does he want to fuckin' hold you so bad? Ain't nothing open after 12:00 a.m. but legs. These fuckin' legs right here are mine. You're trying to get fucked?" I asked. I snatched Yirah's panties off and tossed her on the bed and forced her legs wide open. I shoved my dick inside of her. I gave her long powerful death strokes. Tears were running down her face. "Answer me Yirah, why are you crying? Ain't this what you wanted?"

"Does it matter Lucky? You don't give a fuck about me and Jamal. You want to fuck me now because he's interested in me? You're selfish Lucky, go home to your wife. I hate that I love you. I'll look after your mother," she moaned. Yirah was talking all that shit but steady throwing that pussy back at me, matching me stroke for stroke.

"Answer my question Yirah? I do care about you and Jamal. I love you and I mean that shit. You wanted me to beat this pussy up. You better dead that nigga before I do." I argued.

"Lucky, you know this complicates things between us? I love you too and I only want to be with you. Where does this leave us? It's not fair to me that you have her. Why can't I have someone?" She moaned. Yirah knows what it is and needs to only worry about that right now.

"What the fuck do you want from a nigga? You want the dick, I give it to you. You want cash, I bust down every week. You want time, I always fit you in. What are you trying to do Yirah? You want to be with that nigga or something? If so, let me know? I just fucked around and cheated on my wife with you." I grunted.

"This wouldn't be the first time Lucky," she moaned. I swear Yirah makes it real hard for a nigga to stay committed. I need her to shut the fuck up and play by the rules. I swear shit would be a lot better. What Kaniya doesn't know, won't hurt her.

Chapter-3

Killian

I'm telling you now, MOTHERFUCKAS gone learn to stop fuckin' testing me. Starting with my wife and my daughter. Don't believe any of that shit Kaisha spitting about us being divorced. I'm contesting that shit. I didn't agree to none of it. I will body Kaisha my damn self before I let another man wife her, but she continues to fuckin' play with me.

I received a call from Cynthia. Lucky's mother she said that Kaniya refuses to let her see her grandchildren and Lucky allows it. She also told me that Kaisha was over their house with Kodak and they were having a family brunch. That's the first red flag and trap music to my fuckin ears. Kaisha won't be satisfied until I kill her fuckin' ass.

Kaisha loves to dance with the devil. I wanted her to dance with me today. I've never retired from this street shit. Live by and I'll probably die by it. I fell back, because I was trying to do something different. I told her she got thirty days to bring her ass home and if not, I'm coming for her. She's been gone about ninety days. I hung up on

Cynthia and told her to meet me at Kaniya's house. I'm breaking up all this shit.

———

I made it to Kaniya's house in about forty minutes. Kaniya moved and didn't tell me shit, but I know where all my kids live and lay their heads. I rang the doorbell and Cynthia was right behind me. I heard my daughter yell she was coming to the door.

"What Killian, what do you want, why are you at my house? What are you doing with this old HOE from way back?" She argued. Kaniya and Kaisha will be the death of me.

"Kaniya you can cut that Killian shit out. I'm your fuckin' father. I've never been Killian to you and I'm not about to start now. How many times do I have to tell you I'm sorry? I don't give a fuck how you may feel about it, but you gone respect me." I argued. I knew Kaniya was still mad at me, but that's my baby girl and I love her to death. I fucked up and I regret that shit every day. She needs to let me make shit right between us. She keeps shutting me out, but I'll just force my way back in.

"I don't respect you anymore Killian. It was fuck me and swab her mouth. I'll never forget that or forgive you long as I live. Maybe if you would've done the same thing to Killany, it wouldn't hurt as much. You can leave because you ain't welcomed here." She argued. I made a fuckin' mistake. I need her to move past that shit.

"Kaniya Nicole Miller, you don't have a choice. Is my wife in your house, Yes or No? I heard she was, and ain't NOBODY going to stop me from getting her not even you." I pushed my daughter out of my way as I walked into the house looking for Kaisha and Kodak.

"Kaisha where the fuck you at?" I yelled. I was searching this whole house looking for her. Kodak and I had a few words years ago. I'm a grown ass man. My wife was off limits then and she's off limits now. Kaisha is my wife and that'll never change. I don't give a fuck about murdering a nigga behind my wife. If Kodak wants me to make an example out of him, I will.

Kaisha

I don't know why y'all Queens in the Trap wanted to hear from me? Y'all know my mouth fly as fuck, and I don't mind addressing a bitch or nigga behind my daughters. Y'all already know Kaniya called me and told me about Cynthia. I'll have to be careful with Kaniya and not entertain her. If I give her and inch, she'll take a mile. I have never retired from laying my hands on these hoes, period. What would make Cynthia think she's excluded? I smack bitches for fun. I don't give a fuck how a bitch may feel about me but keep my kids out of it. Yes, Kaniya and Killany are grown as fuck and can handle their own, but I'm their mother. I carried them for nine months. Ain't nobody gone disrespect them period.

Kaniya maybe many things, but calling her a whore and disrespecting her because you don't like me. Come on now, over some old dick. I didn't even get the chance to ride back then. Cynthia silly as hell, but you and I never had an issue. Not until you made it one now. Trust me, Cynthia don't want no problems with me. It has nothing to do with Kodak. It's strictly regarding my daughter. For this same reason I made it clear to Kodak, I can't fuck with you if Lucky is your son. He's married to my daughter and I would hate to kill his mammy. Kodak knows that Cynthia was the one to setup him up back in the day. Fuck that, what are you going to do about it?

Once again, I'm taking a hit on this relationship shit. I like Kodak's black fine ass but shit we just can't be together. To make matters worse Sonja keeps calling me, asking when am I coming back home? Shit I'm not. I'm over Killian. Shit we were separated for twenty years. He tried and disrespected me for the last time, so I divorced his ass. What would make him think that I would consider taking him back? It's not even a thought. He should've thought twice about coming at me indirect.

I gave it all I got and guess what, a bitch ain't got shit else to give. I'm at Kaniya's house right now and Killian's stupid ass is yelling through the house looking for me. Kodak looked at me and laughed. It was funny, but Killian didn't even deserve a laugh from me. I continued feeding Jamel and Jamia. They were laughing too. Killian done lost his damn mind. I couldn't deal with this man today or any other day. He searched every room looking for me.

Why are you looking for me? I can't believe Killian is really showing his ass like this. I just shook my head. He was so fuckin' embarrassing. Killian was really showing his true colors, acting like a clown. Kodak was grilling me hard from behind. I could feel the hairs raise up off my neck. I didn't even want to turn around and look at him because I knew what the problem was. It was Killian. Kodak wasn't here for the drama. He wanted to meet Lucky and establish a relationship with him. I didn't know Killian was going to be here. Had I known, I wouldn't have come here at all. It's been months since we last we saw each other.

I don't appreciate Kaniya setting me up. She for damn sure didn't tell me they were back on speaking terms. I wouldn't have come here with Kodak. He was so DAMN fine. He didn't age a bit the twenty years that he was away. Tall, dark and handsome, with a full beard. I wish he wasn't Lucky's father, but it is what it is. I swear to God I do. I don't know why Cynthia was playing ghetto games with him because he didn't want her ass. I really enjoyed the time we've been spending together. I guess we'll have to remain friends. Killian finally made his way toward the kitchen. We locked eyes with each other. He was grilling me, but I wasn't threatened by him. He was about to say something, but I quickly cut him off. "Save it Killian."

"Oh, so this is what the fuck we are doing Kaisha? Y'all four are having a family brunch without me and I wasn't invited? You're still married to me. I don't want no man around my grandchildren, they only have one grandfather." Killian yelled. He was doing the most. How can you tell our daughter Kodak can't be around her kids? I'm done.

"Killian you and I are divorced. So, whatever I'm doing it's my business and not yours. Kodak is Lucky's father, so he'll be around your grandchildren a lot, rather you like it or not." I laughed. Killian looked at me like I was crazy. Yes, Kodak isn't going anywhere.

"We're not divorced. I contested that shit. Fuck you mean?" He yelled. Whatever, he couldn't contest shit. I'm not trying to hear this shit at all.

"Killian why are you here, making a scene, and showing your ass? We're divorced, so what I do is my business. Understand that. WE are not together, and you know that. Why is she here because she nor you were invited?

Oh, I see what this is all about? Cynthia sent you to do her dirty work? Cynthia, I heard you had my name up in your mouth once again. Whatever your problem is with me, let's address it now. You got my daughter fucked up. You keep coming at her sideways, so now I have a fucking' problem with you. I don't let problems linger.

I'm her MOTHER, not her MAMMY. Anytime a motherfucka that's my age comes at her indirect, I'm the one that's coming DIRECT at that bitch neck about mine. I handle shit accordingly. I'll ask you again, DO WE HAVE A MOTHERFUCKIN' PROBLEM CYNTHIA, BECAUSE I GOT TIME TODAY?" I argued and clapped my hands. I got nothing but time to bust this bitch in her fuckin' face. Kodak grabbed me. I was sick of her ass fuckin' with my daughter. Fuck with me, I don't see how Kaniya does it. I let Kaitlyn's old miserable ass have it one fuckin' time. She may not like me, but bitch, you gone respect me.

"It's not like that Kaisha, Kaniya is very disrespectful. I just want to see my grandchildren, that's it." She explained. Cynthia was lying her ass off. She was looking at Kodak instead of me. I knew she didn't want any problems with me. I just wanted to clarify it. I can't wait to call Valerie when I leave here. She was still mad about

Kodak but that was over twenty years ago. Girl Bye sit your silly ass down.

"Well what is it because my daughter isn't a fuckin' liar? Whatever you say once; make sure you can repeat that shit twice."

"Killian you got a lot of nerve pushing my fucking wife down in my fucking house. If she loses my son I swear to God I'm killing, you." He argued. I looked over my shoulder to see what Lucky was up too. If Killian pushed my daughter to get to me. I'm going to kill his ass.

"Let's go Kaisha, I'm not leaving this house without you." He yelled.

"What the fuck did you do to my daughter Killian? Kaniya doesn't have nothing to do with us, leave her out of it. I'm living and you're living without me. Get that through your head."

"She ain't going nowhere, she came with me." Kodak yelled. Killian looked over his shoulder and grilled Kodak. I notice he patted his side. Killian better not draw down on Kodak in this house. Especially while my grandchildren are right here.

"Do you think you can stop me? You know how I give it up. This has been my pussy for years. Ain't nobody changing that. My nigga, you need to fall back." My ex-husband argued. Oh my God, he is too old to be acting like this. If he wouldn't have let Taliyae get the best of him, we wouldn't even be going through this.

"You know how I fucking give it up. She ain't going nowhere. It may have been your pussy for years, but it's mine now. I don't give a fuck how you may feel. She divorced you." Kodak argued. Killian approached Kodak. Lucky and I stood in between them. Killian grabbed me and pulled me behind him.

"Kaisha, have you given this nigga a sample of my pussy? Kodak you want to go to war with me behind my wife? I haven't made an example out a nigga in long time behind this. Kaisha let's fucking go because if I have to make an example out of this nigga, ain't nobody leaving up out of this bitch Kaisha but me and you. Your daughter ain't fucking safe or her kids." My Ex-husband threatened.

"You got me fucked up. I'm not leaving Killian." I argued. "Don't ever threaten my daughter and her children's life."

"Oh, you're not? I make good on everything I speak on. Watch me work." He yelled and gritted his teeth. He pushed me toward the door and pulled out his sawed-off shotgun. "I came here for you and I'm not leaving this motherfucka without you. If you don't want anybody to get hurt, you'll bring your motherfuckin ass on. If this motherfucka wants to know his son, you don't need to fuckin' be here. I'm not telling you again."

Lucky

I can't believe Killian came to my house with that bull shit and showed his ass. He had the nerve to push my wife down in the process. I wasn't having that shit at all. Killian and his wife had to fuckin' go from my house. I don't want this shit going on in front of my kids, at all. "Kaisha, thank you for introducing me to my father but I need you to leave with Killian. I'll make sure Kodak gets to wherever he needs to get too." Kaisha wanted to object but Killian got me fucked. My kids are here, and my house isn't the place to beef with my father behind your wife.

Kaniya grabbed Jamel and Jamia and took them upstairs to lay them down for their nap. It was just my mother, Kodak and I left. It's crazy because I look exactly like this man. I can't believe she did this shit. My father was grilling my mother, trying to get her attention. I could feel the hateful glares myself. I know he had a problem with her. I could tell he had some shit he wanted to say. Long as he doesn't put his hands on her, we won't have any problems.

"Jamel, I don't know what your mother told you about me, but I always wanted a relationship with you.

Your mother's and my past weren't pretty. I've done some things that I shouldn't have, and she's done some things too. I laid down prison for over twenty years because of her. Yes, she setup me up because she's vindictive. I lost out on getting to know you in the process. I'm passed that. I want a relationship with my son, if it's not too late." he stated. I was open to that. My mother was petty as hell for that shit.

"Kodak, what you won't do is make this shit about me and you. I thought jail would've wizened you up? Years later you're still running up behind Kaisha and she's still with her HUSBAND. If you want to get to know Lucky, leave me the fuck up out of it," she argued.

"Look, I don't want the two of you going back and forth about some shit that happened twenty years ago. I do want to get to know my father." I argued. My mother was mad, but I don't care. She needs to put her feelings to the side and think about me instead of herself. I'm not dealing with it at all.

"Lucky, I'm your mother and I raised you without any help from him. It seems like you're choosing your new family over me?" She asked and argued.

"Momma don't do that, it's not like that at all." I explained. My mother grabbed her purse and stormed out. I started to run after her, but my father stopped me. I looked at him like he was crazy. He doesn't know me to stop me from going after my mother. She's my mother regardless and I don't ever want her to feel out of place.

"Jamel let her go. I know you don't know me, but you've done nothing wrong. She's done a lot of shit wrong and she needs to own up to it. I know that your mother. Don't lose your family trying to pacify her feelings trying to please her. She's not right within. You don't know your mother, but I do. Her true colors will surface. She doesn't have shit lose because you're grown with a wife and kids." He stated. I soaked in everything he was saying. He wasn't credible. He knew how to get in touch with Kaisha, so he could've got up with me years ago. We've been together for seven years almost eight.

Cynthia

J ail did Kodak's body damn good. It's been years since I've seen Jamel Lee Smith Sr. I couldn't keep my eyes off him. Kodak was giving me evil glares the whole time. Nigga get over yourself. He was trying to intimidate me, but it didn't work. It's funny how history repeats itself. My plan worked. Killian did everything I thought he would do. I wanted to laugh so loud when he walked Kaisha up out the house. Kaisha is still a whore. Kaniya is just like her mother. Kaisha thought she was bad, but I'm way smarter than she would ever be. I knew her and Kaniya would jump me, so I kept my comments to myself.

I was hoping the two of them would try to jump me, because I would catch the two of them slipping real soon. I would run the two of them off a cliff. My grandchildren were so beautiful, too bad their mother wasn't shit. I started to bring the real Mrs. Williams to the brunch. I decided not to because in due time, the cards will fall where they need to lay. Speaking of the devil, she's calling me now.

"Good afternoon momma, how was it? How did my father in law look after all these years?" She smiled through the phone. I loved Yirah, she was my biggest supporter and I was hers.

"Good afternoon to you too. Yirah, it was a fuckin' mess. Your father in law was still fine as hell. Jail did his body GOOD. I wanted to jump on him and make another Lucky. My cat was screaming through my cat suit for him to scratch it." I sassed. I meant that shit. After all these years he still has my heart skipping a beat.

"Okay ma after all these years, you still love him? What do I need to do to help you get your man back? After all, you helped me get mine back. I appreciated everything you've done for me. I refuse to let Kaniya and her mother win."

"I'll figure it out. Yirah that's why I love and fuck with you. Be patient with Lucky, I mean real patient. Your time is coming. If Kaniya is anything like that whore that birthed her, she'll drop Lucky if she gets a whiff that he's cheating. All I'm saying is stick it out. You know I don't mind rubbing it in her face about you and Lucky." I stated. I wasn't a Kaniya fan, never have I ever been.

"I appreciate you for going so hard for me. I swear I felt like giving up so many times. I love Lucky so much and he knows it. I love him a lot better than she ever could.

I really want us to be a family." She explained. Yirah loves Lucky. Kaniya only wanted him for his money and what he could do for her. She's a gold-digging bitch, just like her whore ass mammy. I wish Lucky would've never laid eyes on her.

"I know you love Lucky, Yirah and he loves you too. The two of you can't stay away from each other. You have a part of him too. In my eyes you have his first-born son and Kaniya can't change that. I don't even know why he lied. She needs to deal with it. It'll work out, you got Lucky in the bag."

Chapter-4

Kaniya

I've been getting these strange phone calls from a 770 number for the past few weeks. I do NOT answer numbers, that I don't know. I checked my voicemail, not a single message was left. Every time the call comes through, I'm either asleep or I missed the call because I was handling my business. My schedule is open today. They don't even let the phone ring more than three times and they never leave a message. The calls come through at the same time every day. I googled the number, and nothing came up. I was a little curious to see who was calling me from this strange number. Today I made sure I was up, I was trying to keep busy.

I've been sleeping a lot lately. As soon as I get up. I'll shower, bathe and feed my kids. I'll handle my work load for Work Now Atlanta. After that, I usually help Killany with her Accounting Firm she's trying to setup in Atlanta, that she wants me to run. I've been looking at a lot of Office Space properties for her every week. I wish she would move here, but Yung will never let that happen. Killany and I couldn't live in the same city because it's dangerous. It's crazy how we got pregnant around the same time. It's almost time for Jamia and Jamel's morning nap. Usually I would get my morning nap in also before Jeremiah starts cutting up in my stomach but not today. It's 10:45 a.m. and I'm trying to stay up, so I could answer the phone.

Normally I don't sit by the phone at all. The last thing I need is for that number to call me and Lucky was to answers my phone. He's nosey and been going through my phone every day. I notice a lot of read message on my phone that I never opened. I don't know what he was looking for. I wish he would stop because I for damn sure wouldn't go through his phone. I should but I'm not. I don't have time to be doing all that. What's the worse he could do to me? We're married now, it's just me and him and no one else. I can assure that.

Lucky knows, I would kill him if he's cheating on me. Especially after his hating ass ran Dro off. He KNEW he didn't want me to get serious with him because BABY it would've been a motherfuckin wrap. I don't even want to mention Tariq.

If Lucky was fuckin' off and got me pregnant again to still cheat and be up to his old ways, I swear to God he will FUCKIN' regret it. He thought I was a SAVAGE before; he will meet the fuckin' DEVIL. Let me stop thinking about negative things. I'm in a good place and I have been for a while. I can't even imagine a life without Lucky. I love him. He's my first and last everything. I know it's meant because we keep coming back to each other. I can't wait to have Jeremiah. He's been wearing me out and I still have a few months to go. It's 11:38 a.m. and the number is calling right now. I answered the phone on the first ring.

"Hello" I sassed. I rolled my eyes. It's so loud, I here static and a lot of people in the background. I wanted to know WHO was calling me from this number and not leaving messages? My time is precious and way past nap time for me. A bitch is getting tired and restless, my eyes can barely take it. "Hello, are you there" I asked for the last time. I was about to hang up.

"Good morning, I'm sorry we're having some technical difficulties. I'm trying to contact Kaniya Miller. Is she available?" she asked. I looked at my phone. WHO the fuck is this? What do they want with me? I hope Yashir and Kanan Jr. ain't killed nobody, was sloppy with it, and has the police is looking for their bad ass'? I told them little motherfuckas to stop putting my name on shit. I guess they had the right number. I didn't recognize the voice at all. Damn they know my government name. I know it's not a bill collector. I don't owe anybody.

"Who wants to know?" I asked. Clearly this was someone that I didn't know but they knew me. I hear a shit load of papers being shuffled around. It had to be a detective. I need to send my attorney a text to see what's going on.

"Good morning! My name is Audra, and I work for the Piedmont Rehabilitation Center in Atlanta, Georgia. Tariq Harris wanted me to contact you. Ms. Miller the purpose of my call is to inform you of his condition. It's really against our company policy to even disclose this but Mr. Harris wanted me to contact you. I'm not sure if you know or not but he was shot several times and he was in a coma for a month. He just came out of the coma two weeks ago. The police don't have any information and he refuse to cooperate with them and us, so we can treat him properly.

He's in a very bad condition and could do SO much better. Look Ms. Miller, what I'm trying to say is, he's been here for forty-five days with little to NO progress. Could you please come in for a minute to speak with us? We would really like to get him back on his feet, but he's making it extremely hard for us. We may not be able to help him because he's not even trying," she explained. She had so much pain in her voice and I could tell she wanted to help Tariq. Ugh he needs to pull through. He's a fighter, he always has been.

"What do you want me to do," I asked. Why are they calling me? I don't have any dealings with Tariq. Where's Gabrielle? I would always care about Tariq no matter what. Damn I almost passed out hearing about Tariq's condition. Vomit sat at the back of my throat. I was sick to stomach. Lord have mercy on his soul. God please forgive me for my sins. Thank God Lucky wasn't here. My heart hurts so bad and my chest was caving in. Why is this happening to me? I can't blame nobody but myself. I should've never taken it there being vulnerable because of Lucky. We've always had a thing for each other, our chemistry is amazing. We never acted on them and when we finally did, for some reason we can't let go. It's unfinished business, but what business?

"He wants you Ms. Miller, he refuses to let anyone come near him. Could you please come in and speak with him? Could you please help us, help him?" She asked and begged. Tariq was really giving these people a hard time. I'm pregnant what could I possibly do? I would never be able to pull this past Lucky. I wouldn't even try. He would smell me over here from hell, are you shitting me. He always said I was sleeping with enemy.

"Audra, have you tried reaching out to his aunt Sonya or sister Raven? I won't able to come. Where are you guys located?" I asked and cried. Why did I just say that? I still cared about him and never wanted to see him like this. We both provoked each other. Lucky was the cause of this. I know what he did to Jamia wasn't right, but I forgave him, and we moved on. We were cool. He's loving Gabrielle, I was loving Lucky, and we were okay with it. Tears were pouring out of my eyes. My conscious was getting the best of me. I guess this is my karma.

"Ms. Miller, are you okay? Do you need a minute," she asked?

"I'm okay," I sniffled. I had to stop these tears from falling some type of way. I threw cold water on my face, that's better.

"Raven has been here, but she's no help. We haven't been able to contact Sonja. He doesn't want Gabrielle here. He listed you as next to kin and to contact in case of an emergency. That's why I've been calling you repeatedly. I wanted to give up, but he wouldn't let me. I hate to bother you, but do you think you may be able to come in today? The sooner the better. Mr. Harris X-rays shows a lot of strength and healing in his back and torso. We're unable to find out how much, because he won't let us touch him."

"Okay Audra, I'll see what I can do, but I'm not making any promises. I'll try to reach out to Sonja. If I can't reach her, I'll try to be there in about two hours okay." I hope Sonja is somewhere to be found. I called her phone twice from my house phone and she didn't answer. She was probably still mad at me about what happened.

"Thank you so much Ms. Miller. I'm sure Tariq will be happy to see you." She stated. We ended the call. If she only knew I'm the reason he's in there. What the fuck does Tariq want from me? I knew it was some reason the call kept coming through. It was him. How was I going to sneak and see him? I feel so bad about what happened to him. I remember that day like it was yesterday. I'll never forget that day long as I live.

"Yeah, you're surprised to see me huh? It's me in the fucking flesh Kaniya. I caught you with your fucking

pants down and no panties on. Bring that ASS here, it's still fat? I want to fuck you, right before I kill you. Bend that ass over and put your hands over your head. They say pregnant pussy is the best pussy. Yeah, I've been watching you. You had the nerve to marry that nigga right after you attempted to kill me? Is that how you doing shit now? You know you fucked up right? Your lil marriage don't mean shit to me.

Bitch you gone fuckin' die TODAY, since you left me for dead and threw up on my body. I loved your trifling ass. A motherfucka always told me, the one you love will be the one to kill your ass. I didn't want to believe that shit until now. You are that motherfucka Kaniya, you told me that shit. You did, I left you everything and this is how you fuckin' repay me? Killing you is too fucking easy. Taking you from that nigga, means so much fucking more. How could you leave me for dead bitch answer me?" He argued. Tariq had my breasts up against the wall. He was breathing heavy. I could feel his breath touch my neck. He was angry.

He was my worst nightmare stated. He picked me up, by my vagina. Tariq finger fucked my pussy wet. I had to stop myself from cumin'. I hated my body responded to him this way. He threw me up against the stall. He dug his two fingers inside of pussy, then placed them up against his nose. He licked his fingers. Tariq then wrapped his hands around my throat. We were eye level with each other. You could hear our hearts beat. "Kiss me Kaniya, I want you to taste yourself, before I kill you. It's a shame I can still get that pussy wet and you're married. Too bad that bitch ass nigga gone miss this pussy. I'm going to kill it twice, I'm fuck the pussy than kill it. What you think about that Kaniya? You want that, you always liked it rough," he argued. Tariq was way too aggressive.

"They say the good die young Tariq? I ain't never been afraid die, but I refuse to beg. Do what you have to do. If it's my time to go, it is what is. Let me say this to you, real bitches do real things. I'm a stand-up girl. If I would've known that was you, I wouldn't have killed you. Your back was fucking turned. I was called to assist on a job and I don't ask questions but do you. Go ahead and get this shit over with."

"Kaniya, you're motherfuckin' lie. You know my body as well as I know yours. You know me motherfucka. I wasn't a threat. I ain't never known you to lie."

"Kaniya, what fuck is going, on are you ok." My sister asked. Killany was so scared. I could hear it in her voice. She didn't know what was going on. It's her baby shower for God sake. She didn't even want to have one because of shit like this.

"I'm good Killany. Get up out of here please and take care of my kids. If I never see you again, know I love you with all my heart and I'll save a spot for you on the other side. I'll be your guardian angel. I love you Killany, tell momma I love her, and daddy too." I cried. I would miss my momma more than light itself.

"What the fuck is going on, who is that?" she cried. Killany cries mixed with my cries made my heart hurt even worse.

"My ex." I cried. She already knew who that was.

"Who Tariq?" She yelled.

"Yes." I cried.

"Kaniya I'm not leaving you." She cried. I didn't want to leave Killany. I know we talk shit about each other, but we're twins we can't live without each other.

"Go ahead I got it. Kiss my babies and tell them I love them please. Tell momma I love her too. Please Leave Killany please." I cried. I couldn't let Killany get caught up in my shit.

"Do what you got to do Tariq, because if you don't we gone shoot it out in this motherfucking stall. You ain't got long because, if she leaves and comes back without me. They are coming up in this bitch. Your baby momma is out there right now, pregnant with your child. I'm sure she'll be glad if you're alive and well to raise your child. If you kill me this shit ain't gone never stop. Lucky and my mother will hunt you down and kill you, so I'm waiting. I'm not gone beg you for my life."

"Do you think I give a fuck about any of that shit you are saying? We can both go, at least will be together. I'm a selfish ass nigga. He took you from me, so I'll take you from him forever." He argued and gritted his teeth. He started shooting in the bathroom stall. Bullets were flying everywhere. Pop, Pop, Pop, Pop. He let that bitch loose. He held me in place with so much passion. His touch used to feel so good. He had a tight hold on me, so I couldn't move. He was trying to scare me. I wasn't afraid to die, I started laughing and that enraged him. He picked me up

and slammed my body into the wall. I bit the insides of my
jaw, he was trying me.

"That's all you got Tariq? Kill me, if that's what
the fuck you came to do." I yelled. I'm tired of this.

"Bitch you ready to motherfuckin' die? You're loyal
to the wrong nigga. After everything he's done to you
Kaniya, you still chose him?" He argued. Tariq gritted his
teeth. He banged his fist up against the bathroom stall. A
few tears fell from his eye. The tears that dropped from his
eyes landed on my forehead. I peeked up at him, trying not
to stare too hard. He caught me looking at him. I wiped his
tears with my thumb. He probably didn't want me touching
him.

We locked eyes with each other. We were face to
face and mouth to mouth. After that things went left and got
ignorant. It was a mess, my heart ached for months because
of that. It's still aching. I grieve behind closed doors when
no one is around or I'm alone in my car.

Tariq and I have been friends for a very long time,
way before Lucky and I ever met each other. None of this
was supposed to happen. I didn't want to cross the line with

him for that reason alone because we had a friendship. Ugh and we don't even have that anymore.

———

I finally made it to Piedmont to see Tariq. I approached the front desk and asked for Audra. She came out and greeted me. We made small talk then she escorted me to his room. I was so scared to see him. He got hit up bad. What could we possibly say to each other besides I'm sorry? I couldn't help Tariq. Why would he even want or need my help?

"Audra, do you mind if I speak with Tariq alone please," I asked. Audra could be the fuckin' police for all I know. I would never incriminate myself. Tariq knew to keep his mouth shut. He wouldn't dare tell about what happened and he's a convicted felon.

"Sure Kaniya." She stated. I watched Audra walk down the hall. I had a scanner that could detect wires and recordings. Tariq's room was good. I entered Tariq's room slow and stood in the door for a minute. I can't believe I'm about to face him after what happened. I had to blink my eyes for a few seconds to stop the tears from falling.

"Are you going to come in or you're going to stand in the door," he sighed. He sounded fine to me. If Audra set me up, I'll be at her fuckin' car to murk her ass. I walked around to see Tariq. He was laid up in the bed, giving me hateful glares. I'm not doing this.

"Don't look at me like that Tariq. I'm sorry I didn't come here for that. What do you want with me? You and I both know I shouldn't be here. If you called me up here, on some revenge and bullshit, I can leave right now. I'm sorry I swear to God I am. I don't know how much more you want from me." I cried. I couldn't help myself. I tried to keep it together, but I couldn't. The tension between us is too thick. We couldn't be around each other like this.

"I shouldn't look at you like this Kaniya? I FUCKIN' should. How else am I supposed to look at you? Help me move pass this shit. I said if she came, I wouldn't even do this. I almost gave up on you. I always had faith in you. I've never known for you not to come through.

Damn we weren't even supposed to get like this Kaniya. How did we get to this point right here? Nothing we went through should've led to this. I LOVED YOU. I'm the one that's laid up in a hospital fighting for my life. I don't have anybody by my side. I always made sure you were straight. You're the only motherfucka I want, it's you. I fuckin' love you, no matter what we went or been through. Shorty, I love you. Even after this I still love you. I can't change how I feel for some reason.

I'm laid up here, in this hospital bed because of you," he explained. He pointed at me. "I'm confessing my love to you. Your love led me here. I don't want to be here, help me get out of here. I need you mentally and physically. Damn Kaniya what about my feelings? You ain't never took those in consideration for once. I got those motherfuckas too and I hate it because a nigga still got it bad for you. You hurt me for real." He argued. Tariq just ripped my heart out of my chest and gave it back to me in so many ways.

"I gotta go. Good bye Tariq."

"Come here Kaniya stop crying. I'm not trying to make you cry. I'm telling you how I feel. Unlike yourself, I've always been opened with you. You hurt me bad shorty. The whole time I was in a coma, I kept replaying that shit. Mac said your name, but he dies. It's only one fuckin' Kaniya. I'm glad you came; I wanted you to come." He stated. I was hesitant at first. He held his hands out for me. I gave Tariq hug. He smelled so good. He wrapped his arms around me so tight and was holding onto me for his dear life.

He stroked my hair, and the side of my face. I jumped at his touch. He cupped my chin forcing me to look at him. I took a small gaze into his eyes. His eyes, held, pain, anger and sadness. We were mouth to mouth. The only sounds you could hear were our hearts beating. We were searching each other's face for an explanation. He's making me so uncomfortable. I shouldn't be here.

"Tariq I can't do this." I started to walk off. This was too much for me.

"I'm asking you a question. I need you to be honest with me? Listen to me Kaniya. Love was the only thing that kept my mouth shut. I don't owe Lucky any loyalty. I can make that nigga disappear if I want too. I want to raise his kids too. He knew I was going to marry you. Word to my mother I was gonna make that shit happen. I didn't say shit to the police because of you Kaniya and your kids. I owe Lucky one and I don't give a fuck how you may feel."

"Tariq, I'm here, right now. I don't want to hear anything about Lucky. That's my husband and he's not up for discussion. I know y'all got y'all differences. I can't change that but I'm sorry. I shouldn't even be here, but I'm here despite everything. I will try to do whatever I can to help you. I can't make any promises, I'm pregnant."

"I need you to be here for me physically. I need your help with my physical therapy. You're my motivation. If I got you here for a few weeks, maybe two out of a week. I can knock this rehabilitation out the park," he explained.

"I don't know Tariq," I sighed.

"Come on Kaniya, say yes. I just need you here, that's all I'm asking. You want to see me down bad? I ain't got nobody, but you and Raven. Raven got some shit with her. She's not herself anymore. I'm not feeling her vibe. Sonja don't fuck with me like that. Gabrielle is stressing me out more than she's helping me." He explained.

"Alright Tariq." I sighed. I hope I don't regret this. He didn't deserve this. I left Tariq. I spoke with his nurse Audra to get his schedule. I could only come one day a week. Lucky would be to suspicious with two days. I don't like sneaking around, it's too much work. I'll get caught that's why I don'

Gabrielle

What was it about her? This isn't the first time that he's chose her over me. I love Tariq I really do. I'm in love with him and I can't shake it. I've been with Tariq since the beginning. Yes, I've been in the background, but I've always been here. When Kaniya left him because she found out that he was with Jassity he ran his ass back to me.

He left me again for her and proposed to her. I was so heartbroken he shitted on me again. When Lucky broke into his house and had sex with Kaniya in his fucking bed, it was me that he ran back to again. When she saw me fucking him in the club raw, it was me that fucked the pain away. It was my wet and warm tunnel that made you forget about her. It was me that took the wrath of Kaniya's hands when she caught us.

It was me that nursed your dog ass back to health after they shot you in the bathroom numerous times. My tears saved you. It was my sorrow and my prayers that stopped Kaniya and Lucky. She felt sorry for me because no child should grow up without their father. If it can be prevented. I guess she did have heart, but instead he still yearns for her. Even though he can't have her. I'm so tired of this shit. I don't know what to do and no I'm not staying with him because he has money and what he can do for me.

I stayed with him because I thought we could have something solid since Kaniya was out of the picture. Do you know this disrespectful motherfucker had the nerve to let me smell his fingers after he got shot and it smelt like her pussy? Sweet pussy is what he called it and it drives him insane. Tears filled my eyes just thinking about it. I've lowered my standards fucking with him. Love will make you do some crazy shit. I can't compete with her. I refuse too. I can't keep doing this. I'll have to let him go and find myself.

I won't keep his daughter from him, but I can no longer continue with this toxic relationship. I have a lunch date with Kaniya later. It's more of a woman to woman. We have never sat down and talked. It's not that I'm seeking her approval or blessing to be with Tariq. I'm looking for advice and I feel like she can give me some.

He always runs back to me and he doesn't want to let her go. I'm fed up if it takes him to really lose me to find himself than that's what's about to happen because I'm tired of this. Some may say it's crazy, but why not ask her what to do since she knows him better than anybody and he refuses to let her go.

Chapter-5

Kaniya

G abrielle called me? It caught me by surprised. I had to look at the phone to make sure I wasn't tripping. She wanted to have lunch and talk. I didn't care, I just had to run it by my husband first to see if it was cool. He said I could go, but of course he was coming with me. I got dressed. I had a white pencil skirt and blazer and nice nude blouse. My hair was braided in two French braids to the back. My shoes consisted of some nude open toed Chanel sandal.

"You sure you're going to meet with Gabrielle and not Tariq." My husband yelled.

"Lucky, you' going ain't you. I had this outfit laid out before I received the phone call. If you don't want me to go just say it, we can finish what we were doing."

"I don't like the way that shit looks on you. Where are your maternity clothes? You're pregnant with my son. I don't want you wearing that shit." My husband stated.

"Lucky shut up, anything I put on it's going to still show my curves. I know I'm pregnant with your son, how could I forget." Some shit never changes, he still crazy as I don't know what. I didn't have any plans today. I wanted to go to work but Lucky refuses because Dro stopped by to say hi and he didn't like the way he was looking at me.

I couldn't wait to have my son Jeremiah. As soon as he hears his father's voice he acts a fool in my stomach. My son was driving me insane. I can't wait until he gets here because he has a mind of his own already. I dressed casually because you never know if some shit was about to pop off. Tariq and Gabrielle could be out for revenge. The only thing that I want to do is fuck my husband and be a great mother to my kids, that's it.

———

We made it to the restaurant and Gabrielle hasn't arrived yet. She has ten minutes and I'm out. I was so busy exchanging texts with Lucky and smiling. I didn't notice her walk up.

"Hey Kaniya, sorry I'm late." She stated.

"No problem, you're good. What's up?"

"I wanted to sit down and talk with you. You and I have never had a sit down and I need some advice." She stated.

"We can sit down and talk. I don't have a problem with that. What type of advice do you need?"

Gabrielle

"**K**aniya, I brought you here today because you understand him. I've always been in the picture since he was released from prison, until now. He chose you over me time and time again. I nursed him back to health, not you. Do you know he let me smell your pussy after he was shot, and we rushed him to the hospital? He had your scent on his fingers. He called it sweet pussy and put it up to my nose and forced me to smell you. Tears poured down my face."

"You need to lower your voice. My husband is close and I'm trying to live another day and I'm sure you want your man to live too." She stated.

"I know you said in the bathroom that y'all didn't fuck but why did his hands smell like you and he was going crazy behind it. Your scent, it had kept him alive." I cried.

"Look Gabrielle, I didn't fuck Tariq in the bathroom. He picked me up and grabbed my vagina and slammed me against the stall. That's it." She stated.

"Why do I have to compete with you? What's so special about you? I'm tired Kaniya, I can't do this shit no more. I refuse to." I cried.

"Listen Gabrielle. I'm going to keep it real with you the best way I know how, and you can take it how you want too. I loved Tariq, we shared something special. We were supposed to get married, but it didn't work out that way. God well better yet Lucky had other plans. We had a bond that couldn't be broken. Prior to him getting shot the first time we were cool, but my husband thought it was more than that and it wasn't.

Tariq loves you too. He told me that he does. You only think he chose me because you need somebody to blame. He chose you a long time ago. If he was comfortable enough to fuck you in the club and cater to you and not me, then it was you. He brought you to our home that we shared. None of that shit matters right now Gabrielle, don't lose yourself behind him.

Don't ever ask to smell a man's dick in front of anybody but in the comfort of your own home. Never smell another woman's pussy because he forced you too. You should've smacked the fuck out of him for doing that disrespectful shit. Don't take his disrespect at all.

He loves you but give him something to miss. Don't take his bullshit. Leave. When he's ready to be the man he's needs to be, he'll change for you. Replace him. If he sees you with another man he'll get some act right." She explained.

"I can't Kaniya, I'm not you."

"I know you ain't me Gabrielle because if you were baby girl, you wouldn't be here. Leave him and find yourself. You don't have to get another man but make that nigga respect you like he respected me. Let him miss you and come back to you. Not just to fuck or whatever else. Not because he wants to, not because he can, but because he wants to change." She argued.

"It's easier said than done. Can I call you sometimes just to talk?"

"Sure, are we done here?" She asked.

"Yes."

"Take it easy okay and don't stress yourself out behind him okay." She stated. Kaniya was nice person. She's not a monster like Raven painted her out to be. Her whole presence screamed boss. I wasn't about to cheat on Tariq, but I would move out his home until he learns to appreciate me.

Kaniya

I can't believe Tariq. I wish he would just leave me the fuck alone. It's that fucking simple. I only agreed to help him because I felt bad about all the shit that happened and we were better than everything we've been through. I feel like I owed him that much when I don't owe nobody shit but my kids. I feel sorry for Gabrielle because they love each other but I'm in the middle and I'm not trying to be.

"What's wrong with you?" My husband asked.

"Nothing."

"Kaniya, you have never been good at lying to me, so stop doing that shit. What's the matter, she found out that you were going to see her baby daddy every day like you ain't fucking married to me. That shit is so disrespectful. You better be glad I know shit ain't going on between you and him because if I felt that it was...I would finish the fucking job. I wouldn't have to worry about you lying to go see that motherfucker." My husband yelled and gripped the steering wheel.

"Dick got your fucking tongue." My husband gritted.

"Nope."

"Make this your last fucking time going to see that nigga and I fucking mean it. I don't give a fuck about none of that shit. You forgot to mention that he grabbed your pussy. I swear to God Kaniya, I'm not beat for this shit. You begged me to not kill him. I don't understand you. Make me understand this shit. Kaniya, am I fucking missing something?"

"What are you talking about Lucky? The last time I saw Tariq was the last time you saw him." Lucky couldn't have known I saw Tariq. See sneaking around to help Tariq is wearing me the fuck out. To make matters worse, Gabrielle hit me up with this bullshit little lunch and Lucky's listening to everything. Lucky knew I was up to something, but he didn't know what. I covered all my tracks. I told him that I was helping my grandmother. Every time I went, guess who was with me talking shit, Kaitlyn Miller. She wasn't cheap. She billed me for her services. Thank God Lucky had to make a move to Savannah.

I couldn't wait to go see Tariq and give him a piece of my mind. He's so wrong for treating her the way he has.

I waited an hour after Lucky pulled off to leave the house. Lucky was up to some bullshit and I wasn't for it at all. I grabbed my purse and headed out. I had pick up my grandmother first and head out. I looked at the clock and it was already after 3:00 p.m., which means Tariq should be in physical therapy. It shouldn't take me that long to make it over there.

———

I finally made it over to Piedmont. My favorite receptionist Gloria was working. I always signed as Raven Miller.

"Hey Raven, you look so pretty," she smiled as she spoke.

"Thank you, Gloria." I made my way to the exercise facility. Tariq was with his personal trainer, Cara. She looked up and noticed me and stopped working.

"Hey Kaniya! Tariq you can take a fifteen-minute break. I'll be back in about twenty minutes." She stated. Tariq looked at me and licked his lips. I looked at him and rolled my eyes.

"I hope them motherfuckas get stuck. What brings you by here today?" He asked.

"Gabrielle and I had lunch today. Tariq, I have a fuckin' bone to pick with you. First, today is my last fuckin' time coming up here. Don't call me no more, you're healing fine. Audra and Kara confirmed it. Why are you pushing Gabrielle away if she wants to be here for you? I'm married, and I've done everything that you wanted me too. Let her be here for you. She wants to do it, but you won't let her. WHY? Stop fuckin' comparing her to me. She's not me. Would you like it if she compared every nigga she fucked with to you? You're so fuckin' disrespectful. Why would you let her smell your fingers after you played with my pussy?" I slapped his ass for that shit. "I'm done with you Tariq. I can't believe you're treating her like that? You cheated on me with her multiple times. Bye Tariq I'll see you around."

"Wait Kaniya, don't fuckin leave. The fuck is you doing talking to Gabrielle. I need you. I was fucked up when I did that shit. I could've died, but a nigga was holding on to you. She doesn't understand me like you do. She can't help me, like you can," He argued.

"I don't care Tariq. You don't know what she can do if you don't let her in. She needs you and you need her. I'm leaving. Lucky is on to me. I'm not trying to create any problems in my home. I'll see you around." I walked off as fast as I could. I didn't even give Tariq time to talk.

Lucky

Kaniya thought she was slick, but she already knew I order her steps. I don't even know why she wanted to lie and play with me. I knew a chick who worked at Piedmont at the front desk. Gloria, we used to fuck around back in the day. She knew Kaniya, but Kaniya didn't know who she was. She saw Kaniya up there a few weeks ago and she instantly hit me up. I knew my wife wouldn't betray me like that. Gloria had proof, real proof. She sent me pictures of Kaniya going and coming. She also sent me pictures of Kaniya and Tariq interacting. Don't get me wrong, I know I was out here living foul, but Kaniya crossed the fuckin' line nursing that nigga back to health.

It took everything in me not to run up in there and finish the fuckin' job. The only reason Tariq is still alive is because we didn't have a fuckin' silencer. The facility was packed to capacity, everybody was screaming, and somebody called the laws. The police swarmed in the bathroom quick, we played it off like we were helping the nigga. He lied right along with us. Kaniya trusted him, but I don't trust no nigga that's sampled my pussy. How could you do that after what happened to my daughter? My phone was blowing up. I took my phone out of my pocket. It was Gloria. I answered quick before the call ended.

"Talk to me baby."

"Your wife came through here today. I don't know what happened between her and Tariq. Whatever it was, it was heated. He's pissed. I have the recording." She explained.

"Send it to me baby." Gloria still wanted me and to taste the dick down her throat. I wouldn't mind giving it to her, but I'm taking Yirah to Miami this weekend.

"Lucky, you need to come on down. I'm not talking about money," she sassed. Gloria she's talking in circles.

"I don't have a problem giving you what you want. I'm headed out of town for a few days. When I get back in town, we can make some plans to see each other. You know I miss you and that THING you do with your FUCKIN'. I want that head sloppy." Gloria was feeling herself. She was giggling.

"Lucky you still remember, after all these years?" She asked. I could tell she was smiling through the phone.

"Hell, yeah I remember all that shit. You gone fuck around and make me cancel this trip fucking around thinking about your freaky ass." I laughed. I was laying it on real thick too. I wanted to see the video. Gloria's audio and video were on point.

"Lucky I got go. I'm sending you the vide and my address. The key is under the mat on the porch. I want to see you soon, so I can do that little thing with my mouth."

"Alright do that and I'll see your fine ass soon." Yirah swung my door open like a mad woman.

"Who the fuck was that Lucky? It didn't sound like Kaniya," she asked.

"Shut up Yirah. I'm handling fuckin' business. Mind yours and fasten my son in his car seat properly. You wanted a vacation, so I'm taking you on one. You can shut the fuck up." I argued. I was sick of Yirah's nagging ass.

"How did you get away from Kaniya," she asked.

"Does it matter? I'm here. You're worried about the wrong shit. Enjoy yourself without worrying about somebody else," I argued. I gripped my steering wheel. Yirah was asking way too many fucking questions.

Kaniya's lying ass couldn't wait for me to leave to go see that nigga.

Chapter-6

Raven

I fucking knew she had something to do with my brother getting killed, shot, or whatever the fuck happened. That's the reason why I asked the bitch to help me plan his funeral, just to see if she could stomach it. Cartier left me because of how I felt about this situation? I'm pregnant with his child, that he doesn't even know about. I told Killany she better not tell him shit. She ruined my life. I wish I never met her. I hate her. I wish Tariq would've pushed her shit back. I would've sat front row at her funeral and laughed, but no he loved her trifling ass. The love he had for her saved her and outweighed everything else. Right is right and wrong is wrong. If I would've lost my brother, I would've killed her. He's all I got. I'm not trying to lose him. I hate to wish bad on someone but Kaniya deserves everything that's coming to her. The moment I found out we were sisters; my life took a turn for the worse.

God is good despite the bullshit. Tariq was shot multiple times, but he was perfectly fine. I knew that was my mother's doing. I can't even look at Kaniya after this.

I'll spit on her and we'll fight every time because she fucking lied to me. How could she do that to me? My brother is everything to me. I will lay my life on the line a million times for him. Tears cascaded down my face and soaked my pillow.

Why me lord, why was I dealt a bad hand? My mother left me three days after I was born. I just met my father almost a year ago. I met a man that I could see myself spending the rest of my life with and he's gone with a blink of an eye. He can't accept me and my opinions. I accept everything that comes with him, all the baggage. Where do I go from here?

"Raven, what's wrong?" My brother yelled. I've been staying at Tariq's house for the past few weeks. I hope he didn't hear me in here crying. I was going through it and Kaniya and Cartier was the cause of it all. I just want things to go back to how they were before all the drama and chaos.

"Everything Tariq." I sighed. My voice still had a little pain in it. I tried to clear my throat to mask it.

"Talk to me Raven, tell me what's going on? I'm here for you and I'm not going anywhere. You know I got you no matter what. I can see you're upset." Why was

Tariq all in my business. I wasn't ready to disclose that I'm pregnant and my baby daddy left me.

"I hate her Tariq, for what she has done to you and too me." I cried. I meant that shit. Hate is a strong word to use.

"You hate who Raven?" Tariq knew who the fuck I was talking about. He just wanted me to confirm it.

"Kaniya who else." I sassed and sucked my teeth. He better not take up for her ass.

"Look Raven, I know I'm probably the last person you want to discuss Kaniya with but let that shit go. I'm not gone tell you to kiss her ass and make up with her because I respect your feelings. I should've kept you out of our business, but I didn't. I'm your brother and she's your sister. She has been nothing but good to you. Don't cut her off based off what happened to me. I should've never allowed you in my business." He argued in her defense.

"Are you serious Tariq?"

"I'm a selfish ass nigga. Two wrongs don't make a right. I'm not a saint and she's not either. Let it go Raven. Call her and have a sit down to get that shit off your chest, so you can move on. Call your baby daddy and tell him to man up before he sees me about you. Where the fuck is he and you're pregnant with his seed?"

"How do you know I'm pregnant Tariq?"

"I just know, you're my little sister. I know everything about you. I know I haven't brought you any pads in months. I know you haven't gotten your birth control shot. I know you've been going to the OBGYN around the corner. I know more than you think I know. I'm pissed. I didn't want nobody knocking my little sister up without my fucking permission." Ugh Tariq knew everything about me. He was my father and until I met my father.

"You're not mad at me?" I asked. I didn't know how I was going to tell Tariq that I was pregnant. Now I don't have too.

"No, I'm not mad at you Raven. I love you. Call Kaniya and talk it out. I don't want you to be stressed out carrying my niece or nephew."

"I'll think about it."

"Don't play with me Raven." My brother gritted.

Tariq

I love Kaniya. I will never stop loving her. I will always have a soft spot for her in my heart. I really loved her more than I loved myself, but I'm in love with Gabrielle too. For me to be with Gabrielle like I need to be I must let her go. I know I did some foul shit to her that I'm not proud of, but I'm hurt, and a nigga scorned. I hope it's not too late for us. Kaniya and I have history that can't be erased. A lot of the shit that we've been through hasn't even been written because what's understood didn't need to be explained.

Out of all the women that I've been with, I would never think she would do me like that. Not once but twice. Despite the shit that happened between us, she's still good in my book. She has made all her wrongs, right with me. We needed closure, well I need closure. Gabrielle nursed me back to health, but it was Kaniya that got me right physically but not mentally.

Gabrielle didn't know that I had the nurse personally call Kaniya, tell her I needed her and that my life depended on it. I was hit up a few times and that shit wasn't looking good for a nigga like me. I heard the nurse and doctors talking.

I was in a coma for a month and she came to my rescue. It was only right she put me there. I don't know how she was able to do that without Lucky finding out, but she made that shit happen. She's the reason I'm able to be here today. She came through for me despite this shit that happened, and she cried every day. She hated to see me like this, but she pulled through. I forgive her. I'm just glad to be amongst the living.

Chapter-7

Yirah

I've been calling Lucky for two days and he hasn't answered. We had an agreement and right now he hasn't lived up to his agreement. I'm tired of playing with him. I love Lucky, but I don't love him enough not to tell his wife what we have going on. If Lucky was smart he would've told Kaniya in the beginning about Jamal. He wouldn't have to hide us and the time we spend together. He's seeing his son period, what the fuck could she do? Cynthia was already Team Yirah. I knew he was spending time with her because it's close to her due date. I heard him say something about it on the phone last week, when we were together. It dawned on me that she fucked up my delivery and pregnancy with Jamal. He was always worried about her and what she was doing. I've been stalking her social media. She always posting pictures of her and my man. She slipped up the other day. The lady at her OBGYN tagged her and Lucky in a picture on Facebook #beautifulparents. It made me sick, but I got the name and the location of the facility she's attending.

I knew she had an appointment today because when I went through Lucky's phone last week it was on his calendar. I rode past the facility and scanned the parking garage a few times and his Maserati Truck was in the garage. I backed in and pulled right beside him. I've been out here for over an hour waiting on the two of them to come out. Kaniya thinks her life is so perfect, NOT. Bitch I'm still sucking' and fuckin' on him whenever I want too. Today she was about to find out. Yes Jamal, is your children's brother BITCH. We share the same baby daddy. Yirah is the one. I wish he would just leave her.

He finally read the text messages I sent him. I heard the alarm chirp and his engine start up on his truck. I immediately scanned the parking lot to see what entrance they were coming from. I looked to my right and I didn't see him. I looked to my left and he was coming through the parking lot by himself. Smiling and looking at his phone. I politely stepped out and stood in front of his truck. My hands were folded across my chest. It was the middle of December and it was freezing. I didn't care, Lucky could keep me warm. He grilled me.

"What the fuck are you doing out here Yirah? You're out here at the fuckin' hospital, my wife is in there.

You want me to fuck you up? You're trying to ruin my fuckin' marriage before I can even leave gracefully? I told you about this crazy shit." He argued. Lucky grabbed me by my arm, shoved me in the corner, and my back hit the brick wall. His eyes pierced right through me. We were shooting daggers at each other. I couldn't read him, but he could read me. He was all up in my face.

"I'm out here because of you Lucky. I've been calling you and you haven't been answering for me. Anything could've happened to me or Jamal and you were nowhere to be found. This shit isn't fair Lucky, why do we have to be a secret? I can't keep doing it. I'm pregnant too and I wanted to share the news. It'll never be us because you're so comfortable with lying. I don't want to keep living a lie with you. I want to live my truth with you." I cried.

"Didn't I tell you I was working out some shit? Coming up here to fuck with her isn't the problem. What the fuck did I tell you Yirah? If you tell her now, you're not going to solve shit. You're going to make shit worse for yourself. So, what's it's going to be?" He argued.

"It couldn't get any worse. How do you think I feel? Do you ever think about that? My feelings don't matter at all." I cried.

"Yirah don't do this shit out here. Come on, don't guilt trip me. You got to raise up out of here before somebody sees us, I'm not trying to see you cry. I care about you. Get up out of here and go home. I'll come through later," he explained. Lucky pulled me in his arms, wiped my tears with his thumbs, and placed a kiss on my lips.

"No Lucky I'm not leaving, where is she? Your answer isn't good enough for me. Come through now. Follow me home now." I argued. He was lying trying to get me to leave. I wasn't leaving here without him. Lucky jacked me up against my car, wrapped his hands around my throat, hovered over me, and whispered in my ear.

"Get your ass in the car and take your ass home before I fuck around and hurt you out here. I mean that shit Yirah. Do you see all these motherfuckas out here watching us?" He yelled.

"I'm not leaving Lucky. I don't give a fuck whose watching, let them tell her." Lucky picked me up and threw me in his truck and pulled off.

Lucky

Man Kaniya is going to kill me. As soon as I stepped out of the doctor's office Yirah's crazy ass was in the parking lot, parked right beside me. I swear to God if Kaniya would've walked outside. I would've shot Yirah dead in her fuckin' head. She would've never had the chance to say anything about what the fuck we have going on. She came out here trying to set me up to lose my fuckin' family. At my wife's fuckin' doctors' appointment. She's in the passenger seat now crying. How in the fuck do she even know this is my wife's fucking OBGYN practice? She needs to fuckin' fall back. What more do she want from me? She knows what it is. Don't get shit confused. I hit my brother Quan up and told him to pick up Yirah's car and take it to my house. I pulled up at Yirah's house and killed the engine quick. She jumped up right behind me. I couldn't check her like I wanted too at the doctor's office. You never know whose watching.

"Yirah what the fuck was that back there? Come on NOW, you don't fuckin' hear from me for two days and you're doing all of this? Why? I got a fuckin' family and

I'm married? If my wife needs me I'm going to be there regardless of how you may feel. If you and Jamal need anything I make sure you're straight. What more do you want? Your living in my fuckin' house. Whatever you want, you have access too. You wanted a fuckin' Benz truck, I copped you one, brand fuckin' new. You have my fuckin' black card, what is it? What the fuck is it? I'll tell Kaniya and then I ain't got to go through this shit. I wouldn't even be spending all this money. I can throw you money and keep my wife. I can stop all of this shit."

"I want you Lucky, that's it. I don't care about the materialistic shit. You can ignore me but if I ignore you, you automatically assume I'm cheating or fucking someone else. You have a wife, but you don't want me with anybody else. You know what Lucky, just leave and don't come back. I'll find a single man with no baggage to fuck me whenever I want." She argued.

"What the fuck did you say? You like trying me when shit doesn't go your way, don't you? Yirah, I want you to call a nigga over here. Who wants to fuck you? Give me your fuckin' phone." I walked up on Yirah and backed her in the wall. She started breathing heavy. My lips were touching hers. "Call him up, I want you too." Yirah placed her lips on mine and my tongue roamed around in her mouth.

We started kissing while I slid her pants down and raised her shirt up above her head. She wrapped her legs around my waist and I slid my dick inside of her. I started pounding away and took all of frustrations out on Yirah's pussy, she tried me. My dick was balls deep in this pussy. She was extra wet.

"Slow down it hurts," she moaned. Yirah started grinding her hips and speeding up the pace. I could tell she was on the verge on cumin.

"Shut the fuck up and take this dick. You've been a very bad girl and your pussy got to pay for all of this shit." I grunted.

"I'm sorry Lucky. I just wanted your attention."

"You got it, when is my baby due?"

"July," she whispered. Damn Yirah, always trying to trap a nigga. She wasn't going to say shit but continue to trap a nigga. I don't know how in the fuck I'm going to get out of this one? I'll have to get back to the hospital.

"I got to go Yirah. I can't miss the arrival of my son being born." I stood to my feet. I had to go home and change clothes.

"No tell her something came up." She argued.

"Look I'm not doing that shit. No matter what the fuck we have going on. I'm not missing my son's entrance in the world because I want to beat up your pussy the worst way. I got to bounce. I'll get up with you in a few days."

"You're making excuses. You missed me giving birth to Jamal because she was giving birth to them. Lucky ain't none of this shit fair at all."

"Yirah she's my fucking wife. Put your feelings to the side. I'll be there for our next child's delivery."

"Just leave Lucky, because you don't fuckin' get it. I'm not going to be your side bitch forever. What's going to happen when she finds out we share two children together? I'm not keeping this a secret forever. You need to tell her because I want too so bad. I'm tired of sparing her feelings for you. You never spared mine."

"You worried about the wrong shit. We'll cross that point when we get there. Stay the fuck away from my wife.

You're not telling Kaniya shit. It's boundaries and she's the boundary, don't over step that motherfucka."

Kaniya

Remind me not to have sex between the months of March through June. The older I get the more I'm learning my body and what months I'm the most fertile. Which happens to be those months. Unlike my last pregnancy, this pregnancy is peaceful because Lucky and I are together. I wasn't scheduled to have Jeremiah until December 26th, 2017 but he has a mind of his own. I went to the doctor this morning and guess who's in labor?

Me. He's two weeks early and I've dilated three centimeters. Jeremiah was ready to meet his mommy. I couldn't wait to meet him also. According to his ultra sound he looks a lot like Jamel when he was a baby. Jamel looks exactly like Lucky. Jeremiah has my nose and lips. Lucky left to go get my other bag, that had Jeremiah stuff in it. Lucky should've been back by now. My mom and dad had Jamia and Jamel. They stated that Lucky hasn't made it over there yet. He's been gone for over an hour and half. If this nurse comes back in and check me one more fuckin' time I'm going to scream.

I've called Lucky's phone at least three times already and it's going straight to voicemail. What the fuck is so important that you're about to miss the delivery of your child? I heard another knock on the door and it was my nurse again. I swear I didn't mean to have an attitude with this lady because she was just doing her job. My problem was with Lucky. If he misses Jeremiah delivery I will never forgive him for this. I'm not holding out because he isn't here. This will be the second time that he's ruined a delivery for me. If he comes too late, I'll have his ass escorted out of here.

"Mrs. Williams let me check you again to see how far you've dilated?" She asked. I did exactly what she asked me too. I'm hoping its time because I'm ready to see him. My hand was placed on my stomach. He was moving around doing his own thing. A young boss in the making.

"Okay." If they check me one more time and I'm nowhere near ten centimeters I'm going to scream. I swear to God I am. Jeremiah is going to be my problem child. I know it. He's always up to some shit.

"We're making progress Mrs. Williams you're at seven centimeters. It shouldn't be that much longer. We'll go ahead and get the room ready for delivery. The next time I come back it should be time to meet your prince," she smiled.

"Thank you." Now it was a waiting game. I looked at the clock and it was a little after 3: 00 p.m., I was tired. I needed to take my nap. I was trying to wait on Lucky, but my eyes wouldn't allow it. Sleep finally took over.

———

I was sleeping well. I turned over on my side and I felt a pair of lips against mine. I opened my eyes and it was Lucky. I closed my eyes because I didn't want to be bothered with him. I politely turned around and gave him back. When he left here he had on a red Gucci hoody and now he has a totally different outfit on. I could tell he just took a shower. I had to count to ten in my head to stop from showing my ass in this hospital. I didn't even want to think the worse of him.

"What's wrong with you Kaniya?" He asked. I wasn't even about to answer because him because he knows me; and he knows what the fuck the problem was. I don't have anything nice to say. "Do you hear me fuckin' talking you? I know you're not sleep, because you're breathing heavy." I still wasn't about to respond. I grabbed my phone and looked at the clock. It was 4:30 p.m. I took a nap at 3:15 p.m. which means he haven't been here that long. Why wouldn't he wake me up, so I would know that he was here?

"How long have you been here Lucky? Better yet where the fuck has you been and why did you change clothes? The only thing you had to do was take the kids to my mother's house and grab Jeremiah's bag. It doesn't take four hours to do that. I got a fuckin' attitude because of you. If Jeremiah would've came into this world and you weren't here, you would've heard more than my fuckin' mouth." I argued.

"Lower your motherfuckin' voice Kaniya. Ain't nobody fuckin' cheating on you, if that's what you are insinuating? I had to handle some business at the club. I got my hands dirty, so I had to change clothes. I couldn't come up here with red paint on me, you feel me?"

"Lucky who the fuck is you talking to? Watch your fuckin' time with me. A hit DOG will always holla. I never said shit about you cheating. I don't give a fuck about none of that club shit. The club is more important than your wife about to give birth to your son? No text, phone call, or nothing. Your phone was off.

We wouldn't even be having this conversation IF I would've known your where about. Catch me tomorrow Lucky, I'll be thirty pounds lighter and not carrying your child. Don't get this shit confused, for your sake. All this shit better check out. I better be the only ONE riding that big black motherfucka between your legs. Lucky, IF I AIN'T you better get baptized. Lord Have Mercy on Your Soul. You don't fuck with me and my feelings this time around. I swear to God you don't." I argued.

"So, what the fuck is you saying Kaniya? Are you threatening me? What the fuck do I have to lie to you for? I'm not thinking about another bitch. Lower your motherfuckin' voice. You're putting motherfuckas in our business and they don't need to be. You're worried about the wrong shit. Focus on bringing my son in this world Kaniya, that's it. Nobody comes before you and my children. Jeremiah wouldn't come while I wasn't here. I'm sorry Kaniya I had to handle that shit. I didn't think it would take that long." He argued.

"You heard what the fuck I said Lucky. I don't make fuckin' threats. I make promises, you're fucking up my vibe. You can leave and come back after I have Jeremiah." I argued. I'm not even about to go back and forth with him. Lucky was lying his ass off. Whatever you do in the dark it always comes to light. He was too defensive. I turned back around. I was ready to get this over with. I swear this couldn't be son's birthday and I'm beefing with this stupid ass motherfucka, lying beside me. I felt him wrap his arms around me. I politely removed them. "Don't' touch me." He whispered in my ear.

"Stop fucking playing with me Kaniya. I love you and I'm not out here cheating on you. You know I wouldn't miss the birth of my son. I don't want you stressing my son out focusing on the wrong things. I'm sorry, can you forgive me? I don't want our son coming into the world and we're mad at each other. We've been good and we're going to continue to be good. I just want to make you happy. I don't want you mad at me." I'm not trying to hear that shit. At all. I said what I had to say. My nurse knocked on the door. She probably heard Lucky and I arguing and was scared to come in. He knows how I am. I don't even know why he would try me like that? Ain't shit changed with me.

"Mrs. Williams let me check you one more time. I'm sorry I'm late I wanted a little time to pass by before I came back. It looks like your contractions have sped up.

Jeremiah maybe ready to make his grand entrance." She smiled.

"I hope so, because I'm not having anymore. He's my last one." I sighed. I was dead ass serious. Jeremiah was running shit, and he wasn't even here yet. I'm on his time. When he's sleepy, I lay down instantly. When he's hungry, I'm feeding my damn face. When he's ready to take a piss, I'm running my ass to the bathroom. Lucky squeezed my ass and I kicked him. I wasn't having any more kids. I meant that shit.

"It's time and you're crowning. Somebody is ready to meet his parents. I see just a little bit of hair." She smiled. Thank God. The doctors came in the room. Lucky raised up from the bed. He stood right in front of me. He was looking me in my eyes and I refused to even look at him. I hate that I love his ass.

"You're too beautiful to have a frown on your face. Smile for me please. I got you, I'm not going anywhere." He stated. He cupped my face making me look at him. I couldn't help but smile. I was still mad at his ass. "That's what I was looking for. I'm ready to meet my son Mrs. Williams."

"Not more than me." Lucky kissed me on my lips and grabbed my free hand.

"Mrs. Williams on six give me a push 1, 2, 3, 4, 5, 6 one more push on six. 1, 2, 3, 4, 5, 6."

"It hurts. Can you pull his ass out please?" I hollered.

"Come on; he's almost out. One more push Kaniya. Mr. Williams do you want to come down here?"

"Hell no, I need his fuckin' hand! He's not going anywhere!" I screamed.

"I have to stay by Mrs. Williams side. One more push baby and it'll all be over." I pushed one more time long and hard. Jeremiah still didn't come out. I swear to God I'm spanking his little ass.

"He has a set of lungs on him. Mr. Williams, you can come and cut the umbilical cord." Jeremiah Lee Williams finally made his grand entrance in the world 12/12/17 weighing 9 pounds and 2 ounces. He looks just like his father. He's the prettiest shade of a warm cocoa brown that I ever saw. His hair was fine and thin, no curls.

He had my dark brown eyes and my lips. He was so handsome I couldn't stop looking at him. The nurses cleaned me up. I had to have a stitch or two. Lucky couldn't stop looking at him. I want my son. I can't wait until Jamia and Jamel meet him. I should be happy I just gave birth to my son. I couldn't even enjoy it because I know this lying motherfucka is up to something.

Chapter-8

Kaniya

"**M**rs. Williams, I hate to bother you, because it's your first day back and you're extremely busy. Normally we have things under control, but we received a few packages from Foot Work. I know the routines are to drop the packages off and keep it moving. I think the owner has hired some new help and she's not familiar with our procedure. What do you want us to do with the packages?" My employee Kansas asked. What the fuck does she mean what do I want her to do with them? I need you to do what you've been doing.

She dropped all the boxes on my floor making a fuckin' mess. I looked up from my desk, at the mess. Kansas was looking confused and waiting for an answer. I already had an attitude, because my office manager hasn't been doing her fuckin' job. What the fuck am I paying her for? Take that shit to Dro's, duh were the fuck it belongs. Dropping off his stuff should never be a problem. It's a courtesy that I'm allowing his stuff to even come here.

"Today is Thursday, and he should be open." I argued and sassed. I wasn't even in the mood to deal with this shit, but if it needed to be addressed I would do so. Despite this is being my first day back. I wanted to look at the sales reports and the new contracts I received from the City of Atlanta. I'm trying to get back in the swing of things. I shouldn't even have to address this.

"We tried to take the packages there and some female told us to come back when he gets there. She wouldn't let us drop them off." My employee Mya argued. I flared my nostrils up and cocked my neck to the side.

"Run that shit back Mya." I'm not believing this at all.

"She said we couldn't leave the stuff." I searched Mya's face for a lie and didn't find one. My employees have shit to do. I don't pay them extra to handle Dro's stuff.

"Follow me." I had to make sure I was hearing her correctly. Dro gets his stuff shipped here all the time. I need to nip it in the bud because Lucky doesn't want me housing shit here for any man that's not him. I can't do shit but respect that. It was the beginning of the winter, and I just had Jeremiah six weeks ago. I really shouldn't even be out.

Lucky didn't want me working. He wanted me to stay at home and be a housewife and work from home. I grabbed my pea coat and slid my feet into my heels and placed my gun behind my back. I don't know who this bitch was that worked at Dro's, but these packages had to get out of Work Now Atlanta. I marched down to his suite and opened the door.

It was a dark skin chick. Her skin was so beautiful that shit glistened. She grilled me, and I smiled at the bitch. I haven't met a bitch yet who I was threatened by. I walked back to Dro's office and he was sitting there eating. I dropped the boxes on his desk. Mya and Kansas had the remaining boxes and dropped them also. The pretty girl, she was right on my heels too.

"Nice to see you too Kaniya." He snarled and gritted his teeth. Dro had an attitude and I don't give a fuck because I have one too. He wasn't happy to see me, and I wasn't happy to see him either. I cleared my throat and he trained his eyes on me.

"Dro, these packages can't come to my office anymore. Please check your help and let her know, how this shit goes." I argued. I didn't mean to be rude, but he needed to understand where I was coming from. We had an arrangement and we've never bump heads regarding this.

"Dro you better check this bitch and let her know what it is. I'm not the help." She argued. I swear to God this must be prank Kaniya day or something. I can't bite my tongue for nothing and I'm not. He should've told her about me.

"Excuse me, what the fuck did you just say to me?" I asked. I needed her to repeat herself, so she can get this work. Dro was looking at me out the corners of his eyes. He knows I love confrontation and shit was about to go left.

"You heard what the fuck I just said!" She argued and yelled. My face turned candy apple red. I flared my nose up. I had a blade in my jaw. I could slice this hoe the fuck up or I could empty a clip in her. The choice was hers if she kept talking.

"Look Kaniya, don't come up in here with that bullshit. She ain't the help." He argued. Dro knew me better than I knew myself once upon a time. I don't give a fuck who she is, you can't talk to me any kind of way. Oh, so Dro is trying to show off and impress a bitch. Dro ain't even my nigga and this bitch ain't my bitch. See the devil was on my back. I wasn't even about argue with Dro. I'll address his bitch first, then him. I don't know who this hoe thought I was, but I'm one bitch that she needs to respect. I turned around and Mya and Kansas were right on my heels. I stopped at the door right by ole girl. I grabbed my gun from the nape of my back and I pointed it at her head first.

"You ain't my BITCH and you should never address me as one. I don't give a fuck if you're this niggas BITCH. Call me a BITCH again. You better ask DRO how real this shit gets when you're fuckin' with a BITCH like me. I don't mind bodying a BITCH right here and right now. I don't tolerate disrespect at all." I argued.

"Kaniya chill out. Back the fuck up." He argued. Dro walked up behind me and pushed me into the corner.

"Nah DRO, I want this BITCH right here to speak the fuck up. I stay at a hoes' neck about my respect. If she got an issue, I'd solve it. I'm waiting. Right now, I'm at this HOES' neck." I argued. I put my index finger on the trigger ready to lay a bitch down.

"Kaniya, put the gun down. It's not that serious," he argued. His nostrils were flared. I turned around and looked at Dro and grilled the fuck out of him. My gun was still pressed at the temple of ole girl's head.

"Nah Dro, it's serious for me because I didn't come down here on no fuck shit. My two employees brought your fuckin' shoes down here. Mya and Kansas IS this the bitch that said bring it back when Dro gets here?" I asked. Mya and Kansas had no clue about Dro and I, so I knew they wouldn't lie just to get me down here to show my ass.

"Yes." The two of them agreed.

"That's not the way shit goes. They drop your packages off and keep it moving. Since it's a fucking problem find someone preferably your BITCH to collect your shit when you're not open. Re-route that shit because Work Now Atlanta is no longer your drop off spot." I argued.

I slammed Dro's office door as hard as I could. I walked off and kept it moving. Fuck Dro and whoever this bitch was. I walked back to my suite. I needed a shot.

"Mrs. Williams, you're bad. That was dope as fuck." Mya gasped and smiled.

"I like to show my ass every now and then because I can. It's not a bitch walking that can see me. I put that on everything." I smiled and walked back to my office. Dro knows better to disrespect me and talk to me like he's fucking crazy. If Lucky knew I went down there and showed my ass, he would go off. I haven't seen Dro in almost a year since Lucky pulled up on us acting a fool.

"Mrs. Williams, you have company." She snickered. I knew exactly who it was. Mya walked in my office and warned me. I noticed her facial expressions. I'm not trying to go there with Dro.

"I'm not expecting anyone." I laughed. Dro busted in my office like he owned this motherfucker. I just looked at him and rolled my eyes. I had to cut the cameras off. I didn't need any problems with Lucky. My husband had this bitch wired, and Dro knew that, but he didn't give a fuck because I checked his bitch. He slammed my door and was all up in my face.

"Kaniya, you're wrong as fuck for doing that shit. You take shit too far. You didn't have to pull a gun out on my girl, press it on her head, and attempt to pull the trigger. I'm not giving you a fuckin' pass. Lucky needs to give you some act right. A lady should never act the way you do." He argued. How am I wrong, and she didn't won't to accept his shoes?

"Are you finished Dro? If so, you can raise the fuck up out of here. The door is that way. I approached you about your shoes and nothing else." I argued. I continued doing what I was doing before I was rudely interrupted.

"No, I'm not leaving. You're going to listen to me." He argued and threatened.

"I'm not, the only man I listen too, is my husband and you ain't him. Goodbye Dro."

"You showed your ass because I got somebody? You're mad that I'm cuffing a female that's not you? It's okay, we all miss a good thing sometimes. I'm glad Lucky finally married you. He should've done it years ago.

I finally found somebody that's for me and no strings attached, no baggage and this is how you do shit? Since I met you, I've always been a good nigga to you. Whatever you wanted, I gave it to you. I've never disrespected Lucky behind you when I wanted too. I kept that shit savage. I had plenty of opportunities to put that nigga to sleep, but I didn't.

You know why, because I didn't want to break your heart and see you cry because of some shit I did. I love Giselle, do you fucking hear me? I will never let anybody disrespect her, not even you. Yeah, I used to lust the fuck out you, but that shit doesn't matter anymore. You picked him and not me. I'm a real nigga and I'm going to correct you when you're wrong." He argued. Dro tried to make this shit about us and it has nothing to do with us.

"Dro or should I call you Roderick? You talk a good game. It's not about you and her. It's about your fuckin' shoes and where they belong. Congratulations on your relationship, I'm happy for you. You deserve it. I didn't mean to be disrespectful, but you know me. Not one time did you correct her and put her in her place. I'm doing you a favor. Since you got that off pressure off your chest, you can leave. Let me correct you, it's only two motherfuckas that'll put Lucky to sleep and that's ME and God." I argued.

Dro wanted to say something else. I put my hand up and pointed to the door. He's said enough. He switched up on me. I didn't even want to do this, but he begged me too. I didn't want any problems with Lucky. He swears I've fucked everybody.

Chapter-9

Lucky

My wife has tried me for the last fucking time. What the fuck am I supposed to do? I love Kaniya, I swear to God I do, but I will fucking hurt her, and she doesn't believe that shit. I don't ask for much but pussy on demand, respect, and loyalty. That's it. Our love is unconditional, and we have a bond that can't be broken. She takes advantage of that shit.

I know I'm not perfect and I've done some foul ass shit to her. A lot of people think that we shouldn't be together, and I don't deserve her. I don't give a fuck what they think. The things that we went through has brought us here today. I watch my wife's back like I watch my own. Any move that she makes I can account for it. Any conversation that she has, I'm listening.

I didn't want Kaniya working at all. We have three small children, Jamel, Jamia, and Jeremiah. I want a fourth one. My youngest son just turned six weeks old. Jamia and Jamel just turned one. Kaniya needs to be at home with them, period. Kaniya can run Work Now Atlanta from home. She acts like she couldn't stay in the house.

Today was her first day back and I left the house early this morning because I had some business to handle with my brother Quan. I came back home and checked the cameras because I didn't see her when she left. She looked nice. She was complaining about her weight because of Jeremiah. I told her she was fine because she was.

My wife brings out the best in me and the worst. I was sitting back in my office at home and the camera feed to Kaniya's office was killed. I had back up and brought it back up. I hit rewind to see what happened and why. Dro walks in and that's the first red flag. I know that's why she killed the camera. I heard the exchange between the two of them. Why would you cut the cameras if you guys don't have shit going on?

Am I mad at my wife, yes, the FUCK I am. It's not about because she killed the cameras. I trust Kaniya, I trust her with my life. I let Kaniya get away with a lot of shit. She had no business going into Dro's period. I told her months ago, to stop signing for shit for him. Did she listen, no.

I'm pissed because Dro handled my wife like he was me. I'm the only man that can handle my wife and check her about anything. Her father can't even do it. Dro was a funny ass nigga. Whoever this bitch was that he was fucking with, she had him feeling himself.

He said he could've put me to sleep. I rubbed my hands across my face, I know this nigga didn't say this shit. Every nigga that I've got at behind my wife, I left them still breathing for a reason. It's always a method to my madness. If they could get at me as I've got at them, then we can shoot it out fair and I'll still win. I'm bulletproof. It's cocky to say, but I AM.

If Dro had an issue with me, it was never addressed. I'll step on anybody's toes behind my wife. Dro was just something for Kaniya to do. She knew better than to cross that line with him. She only fucked with him to get under my skin and the shit worked too.

Kaniya, she'll learn the hard way. She takes my kindness for my weakness, but I'll show her as her husband to never go against my fucking word and what I say do. Watch how this shit unfolds. She's expecting me to come and show out, but I'm not.

I'll get at Dro. Never speak on and mention what you'll do to me, if you haven't done it. Don't ever disrespect my wife.

Kaniya

L ucky thinks he's slick. He should've been home by now. I called his phone at least ten times to see where he's at. He said enough earlier, and I didn't feel like arguing. The same way he tracks me, I can track him. I knew my husband better than I know myself. Any other time he would've pulled up when I cut the cameras off. I wasn't trying to be sneaky. I just know him. He's cocky and does the most. I can bet you any amount of money he's done something to Dro. I hope he didn't kill him. Dro was a good nigga and he didn't need to die behind me.

Giselle is really feeling him. He's a great guy, I just couldn't be with him. I hope Lucky hasn't done anything crazy. My father agreed to come over and watch the kids. I tracked Lucky's phone and it was at a spot not too far from his club. I called his phone again to see if he would answer and he didn't. Since when did he think it was okay to stop answering the phone for me? My doorbell rang. I checked the cameras and it was my father.

"Kaniya, where are you going this time of night and where's Lucky?" My father asked.

"Daddy I'm going to go find Lucky." I sighed. My dad and I have come a long way from a few months ago. I really didn't feel like arguing with my father about what I was about to do and why.

"Where the fuck is he?" He asked. I wish I knew, but I don't. He should've been home. Tianna said he left her house early. Lucky has never pulled a stunt like this. He must be cheating. I assume since I killed the cameras it gives him an excuse to cheat.

"Doing something he has no business doing." I sighed. Lucky and I have come a long way, but I know my husband and he's being spiteful. I'm sick of it.

"Look Kaniya, I'm not babysitting for you to go out and kill somebody behind him. Keep your ass at home with my grandchildren. He'll be home, trust me." My dad argued. He was right, but I just don't have patience.

"Ok daddy." My daddy kissed me on my forehead and left right out the door. He knew I was up to some good bullshit.

Lucky

Kaniya has been blowing up my phone up. I never ignore her because she has my kids. I know she's tracked my phone and probably thinks that I'm out doing some dog ass shit, but I'm not. She's it for me, I swear to God she is. A nigga is in his feelings. I'm an aggressive ass nigga and that shit turns her on. I'm not trying to turn her on.

I'm battling with myself on how to check my wife and put her in her fuckin' place. I've let her slide one time too many. First it was Tariq and now it's Dro. The thing about Kaniya is, if we get into an argument she doesn't give a fuck. She'll tell me that I can leave, or I can go at any time and she ain't going to miss me. If I leave her, trust me, she'll miss me when I'm gone.

We're married how in the fuck are you not going to miss your husband? I swear I don't want to hurt her, but sometimes you'll hurt a person to teach them. What more can I do? I'll never put my hands on her. She doesn't listen, and I hate when she doesn't listen.

I'll leave her just to teach her. I owned up to all my shit before I started cheating on Kaniya. She wasn't like this at all. It's my fault I woke up a beast that can't be put to sleep. Me leaving her could make us, it ain't no breaking us.

––––––

It was a little after 1:00 a.m. I checked the cameras before I came home and Kaniya was asleep. My dinner was on the counter, waiting for me. She made my favorite. If I stopped and ate my food. I'll end up staying and I wouldn't leave. I made my way upstairs and finally made my way to our room.

"You finally decided to come home?" She argued. I knew she wasn't asleep. She jumped out the bed and was instantly in my face.

"Look Kaniya take your ass to bed. I'm not trying to argue with you. Don't wake my fuckin' kids up." I argued. I just want to pack my bags and leave. I'm not trying to make a scene.

"Lucky I don't give a fuck about none of that shit you're spitting. I MARRIED YOU. I GOT PAPERS ON YOU. Answer me, where have you been?" She argued. Kaniya threw the marriage certificate in my face. I wasn't about to answer her.

I grabbed my duffel bag from our closet and started packing my stuff. She smacked the back of my head and I grabbed both of her hands.

"Kaniya, keep your hands to yourself. I need a break from you, so I'm leaving." I argued. "I'm not trying to fight with you at all. I want to make this easy as possible."

"Oh, you're leaving me. Whoever she is, make sure she's worth it. Let me help you pack your shit. Leave an address so I can have you served. It's a wrap." She argued. Kaniya started grabbing my stuff and yanking it out of the closet. I stood back and just looked at her. "This right here, is what the fuck I'm talking about." She doesn't give a fuck. I stopped packing my shit to address her. I turned around and I was all up in her face. I grabbed her face roughly, so she can understand me. I wanted her to feel the heat dripping from me. She needs to feel my heartbeat.

"It's not about a BITCH. You're the only BITCH that I want. I need some space from you because you don't give a fuck about me and my feelings. I will hurt you physically. You don't listen to shit I have to say. You think I'm a fucking a joke." I argued.

"Lucky, you." I cut her off.

"Stop fucking talking to me please and take your ass to fuckin' bed. I'll be by to see my kids and maybe you tomorrow." I argued. It wasn't even supposed to be like this. I shouldn't have come home.

"Jamel Williams, you're really leaving our kids and me? As big as this house is, you can't go to another room?" She asked and cried. I'm not even about to answer her. I swear I didn't even think Kaniya had tear ducts. Not one time did she say she was sorry. Her tears moved me, but not enough for me to stop what I was trying to do. "I'm not leaving my kids. I'm leaving you." I grabbed a few more things. All I wanted her to do was apologize, but she had too much heart and pride to do that. I grabbed my plate and walked back to my truck. I pulled out of our garage and went to my condo in the city. I looked up at our room window, the curtains were pulled back, and Kaniya was standing in the window looking at me. I know she's hurting but it hurts me to leave her.

Kaniya

Lucky left me okay. I wiped the tears from my eyes with the back of my hand. I'm not even mad that he's gone. I pleaded, no, I begged him not leave. He's walked out on me not once but twice. It will not be a third fucking time. He wanted to be in his feelings today and express himself. Keep being in your feelings because when I'm in mine, it'll be an issue for you and not me. If he wanted to separate that's fine with me, but I'm divorcing him. He walked out on our kids and me. It's all good though. I watched him pull away and leave. I was tired but I'm packing up everything he owns and sending it to his mother's house. I didn't even do anything wrong.

He thinks that I don't know he still had his Condo in the city. He wanted to be a hoe; he can be one. I'm done, and he'll see real soon how done I am. I don't want anything to do with him. I needed to vent. Let me call Killany to see if she's awake. I'm sure the boys have her ass up.

"What Kaniya?" She sighed. I swear sometimes I can't stand Killany ass. How is she my twin again? If I'm calling you at 1:00 a.m., It's problem.

"Killany, what you are doing?" I asked.

"BREASTFEEDING." She sassed. She sounded so fuckin dry. I should just hang up in her face. I can't deal with Killany right now. It's a new day and I'm going to start treating people how they treat me.

"Oh." I sighed.

"What's wrong Kaniya?" She asked. Did she really care because it doesn't sound like she does at all? I wish I didn't have a heart sometimes. I care too much about people. Way more than they'll ever care about me. Sometimes I just sit back and watch how people move.

"Lucky left me." I thought those words would never slip from my mouth but that's my reality.

"He what?" She asked. Killany couldn't believe it but it's the truth. We were done. Lucky couldn't leave me without an explanation.

"You heard me. I'm good though." It hurts but I'm good.

"What did you do?" She asked. I didn't do anything.

"Why do you think that I did something? I'm me Killany, that's all I can be. I told you what happened earlier, Giselle and I squashed that shit. I tell you everything. You're my personal diary, even though you tell my business to everyone. I still confide in you. You know what I shouldn't have called you because you are always judging a me. I'm tired of it Killany. It's sad I can't even call the one person I shared the same womb with to comfort me. You never RIDE for me, the way I RIDE for you. Good night thanks for answering." I cried. I didn't even realize I started crying. I couldn't hold it in anymore. I'm tired. Killany ain't never here for me how she should be but whenever she calls me, I'm always there. It doesn't matter what it is, I'm coming if she calls.

"Stop crying Kaniya, this is not what the fuck we're about to do. If it ain't your way, it ain't no way. You can't guilt trip me. Don't you ever let it come out your mouth that I don't RIDE for you, how you RIDE for me. I ain't never judged you Kaniya. I'm not gone pacify you, as our mother does. I'm not gone lie to you. Kaniya the months I spent in the FEDS woke a me up. I stay woke. Let me keep it real with you. Lucky didn't leave you just because, he ain't gone never leave you. You did something, what the fuck did you do? Can you please change your ways Kaniya? Fight for your marriage the same way that nigga fights and wreak havoc behind you.

I'm surprised he didn't leave you months ago. You were nursing Tariq back to health behind his back like, your husband didn't know. You are accepting packages at your shop for Dro like your husband didn't know. If he did what you did, how would you feel? Do you see what the fuck you caused?" She cried and argued.

"How do you know all of this?" I asked. I was curious. Lucky always threw out hints but he never spoke on it.

"My husband of course." She argued.

"Lucky talks to Yung like that?" I asked.

"Everyday."

"Look Killany, Lucky is in his feelings about a lot of shit. If he didn't do what he did to Tariq, that situation would've never happened. He should've taken the high road and left it alone. My sister and I don't even speak because of that shit. I miss Raven so fucking much, and I want to see my niece, but I got too much pride, to even reach out. Dro, was there for me when Lucky wasn't, he was with me at doctor's appointments, and I was pregnant with Lucky's kids. If I ever need Dro, he'll be there, not that I need him too. Some relationships can't be severed, so me accepting packages for him is minor. He would never cross that line with me again. I trust Lucky, but he doesn't trust me.

Yirah lives with Lucky's momma, and he always over there. Do you see me tripping? No, and trust me that bitch is trying to throw pussy at him every chance she gets. Has he fucked her, who knows. I refuse to stress myself out wondering if he's still fuckin' her. Am I not supposed to have any feelings about that shit? His mammy will keep Jamal but won't even acknowledge my three or anything, but he's in his feelings.

When I said I do, I was done with the games. I have three kids and he ain't one of them. If he left, let the nigga leave. I'm not running up behind him. Eight years is a long time to be with someone. Maybe it's time for us to go our separate ways. Trust me, I'm okay with that. We can co-parent." I argued and cried. I'm tired and some shit ain't meant to be. After everything he has ever done to me, I always forgave him and moved on.

"Kaniya are you up to something? You sound really sincere and chill about the shit."

"I'm not Killany, I've been with Lucky for a very long time. I just want to be by myself and with my three. I need to get back to the old Kaniya. Lucky took that from me two years ago; he woke up a beast that can't be put to sleep. I need to find me again. I just want to be alone."

"I got your back no matter what. Take some time for yourself."

"I am, I love you, but I got to go because Jeremiah just woke up." For the first time in a long time, I was tired. I love Lucky, but I love myself more. I'm glad that he's gone. I'm tired of the arguing and the small fights and the shit that he accuses me of.

If I walked out on him I wouldn't have made it to the hallway. He would've shown his ass, and probably beat mine, believe or not. I'm not on no get back shit. Any other time I would be glad to show my ass and bag another nigga just to show him. I don't have to do all of that. He knows what it is. He's free to do him. It's over...

Chapter-10

Killany

Leave it to Kaniya to bring me out of hiding. I'm secretive and a very low-key person. I'm only in Atlanta for a few days. Yung's cousin is getting married this weekend. It just so happens the weddings in Atlanta. I get to spend some time with my family and both of my sister's. Kaniya has asked about Raven a few times. Raven hasn't mentioned Kaniya at all. Life is too short to be living without each other and the two of them are in the same city. I invited Raven over to Kaniya's house, so we can sit and chill. Armony was with us. Kaniya cooked hot wings and Chipotle Rotel dip. Armony made the drinks. We were going to kick back and chill. The boys were asleep and Jeremiah's spoiled ass too. Kacia was lying on Armony's lap about to fall asleep. Jamia was lying up under me, snatching my earrings out my ear. I popped her little ass too. Jamel was playing with Kaniya phone.

Kaniya's doorbell rang. I opened the door and it was Raven and her daughter. Caria was so pretty she looked like her mother and father. I didn't tell Raven this was Kaniya's house. Kaniya walked down the stairs and asked, "Who was that at my door Killany?"

"It's Raven," I yelled. Raven looked at me and grabbed her purse and headed for the door. Kaniya was coming down the stairs. I stopped Raven right in her tracks. I'm sick of the two of them.

"Raven don't do that. She's your sister. I'm sick of it. Y'all are better than that." I argued.

"We are better than that Killany. I ain't never did shit to Raven, but love her like a sister should, but if she doesn't want to be in the room with me or us. I'm okay with it because I've said I'm sorry a million times. I've righted all my wrongs with Tariq." Raven turned around to face Kaniya. She handed me Caria."

"How can you even say that Kaniya? If you loved me, you would've never put my brother in the position to die. You were willing to hurt me for your happiness. You know how much I love him. You know he's all I have. You're not even with Lucky anymore," she cried.

"How can you continue to hold that against me Raven? HOW? He's alive. I lost everything I had nursing him back to health? How do you think I felt, when I realized it was Tariq that I shot? I was fucked up too. I care about him and I always will. I risked my family to make sure he was straight," she argued and cried. "But you don't won't to acknowledge, that I'm not talking about Lucky. I'm talking about you. I don't even know my niece because you let this little petty shit come between us." Lord Kaniya and Raven were going through it.

"You're not the only one that lost something Kaniya. I lost Cartier behind this. My child doesn't even know her father because of this. He left me because he didn't agree on how I felt about you and Tariq. I'm raising my daughter by myself," she cried. "I just want things to go back how they were. I miss my sister," she cried. I'm glad they both missed each other, because I was tired of being in the middle. Kaniya and Raven hugged each other for what seemed liked eternity.

They really needed each other, because they both missed each other. Raven ended up staying the night with us. It was like old times, just with children. Raven was lying up under Kaniya, like the baby she was. Kaniya always babied her, that'll never change. Caria was pretty, Jamia and Kaycee had somebody to play with.

Ms. Angel would kill Raven if she knew she had a granddaughter out here that she knew nothing about. We caught up with each other. I wanted Raven to tell Cartier about his daughter, especially since he's in town this weekend. Armony and I both agreed, he needed to know and I'm sure a daughter would slow him down. I didn't want any parts of it, Yung had the impression that I didn't talk to Raven, and I wanted to keep it that way. The last thing I need is my husband tripping on me about Raven, and a niece I knew nothing about.

Raven

It felt so good to be back in the good graces of my sister. Going forward I would never get in my siblings' business. Tariq was cool and Killany was too, but Kaniya was here. We've always been close. I needed her for other things, she's always had a mother's touch. I was missing that because I was so stubborn. It was taking a toll on me. Kaniya and Killany convinced me to tell Cartier about Caria. It's been hard on this journey without Cartier in my daughter's life. She's looking more like him every other day. He was my first everything and he just abandoned me. Our babies were sleep and we were sitting around in the family room tipsy. Everybody was texting their husband or boo. Kaniya looked up at me and smiled. We shared a laugh.

"Do it Raven, I know you want too. We're here for your support." They cheered me on. I was skeptical because. I would never forget how he talked to me when he walked out on us. He was my first and I gave him my virginity. I feel like he played me, just to get that from me. I dialed his number, it rang a few times. He finally answered. "Hello," he yelled and slurred.

"Cartier, can you talk?" I asked. He must have been in the club or something because his back ground was loud.

"Who is this?" He slurred.

"RAVEN, what's up, what you want?" He argued and slurred. Cartier was tipsy I knew this shit would end well tonight.

"I need to speak with you about something. Can we talk in person?"

"No, but you can say it over the phone. I got some shit going."

"What about tomorrow?"

"I'm not trying to see you Raven, you could be trying to set a nigga up." Fuck him. I hung up in his face. I wish I never fell for his ass. I sent him a nice long text with a picture of our daughter.

Raven - I can't believe I fell you for you. I wish I would've never given you a piece of me. Everything I thought you weren't, you proved to me that you were. I've been keeping this a secret for a year. I'm tired of holding it in. You deserve to know. I didn't reach out to you, to set you up. I reached out to you because I

wanted you to meet our daughter Caria Rie're Miller. I attached a picture of her. You couldn't deny her if he wanted too.

Cartier read my text message, he instantly started calling my phone and blowing me up. I answered, "I don't want to talk now, I said what I had to say." I hung up in his face, he called right back.

"Where the fuck is you at with my daughter," he asked and argued?

"Does it matter Cartier?"

"Bitch you better tell me where the fuck you and my daughter are laying y'all heads right now. I'm own my fuckin' way," he argued. I looked at the phone because I know he wasn't talking to me.

"BITCH? Get your pussy ass off my phone lil boy, learn how to talk me." I argued and hung up the phone in his face.

"Oh lord Raven, they're on the way Yung just called me and they're pulling up in about twenty minutes. I think you need to run for it," Killany laughed.

"No fuck that Killany, let Cartier pull up. I owe his ass one anyway, when he showed his ass the last time. It won't be any more of that." Kaniya argued. See this is what I missed? Shit is about to get real and I needed my support system. I knew things were about to change the moment he pulled up. At least Caria gets to meet her father for the first time. Oh my God they pulled up fast too. Somebody was banging on Kaniya's door and she jumped up from the couch. She grabbed the AK from underneath the couch. She swung the door open pointing the gun in their faces. It was Cartier, Yung, and KC. Kaniya grilled all three of them.

"Move Kaniya, this ain't got shit to do with you," he argued. He was searching the room for me, our eyes locked with each other. He gave me a menacing stare. He was trying to intimidate me.

"It doesn't but you're at my house, banging on my door like you're the God damn police. Don't come at my sister crazy I'm telling you now, because these two niggas will be carrying your ass out of here. Try me if you want too." She argued. Kaniya allowed Cartier entrance to her home. He approached me. I was playing with my phone to avoid looking at him. He snatched my phone out of my hand. I grilled him.

"Where is she Raven? I want to see her," he asked. I stood to my feet and led Cartier to the guest room, so he could see her. Caria was asleep. As soon as we got in the room Cartier slammed the door and backed me in the corner. I pushed his ass off me. He stood in my personal space. Cartier and I couldn't be in the same room with each other. I can't believe I was in love with him. "Get your hands off me."

"Lower your fuckin' voice before you wake my daughter up. You got life fucked up, keeping my daughter from me Raven. I've killed bitches for less. My own flesh and blood? You know how bad I wanted a child? I got one out her that I knew nothing about? You could've told me that shit Raven. I would've been there for you and her, no matter what we were going through. I got some issues with you. A year later, you denied me the chance to be there? You're foul as fuck," he argued.

"It's my fault Cartier? Don't put that on me, you met your daughter. We can work out some arrangements, so you can get to know her. I'm not about to sit up here and argue about what I did, because it takes two. Me and you." I argued. "Get the fuck out of here."

"I'll keep her for a year and we'll see you next year." He argued. Cartier woke Caria up and she was smiling at us. He picked her up and walked out of the room. He headed to the door and Yung and KC was right behind him.

"Bring my daughter back, I was running out the house behind him. He jumped in a black Escalade truck. I opened the door and Yung pushed me inside the truck and the driver pulled off.

"I'm going to fuckin' hurt you Raven."

Chapter-11

Kaniya

My life has been crazy these past few weeks. Lucky leaving is a sore subject for me. I feel like I fucked up. I'm trying to keep it together for the sake of my children. The three of them are the only things that are important to me. It's all good though, you live, and you learn. I'm learning to live my life without him. I took my ring off my finger weeks ago and placed it in my jewelry box as soon as he left. Next step getting these Lucky charms removed off my stomach. I decided to get a few renovations for Work Now Atlanta.

Every camera and piece of recording equipment had to go. Lucky would never have that type of access to me again. Dro referred me to Mulsane Construction, they renovated his shop and it looks good. The contractor was supposed to be here over an hour ago. I'm leaving to pick up my kids from my grandmother. She's called me a million times already. I answered on the first ring."

"Hello, Kaitlyn I'm on my way traffic is bad and it's raining.

"Kaniya, bitch, you got an hour and thirty minutes to get here. Please pick these bad ass kids up or else I'm putting their asses outside on my porch. I know Jamia's bad ass hid my high blood pressure pills. I need an extra 100.00 since you're late, it's your late fees." She argued. She slammed the phone down in my face.

I told her I would send Yashir over there to pick them up. She didn't want to hear that shit. I'll meet this contractor another day. I cut the lights off in my office. It was 5:45 p.m., I had to leave. It was pouring with rain outside. I heard the door open. I forgot to flip the sign to closed. "Excuse me I'm closed." I yelled.

"I'm the contractor." He yelled. He would come when I'm about to leave. I really had to get my kids before I end up killing her ass. I walked up front to meet the contractor. Damn he was fine.

"I'm sorry I'm late. I'm the owner. One of my employees had an accident, so I'm here to assist you. I won't take up too much of your time. If you can give me a walk-through of your office and tell me everything you want. I'll sketch it and send you the layout tomorrow." He explained.

"Okay." I sassed. I had an attitude and I was ready to go. We need to get this over with quick.

"I didn't get your name."

"Kaniya Miller."

"It's nice to meet you Ms. Miller. I'm Khalid Mulsane." He stated. He had a deep voice, but he spoke with so much confidence. He demanded attention. I gave Mr. Mulsane a brief tour of my office and everything I wanted done. I knocked down the wall myself. I yanked all the wires and cameras out of the walls.

"Ms. Miller, what happened to the wall," he asked.

"I started knocking it down myself." I chucked.

"Okay," he chuckled. Mr. Mulsane finished taking his notes. I hit the lights off in my office. I grabbed my briefcase and umbrella. I waited on him up front, so I could lock up and leave. Mr. Mulsane waited by the door for me. I already had an attitude he could leave with his late ass.

"Ms. Miller, can I walk you to your car just to make sure you get in safe?" he asked.

"I'm okay. I got it. Nobody out here will bother me. Thank you." Mr. Mulsane grabbed my hand. He took my briefcase and raised my umbrella over our heads. Let me find out he was using me for my umbrella. I looked at him and he looked at me.

"I asked you nicely the first time, but I'm walking you to your car regardless of what came out your mouth. Lead the way," he stated.

"If you say so. I'm parked in the Black BMW X5." I sassed and sucked my teeth. I hit the push to start button. No words were spoken between us. We finally made it to my car.

"Where do you want this bag Ms. Miller?"

"In the back."

"Triplets," he asked.

"No, one set of twins and a new born!"

"Married?"

"Separated, filed for a divorce."

"Alright Ms. Miller I'll see you soon."

"Alright Mr. Mulsane I'll see you around." Damn he was fine and very manly. He was all up in my business.

Why though? I'm good on men any way. Let me get him out of my thoughts. I had to share this experience with Killany. He left a good impression on me. She answered on the first ring.

"Kaniya, I hope you're on your way to your grandmother's house. Girl she's called you everything but a child of God," she laughed. Tell me something I don't know. I think she likes hearing herself talk. Soon as I pick them up she'll tell me they can spend the night.

"I'm own my way. I told her Yashir will pick them up. She totally ignored that shit. I met someone." I smiled.

"You met someone? I thought you were good on men for a while?"

"We didn't exchange numbers, we just crossed paths Killany. Remember I told you earlier about the contractors. I was waiting all day and as soon as I was about to close the owner shows up. BITCH he was fine as hell. He was aggressive with his words, very manly, and grown. He could've baptized me."

"Damn Kaniya, how did he look? Why didn't you get his number? You may never see him again."

"Well first. I would never come off as thirsty. He walked me to my car. He inquired about my children and asked was I married. He was the prettiest shade of brown I ever seen. He was cut nice. He works out. His hair was pulled up in a man bun.

I wouldn't mind running my hands through his hair. His hair was nice. He had dark brown eyes. He had small lips they fitted his face to perfection. His nose was small too. His irises and brows gave him a real intriguing look. He was HANDSOME.

Khalid

Time was on my side today. Damn I'm glad Mase got into an accident. Thank God he's straight. I probably would've never ran into her. She had an attitude and I liked it. I could tell she was mean as hell, but I could tear those walls down. I wanted to ask could I call her, but I didn't want to come off as thirsty. It's been years since I've opened a door for a woman, let along walking her to her car. Maybe it was because, she wasn't interested in me or didn't pay me any attention. I haven't found anybody that was worthy of doing it.

Dro and Alonzo didn't tell me Kaniya Miller, was packing like that. Three kids and divorced. I got to get up with Dro and Alonzo in a few minutes. I got to drop off this work to Alonzo. They're supposed to meet at the storage. I wanted Kaniya's story and to know who was her husband? Damn you're divorcing that? She wasn't trifling, she owns her own business, she's knows how to speak properly. He cheated.

I pulled up to the storage unit. Dro and Alonzo was sitting in the car blowing some of the loud super lemon haze. I dropped off yesterday. I could tell they were super dumb high. I had to slam the door shut. If the police would've pulled down, they were done. More of the reason I'll have to get back home. I hate the states. Four of my workers started unloading the ambulance with the work inside. Dro, Alonzo and I made it inside and started lining everything up.

"Let me ask y'all something? Dro the chick whose shop that's next to yours, she wants us to renovate her suite. What's up with her, who was she married too?"

"Damn Khalid, slow down. It's Kaniya, she's cool. She's my lil buddy. She's not divorced yet, separated. That nigga a clown, he ain't gone divorce her though. She a real one, he stupid as hell. You'll have to kill him. He grimy as fuck. You wouldn't know him."

"Why are they getting a divorce? She said she had a new born, he left her with a new born?"

"Man, it's a lot of shit, if you want to get to know her; ask her. You my nigga Khalid, I used to fuck with her. We didn't get serious, but we kicked it."

"Damn Dro, you've fucked already? I'm not fuckin behind you, nigga."

"I didn't fuck but I did taste that pretty motherfucka a few times." He chuckled. I didn't find shit funny.

"Aye I need you to forget all about that. Ain't you about to marry Giselle. Let me have my momma ship you something to erase your memory." I was dead ass serious.

"Chill out Khalid, I'm higher than a Giraffes pussy. I don't think about Kaniya like that. We just happened. We met at the wrong time. If I wanted her, I wouldn't have said shit. I met my soul mate. I can't wait to marry Giselle."

"Good, coming from a wild ass nigga like you. I might see what's up with your lil buddy."

"You do that, she's a real one and she's loyal." Dro spoke highly of Kaniya. I could fuck with her despite what little dealings she had with him. I got to make some moves, I'll get up with them niggas tomorrow before I go back home. I want to call her before it gets too late. I don't want to wake her kids. I respect mother hood. I dialed her number and hit the Bluetooth in my car. I can't believe I'm doing this. I'm trying to get to know Kaniya. I got to find out who her husband was. Dro told me enough. She answered on the fourth ring.

"Hello, who is this?" she answered. She sounded exactly like she looked. That's rare.

"Khalid."

"Hey Khalid, what's up, how can I help you?"

"Kaniya is what's up. You can help me in a lot of ways."

"Is that right, that's what's up. Well it's after business hours, so is it personal or business?"

"It's personal."

"Okay, how can I help you Khalid on a personal level? I want to say something else, but I'm not."

"I want you to speak up, never bite your tongue, ask me."

"Do you contact all of your business associates after hours? Let me stop you right now. I'm not that type of woman." She argued. Damn she snapped on me. I would've never known that soft voice was mouthy and reckless.

"Nah I don't do that. If I start you'll, be the first. I don't even live in the states. I'm trying to get to know you. Can I get to know you?"

"Why do you want to get to know me Khalid? I'm mean and rude as fuck. I break all the rules. My mouth is deadly, it'll run you away. You don't want to get to know me anyway." She stated. I knew she was bluffing, she looks too soft and delicate.

"You heard what I said lil baby, I do want to get to know you. It's something about you. I'm digging you. I like that shit that you said about yourself. Tell me some more. How did you get a divorce? I always acknowledge Queens when I see them, you're beautiful as hell. You're a Boss. You own your own business and you're holding down for your little ones.

I salute that. Who would want to divorce that? I want to know about that. It doesn't add up with what I see?"

"Thank you, Khalid. You're on the outside looking in. You don't know me, so you really can't judge me. You may have an opinion, or we can agree to disagree. Having a heart is a gift and a curse for me. It's always loyalty over royalty. Money will always come to me because I'm going to grind regardless. Blood don't even make you kin, they'll cross you in the end.

You can love a person so much, you'll end up losing yourself because you're not loving yourself. To love someone, you got to love yourself. I know how my hearts works. If I'm nothing I'm loyal, and people play on that. If I fuck with you, I fuck with you period. Let me ask you this Khalid. If you've known someone for a short period of time, and they've always been there for you since the day you met them, no matter what. If they needed you, would you be there for them? Wouldn't you be there for them if they're always there for you?" she asked.

"Yeah."

"Okay, if you were hired as an assassin on a job and you didn't know the mark until after the job was done. If you knew the person after the fact. Y'all had a past and was cool minus a few hiccups, but they were always there for you too. Would you nurse them back to health?"

"I don't agree with that. One hiccup is too many, you're in that position for a reason. But you shouldn't be that loyal at all. Why would you give a person a pass on fucking over you? Would they keep doing it because you allowed it?" I argued. Kaniya and I stayed on the phone for hours. "Ms. Miller it's getting late. I'm going to let you get off this phone. Tomorrow is my last night in the states. Can I take you out or treat you to dinner? I'm trying to get to know you lil baby."

"Sure, that can be arranged. Send me an email or text with the location and I'll meet you there."

"Okay I'll see you tomorrow, Good Night." We were on the phone for a few hours getting to know each other. It felt like some high school shit too. Her husband wasn't an issue. He had some shit with him. Why would she need to assist you on killing and nigga? If he makes himself an issue than I'll be his kids' father.

Kaniya

Ali and I stayed on the phone until 3:00 a.m. I can't believe he called me. I was surprised and excited. I was scared to answer at first because it wasn't a Georgia area code and I don't answer numbers that I don't know. We have a date later and I couldn't stop thinking about his fine ass. His voice was mesmerizing. It was deep and a little raspy, but I liked it. You could tell he was from the islands by the way he said certain words. I had to call Killany and tell her about my little encounter. She answered on the third ring. She knew she wasn't doing shit, petty ass.

"Hello, Kaniya are you on your way to work?"

"No, I'm working from home today. It's too cold to take them out. I slept longer than I would like too. I'm about to start working in a minute. Girl guess who called me last night?" I smiled through the phone. I was blushing behind Khalid Mulsane.

"Who called you last night, Lucky?"

"No BITCH. Khalid Mulsane. The man I was telling you about, that I met yesterday."

"I thought you said that you didn't get his phone number Kaniya? Bitch you be lying. Don't you think it's a little too early for you to start dating again since your divorce isn't finalized. You're still married LEGALLY. You and I both know Lucky isn't going out like that. Nor is he going to grant you a divorce."

"Fuck Lucky, he's the last person I'm thinking about. Fuck you too with your cheerleading ass. I didn't give him my phone number. He called me last night and we stayed on the phone until 3:00 a.m. getting to know each other. He said he wants to get to know me. It was a neutral conversation. Killany he's a grown ass man. Something Lucky knows nothing about. The conversation was different. We were filling each other out. He stimulated my mind. He put a lot of things in perspective for me. I stimulated his as well."

"Damn Kaniya, this man got you talking different. I forgot you knew how to use big words. My little hood rat is expanding her vocabulary. What did y'all talk about?"

"Everything! Me, my divorce and my children. He asked me out on a date tonight? He's not from here, he's from the islands."

"Alright hot ass, he isn't any kin to the BumBiyae is he? Are you going on the date? How did he get your number? It's a little creepy and mysterious. I hope he's the one, you deserve nothing but the best."

"I'm not looking for the one Killany. I'm cool by myself. It was just casual conversation. I can't think of the last time I was single with no strings attached. It's been years."

"I know but you deserve to be happy. Third times a charm." Killany and I finished chopping it up. I had a ton of work to do. Khalid sent me a Good Morning text, with the address to the location. I guess I could get cute tonight. Khalid Mulsane, this man is too fine to be single. I can respect that and he's a few years older than me.

——

It was a little after 6:00 p.m. Our date was scheduled until 7:00 p.m. and traffic was heavy in the area. I had to pay Kaitlyn again to watch my kids, her great grandchildren? What happen to the real grandmothers? Kaisha is always on the go. FUCK Cynthia she couldn't keep a picture of my kids. Kaitlyn charges more than a fuckin' daycare. My dad would get them, but all our conversation is about my mother. I had to pay Kaitlyn a

$300.00 to babysit while I go on a date. I swear she was wrong as hell for that. She knew I was paying.

It took me over an hour to get dressed. I found a cute little Smoke Grey dress. It had the warmest material, sweater shirt fabric. It was fitted too. I had the same color Uggs to match. It was cold outside too. My face was free of makeup. The cold air gave me a nice red cheek beat. I applied a little mascara to give my lashes length. My lips were nude with a hint of gloss. My hair was flat ironed bone straight. I can't think of the last time I've been on a date. It's been awhile. I typed the address in my GPS. It was a spot in Sandy Springs. It wasn't too far me about thirty or forty minutes depending on traffic.

Finally, I made it to the location Khalid sent me the text too. It's a nice town house, the properties start at $400,000.00. Private location, his house. I rang the doorbell. He opened the door. He was dressed down. I wish he would've given me the heads up. White Ralph Lauren Polo shirt and gray night jogging pants too match. His dick print was on display and he was packing too. His dick touched the middle of his thigh. It was thick too. I wish I had my shades on, but I couldn't stop openly looking at him. He pulled me in for a hug. I almost melted in his arms, he smelled good. His Jimmy Choo cologne invaded my nostrils.

"It's good seeing you again Ms. Miller."

"It's good seeing you to Mr. Mulsane."

"I like the way you say that." If he only knew I love saying it. Khalid was a man of words. I could tell he was educated and a gentleman too. He grabbed my hand and led me into his home. I sat my purse and phone on the sofa. Khalid led me into the kitchen. I took a seat at the island. He had few pieces of fish scattered on the cutting board covered in spices. His onions and peppers were cut to perfection. I could smell the aroma of the spinach. He was cooking for me.

"Ms. Miller would you like a glass of wine or water?"

"I'll take a glass of wine." Khalid poured me a glass of Pinot Grigio. His eyes were trained on me the whole time.

"Why are you looking at me like that? You're making me nervous." I blushed.

"You're beautiful and attractive Kaniya. I like your personality. I'm trying to get to know you. I want to know your weakness and strengths. Are you allergic to fish? I don't eat beef or pork."

"Thank you. You're handsome and VERY attractive. I'm not allergic to fish. Do you want me to help you cook anything? I can't eat your food and leave, that's rude." I laughed.

"Oh, she can be honest too? Trust me you weren't about to eat my food and leave. I got it in the kitchen, but if you insist. Do you."

"I insist, let me see what you have in here. I know I can whip up a desert quick. Whip game real proper." I sassed.

"I see you lil baby. Let me see what you can do." I nodded my head at him. I took my Uggs off. I grabbed Khalid's apron from out the pantry. He had a few green apples on his kitchen table. I can make an apple pie. He had everything I needed. I made my crust first from scratch. I sliced the apples last. I made my filling then sprinkled the brown sugar, ground cinnamon and flour evenly across the apples. I mixed it evenly. I added a few extra spoons of sugar, so it'll be sweet. I don't use cook books. I taste for perfection. Right now, this apple pie was about to be so good. Damn, I wish he had some vanilla ice cream. You could smell it and I haven't even placed it in the oven yet. Khalid's food was smelling good too. He was grilling the fish. I took a seat by the island and hung my apron up. I had no plans to cook tonight.

"Ms. Miller, you have flour on you dress."

"It's okay, I was putting in work."

"I have a shirt and some shorts you could change into."

"Okay cool, I'll do that." I had flour everywhere. Khalid led me to his bedroom. He took a bath in Jimmy Choo. His room was engulfed with the scent. He handed me a pair of basketball shorts and a wife beater. I had way too much ass for these shorts.

"Ms. Miller your food is ready," he yelled. I made my way back to the kitchen. Khalid had my plated fixed nice. Cajun fish, spinach, rice and peas. A real, Island man. I joined Khalid at the table. He grabbed my hand and we prayed and said grace. His parents raised him right. The food was amazing. The fish danced in my mouth, the spinach melted on my tongue. After eating the rice and peas I'm sure my butt has gotten a little bigger. Khalid and I finished eating.

"I want to see what this apple is hitting for. It smells good, but does it taste good?"

"Go ahead and taste it," I laughed. I don't know why he was trying me. He knows his food was the shit. I know my pie is the shit because I can cook.

"I want you to cut it for me Ms. Miller, please?" Begging looks good on him. I grabbed the hand MIT, so I could take the pie out the oven. Khalid pushed up behind me, when I bent over. I sat the pie on the oven. Khalid rested his face in the crook of my neck. I cut a slice of the pie. I gave him a tiny piece on a fork. I fed it to him? What am I doing? Why does this feel so natural?

"It's good but I need more." I fixed Khalid a bigger slice of pie. My phone starting ringing. I ran to the living room to grab my phone. Ugh speak of the devil. It was my grandmother Kaitlyn. I put the phone on speaker, just in case my babies were saying mommy in the back ground. "Oh hell."

"What's wrong?" he asked.

"It's my grandmother; she's wild and crazy." I laughed. I put the phone on speaker, secretly praying she doesn't say anything crazy. "Hello grandmother?"

"Grandmother? Since when hooker, it's always KAITLYN. You're really showing out for this date. Give him the real you hooker." She laughed.

"What's wrong, grandmother?"

"How's the date going hooker? It's getting late, the only thing up after dark is legs. I was calling to see if you had those big red legs up? Don't open your legs up on the first date," she laughed. I swear she likes fuckin' with me.

"KAITLYN why are you being messy. Where are my babies?" I laughed.

"I'm not, they're asleep. I called you because I need an extra $300.00 from you. Jamia your demon child, fucked up my wig. She threw it by your damn fire place. It melted." Khalid looked at me and busted out laughing.

"Yo your grandmother is too fucking wild,"

"I know, and she loves to fuck with me."

"Come on let's wrap for a minute, before you leave me." Khalid and I took a seat on the sofa. He was on one end of the couch and I was on the other end. Khalid grabbed my feet and placed it in his lap. He pulled my socks off and started messaging my feet.

"You have nice feet."

"Thank you."

"I really enjoyed you this evening Ms. Miller. I appreciate you for letting get a moment of your time. I want to do this again one day soon. Come here, why are you at the end of the couch. I won't bite you if you don't want me too. You're too far away from me. I raised up and moved closer to Khalid. He pulled me into his arms and held me. It felt good to be wrapped up in his arms.

"I want to see you again too. How are we supposed to do this if you don't live in the states?"

"Give me a reason to come back Ms. Miller."

"I will Mr. Mulsane." A text came through on my phone. It was Killany telling me to call her when I leave.

"You have a beautiful family. I want to be a part of the picture one day. Take one of us, so you can think about me, when I'm gone and send it to me. I'm serious, I want to get to know you." Khalid and I snapped up a few pictures. I loved them all. "How do we look," he asked.

"Good." Khalid and I finished talking. I loved the way he held me. I could get use to this. I tried to change back into my dress, but he wouldn't let me. He gave me a jacket to put on and walked me to my car. He sealed the date with a kiss on my forehead. I couldn't wait to pull off and call Killany. I sent her the picture of Khalid and me. I hit the Bluetooth button as soon I pulled off. Killany answered on the first ring. I knew she would. Nosy bitches keep their phone at their disposable.

"Kaniya we're going to have to have a long talk. He's very handsome. Y'all were a little close tonight. The two of you look good together. You described him to perfection. How was it? You didn't respond to my text message. Since when you leave my messages on read?"

"Shut up Killany, you do it all the time. You respond days later. It was amazing. He cooked a Jamaican dish and I baked him an apple pie. It was different, and he was romantic as fuck. I like him. I can't believe he's single. I got flour on my dress, so he gave me a wife beater and some basketball shorts to put on."

"Damn Kaniya, you got me over here blushing and I haven't even met him yet. He sounds different. My little hood rat finally met a real boss. Don't fuck it up, he may be the one. I pray he is especially if you're using words like romantic in your vocabulary."

"Fuck you Killany. How is he supposed to be the one if he lives in another country? I don't want a long-distance relationship. I like the way he held me." I blushed.

"Hold up Kaniya, how is this man already holding you?"

"We were getting to know each other. He wanted me in his arms."

"What am I going to do with you?" I finished giving Killany the run down on our date. I like Khalid, but I don't want to get to attached if he doesn't live here.

Khalid

Ms. Miller has me feeling her fine, cool ass. She was perfect. I was surprised when I stood behind her and she didn't object. I had to see if that ass was real and it was. The apple pie was my favorite. She made that shit from scratch. I watched her put in work. I miss her little feisty ass already. I need to speak with my OG about Ms. Miller. A woman wasn't part of the plan. It looks like I may have to make a few exceptions. It was time for a nigga to settle down anyway. Kaniya was holding back. You can't put a time limit on love or deny or chemistry. I know she's been hurt a few times. I can see it all, but I'm not trying to hurt her. I grabbed my phone off the coffee table. I need to call my mother. She answered on the first ring.

"Khalid Mulsane, you were supposed to be home hours ago. Where are you?" She asked. My mother's accent was so thick. I knew she missed me. I've only been gone for a few days. I missed her though. I missed my son too. I'll see them tomorrow.

"I'll be home tomorrow. I met someone. I had a date tonight. I might you let meet her one day."

"Pussy kept you in the states for an additional day? Why would I want to meet her Khalid, I told you years ago I don't want to meet a woman if she's not your wife. I don't want to get acquainted nor do I want her around my grandson."

"It's different with her momma. I haven't sampled the pussy. I don't want that from her. I'm not trying to court her to get the pussy. It feels different. She's a different breed."

"How can you be so sure Khalid? You've only known her for a few days? Different? I'm listening Khalid who is this woman that has you caught up? What has she done to my son?" I gave my mother the rundown on Kaniya and our little encounter. I filled her in on our date.

"Khalid if you feel that way don't let her go. I hope she's the one. I want to see you married soon. Your son, he's needs a mother figure. I need to find me a husband." She explained.

"I'm going to try not to. Look ma, you don't need a husband. I'm not in agreeance with that." I finished chopping it up with my mother. My son was already asleep.

I FaceTime with him earlier. I looked at the clock and it was 11:24 p.m. Kaniya should've been home by now. I told her to call me when she made it. She's hard headed. I hit the call button to call her. She answered on the first ring sounding sexy as hell.

"Hello." Kaniya had a low mellow voice. It was sort of deep, but strong and high pitched when she says certain things. Her tone was deadly and aggressive.

"You made it home yet?"

"Yes." She sighed. She knew she was supposed to call me.

"Why didn't you call me to let me know you made it home safe?"

"You want me to be honest with you Khalid?" She asked and chuckled.

"Of course, I do. I always want you to speak on how you feel. Tell me how you lil baby. What I do wrong?"

"You didn't do anything wrong. You've done everything right. I was going to call you, but I started thinking way too much. I don't like the way you make me feel. You're doing something to me Khalid. I'm drawn to you like a moth in a flame. It's crazy."

"I feel the same way. Let me ask you this, what are you going to do about it, besides try to run away from me?"

"Who said I was going to run? I ain't never ran from shit in all my years of living. Maybe I should've ran. You may end up running from me," she chuckled.

"We'll see. It's two sides to Kaniya. I saw one side an hour ago, she was soft and well spoken. It's that other side that I want to see."

"One day Khalid, be careful what you wish for, you just might get it." Kaniya and I finished talking. I hate I'm leaving so soon but I'll be back in the states in a month or so.

Chapter-12

Kaniya

If it ain't one thing, it's something else. My heart broke hearing Giselle cry because they hauled Dro away. I was in traffic on my way to pick her up. Dro was a good nigga. Giselle is like a sister to me; everybody is so quick to judge her not knowing what she has been through. She's a good girl that has been dealt a bad hand but she's making a way out of no way.

I can't believe Snake pulled that shit. I told Giselle a few weeks ago to slump that nigga because he was threatening her. She thought I was bullshitting. It's all good though because he'll show his face soon thinking he has one up on her. If I'm training her, she's going to rock that nigga to sleep, clean up her mess, and wait on her nigga to come home. So, they could live happily ever after, without a bitch ass nigga in the background.

The Main Event wasn't too far from my house. Thank God Kaisha was in town for the weekend. I had a babysitter on deck. The police had this place swarmed. I valet parked my truck, I jumped out, and ran toward Giselle. The police had her in cuffs.

"Excuse me, officer, I got her." Damn, she's breaking my heart looking like this. I grabbed some tissue out of my clutch to wipe her eyes. She broke down into my arms. I just held her in place. If she needed my shoulder to cry on, I'm here. I'm not going anywhere. I wouldn't wish this feeling on my worst enemy. I swear I wouldn't.

"Why me Kaniya?"

"Stop crying Giselle, he's coming home. He may be gone for a little while, but he'll be back soon. Dro so gone off you girl, that nigga working as we speak to make his way back home to you."

"How you know?"

"Do you love him? If so, do what you need to do, and make sure that he comes back home to you. I told you weeks ago to kill that pussy ass nigga. You didn't listen. Don't let nobody take your happiness."

"You ain't killed Yirah yet, why is she still breathing?"

"Look Giselle, I love you like my sister, but please don't bait a bitch like me. My favorite game is body for body. I got a trigger finger and I love my sanity right now. This shit ain't about me, it's about you and Dro. Don't miss Dro if you don't have too. I don't miss Lucky, I'm glad he's gone. Look at this fresh beat on my face. Check my DM's. I'm good."

"Bitch you just want to be hot in the ass, where are you coming from all dolled up?"

"Yep, there's that smile I love Dimples. I met someone."

"You're playing a dangerous game. Where did you meet somebody at?"

"Who me? I haven't even started yet. I'll show you how real this shit gets one day. If a bitch reaching, I'll snatch a hoe soul. It's time to teach Dimples to snatch a nigga soul." I'm glad that Giselle is feeling a little better. It probably won't hit her until she's alone to think about what the fuck happened.

"You're going home, or do you want to stay at my house tonight?"

"Bitch you're a little nice today. You got some dick?"

"Not yet, don't do me, take your ass home in that big ass house."

"I'm just playing I'm coming to your house. I can't lay in my bed and smell Dro, and he's not there I'll die." I don't have time for Giselle and her theatrics, we have work to do and bringing her man home is a job within itself.

I pulled up to my home and Giselle was asleep on the passenger side. Poor Dimples, she's tired. I woke her up, so she could be prepared to get out. Lucky was parked in the driveway. He couldn't come in. I had the locks and the garage code changed. I don't care if our kids where in the house or not. He wasn't coming in the day he walked out on me and mine, it was a wrap. He walked up in the driveway.

"Where the fuck you been and why can't I get in my house?"

"Lucky, you left your house. It's after hours anyway. Comeback tomorrow when it's daylight."

"You got me fucked up. I paid for this shit. I'll see my kids when I'm good and god damn ready, it doesn't matter the fucking time."

"Whatever Lucky, I'm not even about to argue with you." I walked off from him. I'm sick of him. I haven't seen him in months, but he wanted to show up today out of all days. I felt him yank my hair. I kept walking. He threw me up against the wall in the garage, took my phone and keys, and emptied everything out of my purse.

"Strip butt naked right here. You want me to beat your ass Kaniya? You got me fucked up. I saw you and that nigga. You can't play me. I will fucking kill you. I said I needed fucking space, it ain't no moving on."

"Are you finished?"

"Are you fucking listening?"

"You left Lucky. Did you actually think that I was about to be sitting around waiting for you to come back? It's cools for you to lay over your momma house and fuck Yirah. Have I come at you sideways about that shit? I'm not tripping. You know why, because you can keep that bitch.

If a bitch can get anything that I had, I don't want it. If a nigga is comfortable enough to leave his wife and kids and lay up with bitch who I despised I don't want him. Take your ass on. I'm good, me and my kids don't need shit from you.

I'm not for the games at all. Tell your bitch and your momma to keep fucking with me, and I'll snatch both of those hoes' soul, and your son's soul too. Yeah, I had Jamal tested too. Something kept telling me to do it, since she was always at your mother's house. He was the reason you couldn't stay way. He's yours bitch. You covered that shit up good, but you left some shit unturned.

As far as for you paying for this house, I brought you out. Your name ain't on the deed to this. I wanted this house. I put the offer on it.

You couldn't stand to see me doing something on my own without you. Check your account, your money is there. Oh, while you're at it, sign those fucking divorce papers."

"Damn you are snooping huh? Yes, he's mine I fucked up Kaniya, I did. I should've been honest with you from the jump, but you fucked up too. I'll take care of all my kids. It ain't no breaking up. Do you see how you flipped this shit on me?

I didn't leave you to be with her and my son. I left you because you're hard headed as fuck. You want to have these side relationships with these niggas who don't mean you any good. You don't give a fuck about me and my feelings. If it ain't your way, it ain't no way. You'll hurt me anyway you can. You actually thought I wanted to leave you?"

"Lucky none of this shit matters to me right now. I'm tired and despite how you may feel, I care about your feelings. All this shit you caused. Own up to it. Lay in the bed you made. Maybe it's not meant for us.

Jamal being your son changes the game. He is the same age as Jamel and Jamia. You cheated on me in the beginning and you have a baby to show for it. Every time we have an issue or disagreement you revert to your old ways. I can't stop you from cheating. I'm not enough for you. You pushed me into the arms of the right nigga because I'm sick of you."

"You don't know when to shut the fuck up."

"I need to shut up now because I exposed you?"

He started choking me because he couldn't handle the truth. Niggas can dish it, but they can't take it. He didn't deny fucking her. If I learned anything from being with Lucky, it was be two steps ahead of him. He shot me when Jamia wasn't his. It hurts that Jamal is his but why do all of that to cover it. I knew it was a reason his mother would act funny toward my kids. It's all good though.

Chapter-13

Kaniya

"Can I keep my kids for the weekend, all three of them?" He asked. I had to look at my phone to make sure I wasn't tripping. I know he didn't say what the fuck I think he just said. I guess I was on his radar today.

"Lucky, you're not playing house with my kids. Your baby momma doesn't like me, and your mammy doesn't. When I can train Jamia to shoot a bitch dead in her head train Jamel to body a nigga, then they can spend the night. Until then it's a no. I'll never keep them from you, but you know where we lay our heads at. You can come and see them before the sun goes down." I meant that shit. I don't trust everybody around my kids.

"Kaniya, I kept Jamel for months. Do you think, I'm going to let anybody do something to my fucking kids? I want them to know their brother. Are you doing this because I don't want you? You're making this shit hard and doesn't have to be this way." Lucky is crazy. I'm glad he doesn't want me. I see what type of nigga I'm dealing with. You seeing your kids has nothing to do with me. If you want to see them that bad come by the house. You left us, it wasn't the other way around.

"We can't even have a decent conversation without me being the topic of discussion. I'm not bothered by you and what you have going on. The day you left I haven't hit your phone or asked you for shit. I'm glad that you don't want me, the feeling is mutual. If you want them to meet him so bad, bring him to my house. You've been hiding him for years. I know you wouldn't let anybody do anything to mine.

Trust me for my three, ain't nobody safe. I'll do FED time for mine and not give a fuck. At the end of the day, any motherfucka that attempted to hurt mine ain't living to speak on it. My mother got them. I'm not making shit hard. I thought you didn't want to be a father anymore. They haven't seen you in three months. You stop fucking with them because of me?"

"She doesn't trust you. I know what you'll do, and you know what I'll do." He argued.

"Well that makes the two of us. Who's running shit you or her? I knew you like pussy, but I didn't think you were a pussy ass nigga. Shit changes though. I get paid to talk on my phone and you ain't the nigga that's paying me, so I gotta go.

You know where we lay our heads if you want to see them. Be here before the sun goes down," I hung up in his face. I don't have time to even argue with Lucky. You haven't seen your kids in months by choice, but you want to give me some demands. Get the fuck out of here.

I'm not even bothered by Lucky and Yirah, and what they have going on. They can have each other but you ain't playing house with mine. I'm not even being petty. It's the principal. Grant me my divorce and child support, that's all I want. Bitch you gone pay me. How could you be with a man that killed your brother? Crazy huh. I killed her brothers, he orchestrated it.

"Jeremiah, why are you always laughing at mommy when I cuss your daddy out? I love you. Give me a kiss." Jeremiah loves to hear me to talk. I swear he does. He's just listens and soaks in everything that I'm saying. He's going to be dangerous but he's so handsome.

He doesn't even sleep because he's too busy watching me. Jamia and Jamel take their naps. He's seven months, looks just like Lucky, and only have my complexion. He's so spoiled. He loves to crawl and approach me. He's fighter though, he hits me and laugh.

He can't stand Jamia. If he sees her next to me, he'll crawl up on her and start hitting her. She hollers like he really done something to her. She'll say momma I'll hit your baby. I'm tired I wish Jeremiah would take a nap.

———

I finally got Jeremiah to sleep. Jamel and Jamia woke up ready for lunch and to play. I fried them some chicken fingers and potato wedges. My doorbell rang so I looked at the camera on phone. It was Lucky and Jamal. I opened the door to let him in.

"Hi Lucky and Hi Jamal. Jamia and Jamel you have company. Let me go wake Jeremiah up. How long are you going to be here?"

"Until the sun goes down." I can't stand his no-good ass. I really used to be in love with him. I gave this man majority of my twenties and he ends up not being shit. I wish I never said I do. How did we even get here?

"Okay." I went upstairs to my room and woke Jeremiah up. He was mad as shit, oh well your daddy is here. Wear him out, I'm taking me a nap now. I tapped Lucky on his shoulder. He turned around and grilled me until he saw Jeremiah. I don't want him. I'm glad his hoe has him trained.

"Here you go." I gave Lucky Jeremiah. I changed the lock code on my gate. I'll be damn if he sneaks my kids out while I'm sleep. I checked my phone I had four missed calls one from Lucky, two from Khalid and one from

Giselle. Let my call my bitch back to see what's she's up too.

"What Giselle, what do you want?" I love Giselle. She's really a sweet heart once you get to know her. We're bonded together for life.

"I called you an hour ago, your legs must be up," she laughed.

"Girl stop, who am I fucking? Nobody yet. When I do get me some new dick you'll be the first bitch to know. I'm going to call you while I'm riding dick."

"Umm, everybody wants to know what's up with you and Khalid." I like Khalid a whole lot' but I'm not trying to be in a relationship right now.

"Who is everybody?" See that's the problem with females they always worried about Kaniya and who she's fucking. I only fucked two niggas in twenty-eight years of living. The next nigga I put this pussy on will be the last.

"The crew?" I had to look at my phone to make sure I wasn't tripping. I only talk to two females and that's Giselle and Killany. I don't have a crew.

"What crew bitch, I ride solo?" I laughed. It's the truth I don't befriend to many females.

"Me and you are a crew. Alexis called me and asked what was up with you two. Apparently one of her cousins was checking for him. He curved her."

"Oh well we're just friends with no benefits. Her cousin though? They should've asked Khalid instead of me. He can tell a bitch better than I can." Khalid ain't no friendly nigga. When I met him, I could tell he was conceited and a boss. I guess he was used to women flocking to him. In a room full of women, I was the only one who wasn't checking for him. He approached me."

"Okay I was just giving you the heads up. Where are my little savages? They're quiet." I appreciate Giselle but I ain't never had a problem getting a nigga or keeping one.

"Don't do mine. Their daddy came to visit them. He wanted to be a daddy today, they're in his face."

"Oh, bitch that's why you didn't answer the phone. Your husband was breaking you off huh?" She laughed. I can't stand Giselle's petty ass.

"Girl I wouldn't even let him get a whiff of this pussy. He does nothing for me." I laughed it's the truth.

"I'll hit you back later, Ryleigh has just woken up." Giselle know she's lying. I didn't even hear Ryleigh. Dro probably walked in and she's ready to do some tricks on that dick.

"Cool, I'm going to take me a nap too." I sat my phone on the charger, and it rang again it was Khalid.

"Hello." Whenever he called I put my sexy voice on.

"I called you a few times, why haven't you called me back?" Here he goes, this is the shit I'm talking about. He was so demanding. He wanted to know my every move.

"I was about too, Khalid I had to feed my kids and put one to sleep." I pouted. It gets his ass every time.

"I miss your married ass." He always must be slick and throw his little jabs in.

"I miss you too."

"I'm about to stop fucking with you, until you get a divorce. I can't be fucking off with you like that, and you're a whole married woman to a man that's not me.

What the fuck are you waiting on, are you really done? Let a nigga know something." I like Khalid. I need him to be patient with me.

"What's wrong with you Khalid?" I asked because I really wanted to know.

"You." I'm the problem it must has something to do with Alexis's cousin.

"What I do?"

"You heard what the fuck I said." I hung up in his face. He's used to talking to females any kind of way but not me. Every other day we're having this same conversation. I'm not doing it today. We're friends that's it. He wants to be more than that, I do too, but this man refuses to divorce me. I don't even want to get deep with Khalid until I'm divorced. He's calling back. I picked up the phone and didn't say anything.

"Yo, are you just going to pick up the phone and not say shit?" He argued he knew why I hung up.

"I'm listening."

"Stop playing with me, I'm not like those same niggas you're used to fucking with. Ain't shit pussy about me. I'm real a fucking shotta." He argued.

"I'm not like them bitches you're using to fucking with. Do you think I want to be married to him? He's not trying to divorce me." I argued.

"Do you think I'm about to sit up and keep waiting on you? I'm not like them other niggas. It ain't no back forth shit. I'm not chasing you and I'm not for the bullshit. Divorce him and make that shit happen because I'm not about to keep investing my time in you. Do you know how many bitches out her waiting on me and I'm waiting on you to see if we could be something serious." I knew it was about a bitch. He doesn't have to curve females because of me. He just wants too.

"Khalid if you got a lot of bitches waiting on you, then pursue them. I don't ever want you to feel like you're putting your life on hold for me. I never asked you to wait. I kept it real about my situation. Test the waters and see what's out there." I like him, but he can move on. I don't want anybody to feel like I'm holding them up.

"That's how you feel Kaniya? The difference between you and I is that I don't my mind putting myself out there and telling you how I feel about you. My mother used to always tell me you don't miss a good thing until it's gone. I'm giving you thirty days to handle your fucking business. I don't want to be your friend when I come to Atlanta. I don't want to chill with you on any friend shit. I'm done with the fucking games. I don't play games at all. What's it going to be?" He argued.

"Khalid, I told you how I feel about you and you know it's not that I don't want to be with you. I cherish what we have. I swear I do. I have never been by myself for an extended period. I got baggage and a shit load of issues. Before I can commit to you. I need to commit to myself and get my shit together. If I lose you in the process of me getting myself together than it wasn't meant to be." I explained. It was important that I let Khalid know how I feel.

"Don't fix your mouth to even fucking say that. Take that shit back. I got you and your kids. Whatever you're going through, you don't have to go through that shit by yourself. I want to be there for you but you're pushing a nigga away. What type of man would I be if I see you're going through something and I can't lend you my shoulder to cry on. Every nigga ain't out to hurt you. I want to put you back together again. I'm putting you back together for me. Not your EX. Divorce him because you're slowing up the fucking process." He argued.

"I'm working on the divorce Khalid." I pouted. I am working it on it. Lucky has a whole new life but he's not trying to divorce me.

"Work harder. I'll call you later." I swear I can't win for losing with this man here. What am I going to do? My door slammed. I didn't even turn around I knew it was, Lucky. I had my gun up under my pillow and I grabbed it. I'm waiting on him to put his hands on me. He walked around on my side of the bed.

"I know you holding Kaniya, I didn't come in here for that. I ain't got no gun." He smiled and raised his hands up."

"Okay." I grilled him.

"Raise up, so I can talk to you for a minute." I put the gun down, stood and I folded my arms across my chest. He wanted to talk to me for a minute. About what?

"I heard your conversation. That nigga got hope, don't he? I ain't signing that shit. You belong to me forever. I don't want him around my kids. He might as well get to stepping because that shit ain't happening. You're going to miss your good thing? I listened to your whole conversation. You love that nigga. You'll listen to a nigga you don't know about divorcing me. But you'll fight me on anything and do what the fuck you want?

You so disrespectful. How do you think I feel? It's fucks Lucky and everything we've been through. When I found out you nursed Tariq back to health, how do you think that shit made me feel as your husband? I found out you're signing the packages for Dro. That was minor because you weren't seeing him. You nursed a nigga back to health that could be a potential threat to get at your husband and your family. He played God and dictated my daughter's paternity." He argued and pointed his finger in my face.

"I'm sorry Lucky, I swear to God I am. I never meant to hurt you. I know you have feelings. As your wife I shouldn't have done that, but you put me in a fucked-up situation. It didn't have to go down like that at all.

I have a heart. My sister doesn't even fuck with me because of that. What Tariq did was wrong, but you started it. You paid Jassity $10,000 to fuck him to hurt me. You broke in our home and fucked me in his bed and sent it to him. Justify what you did, because I'm owning up to my shit." He always wanted to flip shit on me. Before he came over, he was screaming he didn't want me to pacify her feelings. Now you're here and you heard Khalid telling me how he feels about me and you're mad.

"You cheated first, Jassity sent me the pictures of you in Tariq's phone way before I even started cheating. He left you $100,000 Kaniya. What man would do that if he's not your man? Did you let him eat your pussy when you were with me, yes or no?" He argued. Why did he want to know that? Does it matter it's the past leave it there?

"I did." He pushed me, and I pushed him back.

"Why do you have to put your hands on me? We can't even talk without you, using your hands. You can leave now? He ran up to me; and threw me on the bed. I reached for my gun. He threw it on the floor. He started choking me and I started clawing at his face.

"You cheated on me first bitch." He argued he kept his hands trained on my neck.

"You cheated with multiple women. Let me go Lucky. We ain't good for each other. I rather be your friend and co-parent. We're not healthy for each other. It's not meant. Let's not force it anymore. Your mother loves Yirah, be happy with her. I'm so tired. We've been going back and forth for the past three years. We didn't work out and it's okay. We got married and we have three kids. I wouldn't trade them for nothing. We're tied together whether we're together or not." I'm tired of the fighting our good days used to outweigh our bad days. It's not the case now.

"You want to be with him bad huh? The judge will never grant you a divorce. We haven't even been to counseling." He argued finally releasing his grip off my neck.

"It's not about him. I'm not worried about him or you. My only focus is me and my three. If he goes than he goes. I'm never worried about who goes or who stays. I can be by myself. I have been for the past six months. As soon as you left me, you're playing house with Yirah. She can have you and you can have her, I'm okay with it." He didn't have anything to say because he knew I was telling the truth. You have a son by this girl to my three. Our kids are the same age which means you never stopped fucking her. I knew it was something about her he liked. She's crazy. He went through drastic measures, so I wouldn't find out.

Chapter-14

Lucky

One night only, I'm from out of town

Ass up, face down

Pound, new rules we ain't waiting on it

And if that pussy good we spend a cake on
it...

I'm leaving Kaniya's house. It was good seeing my kids. I missed them so much. I feel like shit for staying away from them for so long. It'll never happen again. Jeremiah didn't even want me to hold him. I'm fastening Jamal in his car seat, before I pull off. **Yo Gotti Fuck You** song is blasting. I had that shit up loud as fuck. Yeah, I wanted her to here that shit, because that's how a nigga feel right now. It'll always be fuck her, I'm good on her. I meant that shit. Kaniya and I could never be. I don't trust her and too much shit has happened between us. I'm not ready for a divorce just because we're not together. I'm not signing anything.

"Aye Lucky." Kaniya was calling my name. I looked over my shoulders to see what she wanted. I grilled her ass. I know she was on some bullshit.

"Look, this how you pop pussy for a real nigga." She yelled. She wonders why I put my hands on her ass. For one she ain't got no clothes on; a tube top and some little ass shorts. She started dancing and shit fucking with me. Kaniya loves to try me. This is the reason why we're going through this shit right now. I slammed my car door and ran up on her. Before I could even get close, she grabbed an AK from off the ground and pointed it in my face.

"Get that shit out of my face." She wanted to shoot me. She knows I was going to lay hands on her.

"Say I want do it? I'm begging you too. I haven't made an example of a nigga in a long time. I want you to be the first one. Lucky, I want to be a widow.

Keep fucking with me and I will put it on your momma and the bitch you are fucking. Your ass will be on a RIP T-shirt." She cocked the AK back and released the safety on it. Shit done got bad between us if she wants me dead.

"You hate me that bad that you want to kill me?" I argued I was all up in her face. She wanted to make out, so I can't see my kids grow up.

"I hate you and I'll take you out before God does. If you want to keep breathing, stop fucking with me. I'm not bothering you. The same way you hunt niggas, I'll hunt you," she argued. I had to walk away. She had the red beam aiming at my head. Kaniya crazy but her aim is on point. I hopped in my truck and pulled off.

I love my wife, I swear to God I do. Never question that. I swear I wouldn't think that we would be here. I had to leave Kaniya, but I didn't want too, I had too. One of the hardest things to do in life, is to let go or leave something that you loved. I love her. I may have a funny way of showing it, but I do.

I fucked up. I knew Jamal was mine because he looks just like me. I was in denial about that shit for the longest. Yeah, I had some shit drawn up stating that he wasn't mine. Yirah took matters in her own hands and had another test done to confirm it.

I've been juggling this shit for the past year. How do you tell your wife, that a child you confirmed that wasn't yours, is yours? This child was created when we were together. I could never tell Kaniya that. If I did, she wouldn't accept it and we wouldn't be together.

I know she would never let me abandon my son, EVER. I sat up many nights battling with myself. Should I tell her or not. I don't want to lose Kaniya, but I've made some mistakes and I know she ain't going to forgive a nigga. Yirah is pregnant again, three months to be exact. It might be time to let this shit go. I'm a selfish ass nigga. I don't want her happy if it's not with me. I'm not perfect and I've made mistakes. I don't know what to do.

Yirah is submissive to me, she listens and does everything I tell her to do. My mother loves her. I love Yirah, but I'm not in love with her. I keep slipping up with her. We have a child together and another one on the way. I've been fucking with Yirah for about three years now.

Kaniya, my mother hates her, but I love her. She has my heart and three of my children. She doesn't listen to me at all. She does what the fuck she wants. It hasn't always been that way. I can blame myself for her behavior. We've been together for a long time.

Majority of the highlights of my life have been with her. We have a bond that I swore couldn't be broken. I fucked up.

Chapter-15

Cynthia

I'm so glad my son left that bitch. Ugh I can't stand her. Hell, no I'm not keeping her kids. Let her mammy do it. Fuck her and her kids. Yirah was my choice for Lucky and I don't give a fuck who knows it. It's not a secret. I told Kaniya day one that Jamal was his, she wanted to take Lucky's word over mine.

Now the laugh is on you. I love Yirah. When Lucky left her and decided to marry that tramp. I moved her and my grandson in my home, in my mother in law suit. Yirah's and Lucky are expecting again. He moved her out of my house and back into the home they once shared, where they belong.

Lucky needs to divorce Kaniya. I'm this close to signing the papers my damn self for Lucky so they can make that shit official. Yeah, I was with the shit. Every time Lucky and Yirah were having sex, I told Yirah to record that shit and send it to her. Hurt that hoe feelings. Let her know you can get him anytime you want too, it's simple. I'm petty. I sent Kaniya a few texts telling her to come to my house to get him, so she could see what he was up too.

I was waiting on her, she never came or sent a text. I used to care for Kaniya. I never liked Kaisha and Sonja. I couldn't stand the two of them. I asked Lucky for Kaniya's new phone number. I felt like being messy today. I wanted to see how miserable she was without Lucky. I'm sure it's hard raising three small children by yourself. I grabbed my phone and placed a call to her. She answered on the first ring.

"Hello." she sounded pretty good.

"Hi Kaniya, this is Cynthia. I wanted to see if I can come and get Lucky's kids." Yes, Lucky's kids he made them.

"Cynthia, you want to come and get Lucky's kids, why?" I didn't want to, but my son said I needed to do better.

"I want to see them." I lied. I really wanted to fuck with their mother. Yirah called and said Lucky hasn't been home all day.

"My mother I always told me to respect my elders but you're one old bitch that I'll be glad to check. You don't fuckin' like me or my kids. Whatever your agenda is, I suggest you end it. I'm going to tell you one time and one time only. Keep fucking playing with me and I'm going to give you exactly what you want. I'm pulling up and I'm bodying you. I'll let your son know I did it. I'm the grim reaper and I'm in the business of snatching souls."

"I'm not afraid of you. You don't put no fear in my heart. You're a bitter bitch because my son doesn't want you. He's with a real woman now, Yirah. Did he tell you that she was pregnant again, 3 months to be exact?" I argued. I wanted to hurt her feelings I'm not sparing her today.

"Bitter, Yirah can have him. She can have as many babies as she wants by him. The difference between me and Yirah is that I can have any man I want to. I've never been a side bitch to any nigga. I have options. Your son, he knows that. I never had to chase Lucky, he chased me. I always replaced him. I got that come back pussy he always come back to. This time around it ain't no coming back. Lucky trapped me, I didn't trap him. I wouldn't trade my children for nothing in this world. I guess he got that from you. He got his hoe tendencies from you too. You never confirmed was Kodak his real daddy because it wasn't

Deuce." I had to hang up in her face. She kept calling back.
I don't have time to argue with Kaniya.

Kaniya

I can't believe that old bitch tried me. I'm petty and I ain't got nothing but time. So Yirah is pregnant again? This nigga been fucking with her. It's okay though, he's not worth any tears of mine. I don't feel any type of way about it. Let me call my momma. I'm sick of this old bitch. She thinks I won't lay hands on her, but I will. My momma isn't answering the phone, so I kept blowing her up until she finally answered.

"Ma, where you at?" I argued.

"What is it Kaniya Nicole? Damn you are blowing up my phone, what's wrong?"

"Cynthia keeps fucking with me. Come and get my kids, I'm ready to make an example out of a bitch." I explained.

"Slow down, what happen?" I gave my mother the run-down of what happened.

"Kaniya, suit up and give me an hour." She was on her way. She claims that she was going to pick my father up and he was going to watch the kids. Nine times out of ten they were together. I smelled her perfume at his house, she's not fooling me.

Kaisha

Cynthia knows better. I already checked her one time about my child. I'll never check a bitch twice. My pull up game real strong. I'm not even asking any questions. Kaniya said a mouthful. Cynthia is my age. Anytime a hoe my age comes for my child, I'm the one that's coming. I know Kaniya can handles hers, but I got this. I was pushing 100 mph coming down I-85N. I made it to Kaniya's house in about forty-five minutes top. Killian made it before me. I called Kaniya and she answered on the first ring.

"Bring your ass, I'm outside." She ran out dressed in all black, with a ski-mask. Only my child. I couldn't even do anything but shake my head.

"Fuck you need all that shit for Kaniya?" I asked because I was curious as fuck. She had too much to kill a bitch.

"I'm going to torture the bitch." She laughed.

"Let me kill her and keep it moving. I'm sick of her."

"No ma, killing the bitch is way too easy. She said that she's not afraid of me. I want that bitch walking on eggshells. I want that bitch to see how easy it is for me to touch her."

"I hear you, but I'm tapping that ass. I don't even want you touching her. I told her once and she didn't get it. The worst mistake she made is to bring me out of retirement behind you. What about Yirah, what are you going to about her?"

"Nothing, I'm so good on Lucky. Killing Yirah ain't worth it, you know why? Because if I do that nigga will be all up in my face, making my life worse than what it is. I want him to be happy with her, so he can leave me the fuck alone. He likes her, I want him to keep liking her."

"Okay." Kaniya did have a point. I guess she calculated this one out. Maybe she doesn't want him. I could see one kid but two, oh hell no.

———

We pulled up at Cynthia's house. I grabbed my AR out the back seat. I picked up a brick and threw at her window. Kaniya threw another one at the other window. The door swung open. I hit that bitch in the face with the back of my AR and she fell to the ground. I dragged this hoe to the street. I want her to talk all the bull shit she's been talking.

"What the fuck is this?" She asked.

"A homicide."

"Kaniya and Kaisha, what are y'all doing here?"

"My bitter ass, came to lay hands on you, since you came for me."

"Cynthia, I told you about fucking with mine. When you see Kaniya, that's me all day. I don't give a fuck how old she is. I'll never let a bitch disrespect mine and think it's okay. Stand your hoe ass up and take this ass whooping. Bitches love to talk to shit over the phone, but when we're face to face they're on mute."

"Kaisha."

"It ain't no Kaisha, I said stand the fuck up or I'll let Kaniya stand you up." This hoe was taking her time, I don't have all day. Kaniya picked her up and she stood to her feet. I approached her and let her ass have it. I needed her on two feet. This bitch ain't no match for me. I kicked her in both knees, she fell to the ground. I started stomping her ass out. I grabbed her by the hair and rammed her head in the concrete.

"Grab my AR Kaniya."

"No ma, I got it from here. I came to put in work also." Kaniya stood over Cynthia she had a blow torch. Oh shit. Kaniya opened Cynthia's mouth and put fire on her tongue.

"You ain't scared of me huh." Kaniya put the blow torch on her lips.

"Aye bitch spit that hot ass shit you were spitting earlier. I'm a crazy ass bitch. You don't want to keep fucking with a bitch like me. Your lips hot right?" Lord my child is crazy.

"Come on Kaniya."

"I ain't finished ma. Let me put my stamp on her."

"Bring your ass on." I yelled. She waived me off and made her way back to Cynthia.

"Ma did you see her scary ass?" she laughed.

"You know you crazy." I laughed

"Yep, watch this."

"Who are you calling?" I asked.

"Yirah, put my husband on the phone."

"You mean our husband." Yirah's sound silly as hell. I don't see how side bitches could be faithful?

"Funny, he could be your husband, but he doesn't want to sign the divorce papers. Make him sign them, so he can wife you." Kaniya laughed.

"What Kaniya, why didn't you call my phone?"

"I didn't want too. She dead Lucky." She taunted him. I could tell he was frustrated.

"Who dead?" He asked.

"Your mammy BITCH! Tell that HOE, never fuck with a BITCH like me, behind a PUSSY ASS nigga like you." I swear my child is the worse. A bitch will learn her lesson about fucking with mine. I must be careful with Kaniya because she's worse than me. I don't want her to give a reaction every time somebody pisses her off.

Everybody ain't gone like you but oh well. Cynthia
deserved that shit.

Chapter-16

Lucky

I hope she was bull shitting. I knew she wasn't. She wanted me to know she touched my mother.

My mother is off limits. If she killed my mother, she'll regret it every day she fuckin' lives. I'll make her life a living hell. I don't care if she's the mother of my children. I love my mother just as much as she loves hers.

"Lucky, where are you going?" She asked. Why would she ask me a question she already knows the answer?

"I got some fucking business to handle. If Kaniya killed my momma, I need you to call my lawyer, and meet me at Fulton County Jail. I'm going to fucking jail. I put it on the baby you're carrying." I meant that shit too. I play a lot of games but leave my mother out of our shit. I told my mother to leave her alone.

"I'm going with you. I don't want you to do anything crazy. Our children and I need you." She cried. I wish she could go but Kaniya is my wife and Yirah needs to sit this one out. Now isn't the time. Kaniya doesn't even know that Yirah's pregnant again.

"Yirah, I hear what you are saying, but I don't give a fuck." I'm not trying to hear shit that Yirah saying. I know my mother and I know Kaniya as well. I put my clothes on fast. I had to get to my mother's house quick. Kaniya has took shit too far. My mother doesn't have shit to do with what we are going through.

"We're ready Lucky, let me drive since you're on a thousand." I really wanted to be left alone. I appreciate her for being there. The thought of losing my mother and killing my wife was running through my mind.

"Okay." We pulled off and Yirah grabbed my hand to ease some of the tension. I want to be good until I see my mother. I called her phone at least ten times and she hasn't answered. My mother, she's all that I have left in this world besides my kids. Kodak is my father but I'm not trying to get to know him. Deuce will forever be my father.

"I love you Lucky."

"I love you too Yirah."

"I don't want to lose you. I love your mother as if she was my own. If something happened to her I don't know what I'll do. I'll lose my mind, we have a bond. You need to divorce Kaniya if she killed your mother."

"I'm listening."

"What are we waiting on? I've forgiven you for everything that you've done to me. We're about to have two children together. You won't even let me date another man, but you're still married to her. I'm tired of coming second to her. When will I be first?" She cried.

"Not now Yirah, be patient with me." Yirah was in her feelings. Now isn't the time, she snatched her hand from mine, and turned the music up. Tears ran down her face, I grabbed her hand and placed a kissed on it. I didn't want to upset her and she's pregnant with my child. I do love Yirah, but she knew what it was when we started fucking around. I'm separated from my wife but I'm not sure if I want to divorce her.

––––––

We finally made it to my mother's house, it was a little after 10:00 p.m. As we approached her house. I noticed a body laid out in the street. Before Yirah could throw her car in park. I hopped out to see if it was my mother. Kaniya took this shit too far. My mother still had a pulse. She may have fainted or passed out. Meat and blood were seeping out my mother's lips.

"Yirah, grab the water hose and call the ambulance. I'm going to kill her." Yirah ran down the driveway with the water hose.

"Oh my God Lucky, is she dead," she cried.

"No, she has pulse."

"Where are you going?"

"Look, I have to handle some business. I'll meet you at the hospital. Don't say shit to the police. I'll handle it. Momma I'll take care of it." I pulled off. Kaniya got me fucked up. I called her phone and she didn't answer. I kept calling she finally answered.

"Yeah."

"You're a dead woman walking. You want me to hurt you? I don't give a fuck about nothing we're going through right now; my mother is off limits. I'll kill any bitch behind my momma. I don't care if she has my kids or not."

"I'm glad you feel that way. Lucky, this shit is not a game. Think before you talk to me. Fuck YOU and your

MOMMA. You better Thank GOD I didn't kill the bitch. I had to touch her. She needed to feel me because I don't fuck with nobody. Anytime a bitch got the balls to send for me. I'm coming the worst fucking way possible. What I did to her was minor because she's still living.

Oh, and congratulations on your new edition. Your mother told me she's three months PREGANT? You did leave me for her. I begged you to stay. It's all good. I'm glad you gone. I ain't got nothing but time. Keep coming at me with some bullshit. I got some nice hollows with your name on it. I'm ignorant as fuck and I have a zero tolerance for fuck niggas. I'm allowing you to do whatever you want to do with Yirah. Just sign the fucking papers, and we don't even have to keep doing all of this.

You're happy, let me be happy too. Give Yirah everything that she wants. I don't want anything from you Jamel. Just sign the papers please, that's all I want. You don't give a fuck about me, and I don't have any fucks to give." She argued.

"Kaniya." She cut me off quick.

"Goodbye Jamel." She hung up in my face, but I was on my way. My mother ran her mouth telling my business. She wants to hurt Kaniya but she's causing problems for me and what we have.

———

I pulled up to Kaniya's and our room light was on. I knew she was up. I jumped the gate because I didn't have the code. I banged on the door and Killian swung it open. I pushed him out my way. I don't live here but this is still my house.

"Let me in my house." I'm not trying to hear shit Killian is talking about right now.

"Let me holla at you Lucky. Normally I don't get in my children's business but leave my daughter alone. I don't have time to watch your children, so she can go out and do dumb shit. If she wants a divorce, divorce her. I'm sick of this shit." Staying out of our business is the only thing he needs to do.

"You cheated too." I argued.

"I did, but you have two babies by the same chick. It's not the same. I made one mistake, but you keep making them. You got my daughter fucked up. She doesn't have to go through anything that your dishing out. Take care of your kids and step."

"Let me talk to her."

"No, it ain't shit to talk to about and keep your hands to yourself. I don't want to put my hands on you again."

"Look Killian, this is my house and Kaniya is my wife despite what we are going through. I'm not going to put my hands on her, but I need to speak with her." Killian don't put no fear in my heart. He bleeds just like I do. I moved him out the way and went upstairs. Just a few months ago, he was doing the same shit when Kaisha was with my father at my fucking house. Kaniya had her door locked, I kicked that bitch open. She was laid on her back smiling.

"You could've knocked," she had a blow torch laying right beside her.

"Knock for what. why did you do that to my mother?"

"I told you to tell your mother to stop fucking with me. It's cool that she doesn't like me. I'm not fucking bothered by it. She called me fucking with me. This isn't the first time. When Yirah sent me the video of you and her fucking, your mother sent me one too from her phone. I let that shit slide and changed my phone number.

I guess she wanted to be messy. She called and said that I was bitter and Yirah was pregnant again by you. She's three months and he's with a real woman. I don't care if that's what you want, and she makes you happy, be with her. It's that simple let's get a divorce. Here are the papers sign them."

"You had to do all of that, because she was fucking with you?"

"Jamel you don't get it do you? Your mother talks too much. I'm sick of her. I don't need to know about your infidelities. That's your business and you must deal with it. I haven't come at you sideways one time about you and Yirah. I could've, but it's not worth it. You made permanent decisions on temporary emotions."

"I'm sorry."

"No, you're not. Stop saying that. When it comes to me and you, nobody knows their fucking place. The difference between you and me, I'll never let anybody disrespect you or cause harm to you. The way I ride for you, you never ride for me the same way. I want off this ride. You've fucked me over one too many times."

"You really want a divorce?"

"Yes, that's all I want from you. You don't even have to do nothing for my kid's period. I just want you gone out of my life."

"I'm going to take care of my kids regardless. If that's how you feel I'll sign it, but you're going to regret it."

"Here sign it, so we can make it official."

"I don't want to sign it Kaniya, get this shit out of my face." I tore the papers up in her face.

"Jamel, I want you to be happy, even if it's not with me. You're just being selfish. Just sign it willingly. The judge will grant me a divorce because you committed adultery and I got you on tape laying hands on me. I don't even want to do all of this, but I will."

"You know what Kaniya, I don't give a fuck about none of that shit. I'm not signing it. I'm not ready for a divorce yet. We haven't even talked about all this we're going through. What you did to my mother, it ain't no coming back from that. You took shit too far, you should've called me instead of taking matters into your own hand.

You had to prove a point and show how bad and tough you are. You disgust me. I may not have been the best man to you, but I was good to you despite the cheating and other shit. You'll miss me when I'm gone. You know what's funny, you told me to push you in the arms of the right nigga? What nigga is going to put up with you and all the bullshit that comes with you?

You're beautiful, smart, loyal, and you'll ride for a nigga if necessary. You have baggage, you're crazy as fuck, and you don't listen. Your attitude is nasty, your spoiled, and rude as fuck. I blame myself for that. I put you on a pedestal so high that nobody could ever knock you down. When you touched my momma, it was wrap. I want to put my hands on you so bad, but you ain't fucking worth it.

We've been together for eight years. We had some good times and these last three years were the worst. I wouldn't trade my kids for nothing. I married you and I didn't want too. I felt like I at least owed you that much. I'm not even going to fight for us anymore. I gave this shit all I got. I don't have anything else to give. You want to know why it's Yirah and not you?"

"I don't."

"I want you to know. I love Yirah, Kaniya, I'm not going to lie. It's something about her. I couldn't stop fucking with her. It's not how I love you, but I do love her. Yirah is everything you ain't. She listens to me and she's submissive. Whatever I tell her to do, she does. Yes, we argue and fight, but it doesn't last long, we make up quick. She caters to me. She really knows how to treat a nigga. The way she fucks me blows my fucking mind. She got me gone."

"Okay I'm glad that you found that in her, just sign the papers and divorce me, if you feel like that. You can have everything with Yirah and the two of you could be official."

"I'm not done yet."

"We're done here. Lucky, you didn't MAKE me nor can BREAK me. I'm going to keep it ninety-five with you. You want to talk down on me and make me feel bad about this shit. It's not happening. You kept coming back and you didn't have too. We didn't have too. I know my worth. I want you to be with Yirah, that's why I never touched her. I've never been in the business to keeping ANY NIGGA that doesn't want to be kept. Bitch I Play for Keeps. REMEMBER THAT. You ain't shit to keep. I'm me and

I'm not changing for nobody. What you see is what you get with me. I'm comfortable in my OWN fuckin' skin. Don't NO NIGGA make or break me."

"I'm not shit to KEEP KANIYA?"

"Lucky, why do you want to hurt me so bad? Despite everything that we've gone through, I will never wish bad on you. I want you to be happy. I want to witness that. I want to see you love Yirah and the two of you do your thing, that's all I want. You said all these wonderful things about her, but you still haven't signed the papers. If she makes you happy, just sign them."

"I'm not signing them. You want to be with that nigga so bad? It ain't fucking happening. Its till death do us apart. Let me know when you want me to cover you in dirt. That's the only way you're getting a divorce. I'm a selfish ass nigga, Kaniya. I always have been. I'm holding on to you. You'll forever carry my last name." I tore up the last piece of divorce papers in her face. She had the nerve to take my ring off her finger. I put that shit back on her finger. I looked back at Kaniya one last time. "We're not done until I say we're done."

Chapter-17

Kaniya

He still didn't sign the papers. I'm never going to get a divorce. I wish this shit was finally over. My mother always said if they're not helping you they're hurting you. Lucky and his mother were in the business to hurt me. I'm going to protect me, my heart, and my sanity at all cost. I heard a knock on my door. It was my father.

"Are you okay?" He asked.

"I'm fine daddy, I wish it was over. He talked to me like I was just an average bitch on the street."

"I heard him, you handled yourself well. I never get in your business Kaniya, and trust me, I wanted too several times. Promise me you'll never go back to him? You're my daughter and I love you so much. You ain't perfect and I don't want you to be. I love you just the way you are. You have some growing to do. I want you to work on yourself and focus on my grandchildren, that's all I want. I want the old Kaniya back."

"Daddy, that's what I want too. You know I don't bother anybody. My hand was forced. I didn't want to do that, but I was provoked. I knew what Lucky was doing I allowed it because I didn't care anymore. His mother was always disrespectful to me because of who my mother is."

"I know. It's new day Kaniya, move on. Get some rest, your mom and I will be here with you to help with kids for as long as you need us too."

"Thank you." I'll get this door fixed tomorrow. What a day. My babies were already asleep. I grabbed my cell phone and sent Giselle and Killany a still married text, with the papers Lucky tore up and refused to sign. I went to my office and put the papers in the shredder. Something must give because I'm tired of living like this. I just want to be free of all the drama and bullshit. I needed this divorce done ASAP. My phone started ringing and it was Khalid. I haven't heard from him since earlier.

"Hey Khalid."

"What's up, what are you still doing up, how was your day?"

"Nothing, you don't want the answers to the last two."

"I do, I always want you to be honest with me."

"It's a lot Khalid."

"I have nothing but time talk." I gave Khalid the rundown of everything that happened, and he just listened. This maybe my last time talking to him. He might not want to fuck with me after this but it's cool, I would rather be myself anyway.

"Kaniya."

"Yes."

"You know you're wrong, I don't agree with you doing his mother like that. I'm keeping it ninety-five with you. If that was my mother, you'll be dead. It's not a threat. She baited you and you took the bait. He's not trying to divorce though."

"I hear you. I'm tired, I'll talk to you tomorrow."

"Kaniya, so you're really hanging up because I'm telling you some shit that you don't want to hear?"

"That's not why I'm hanging up Khalid. I told you I was tired. I know right from wrong. Everybody wants to make it like I'm such a bad fucking person. That's why I didn't want to tell you. Everybody wants to fuck with me and expects me just to take everything they're dishing. I don't have too. I don't mind showing a bitch or a nigga how real shit gets when you decide to fuck with me. I mind my own business. I'm not supposed to say shit but turn the other cheek," I hung up in Khalid's face because I didn't like where this conversation was going. He's calling right back. I answered and didn't say anything.

"Kaniya, say something. You want to hang up in my face because you don't want to hear the truth."

"Khalid, I don't want to argue with you about shit that doesn't have to do with me and you. I'm hanging up. If you don't want to deal with me let me know. I'm making some changes in my life, starting with this phone number."

"Do what you have to do. I'll be in Atlanta tomorrow. I'll see you rather or not I have your number. You can run but you can't hide from a nigga like me."

Tariq

Damn I've been trying to reach her for a minute. She just up and changed her number on a nigga. What part of the game is this? We were friends before anything. I've been driving around the city with no destination. I hit the Bluetooth. I knew Raven had a number on her. I swore that I wouldn't put Raven in our business, but if she could do me this one last favor. I knew her Kaniya were back on speaking turns.

"What Tariq?"

"What's Kaniya's number?"

"I don't know, why? You know we're back on good terms. I'm not trying to mess that up because of you. If you don't have it, maybe you don't need it Why do you want it?" Raven was giving me the fifth degree about getting her number.

"Because I need to know what she wants to do with this house?" I argued.

"Oh, hold on let me text Killany and get it from her." She sassed. She knew she had it all alone. Raven sent me a text with Kaniya's number. I swear I'm glad they squashed that little petty shit they had going and moved on. Raven missed Kaniya, but she wouldn't admit it first. Now that's all she talks about, her sister this and sister that. She had the nerve to change her number and not give it to me. I hit the Bluetooth and called her.

"Hello."

"I heard you was single again?"

"How did you get my number?"

"I know some people, who know some people. Answer my question."

"I'm in the middle of a divorce and your part of the reason."

"You should've never said I do anyway. It was supposed to be me and you."

"Tariq, we could never be."

"We could. You and I both know that. I had to confirm to see if the rumors were true."

"They're true."

"Are you good, do you need anything?"

"I'm great, it's 10:00 p.m. where's Gabrielle and the baby?"

"We're not together. I gave my daughter and her the house. I copped me a bachelors' pad in the city. You need to figure out what you want to do with the house that we had. Sale it or rent it?"

"We can sell it Tariq. Gabrielle was a good girl you, should've worked it out."

"True but too much has happened with us. She'll never forgive me or forget, so it's best that we just co-parent."

"I hate that, but I understand. You're a great guy. I thought she was the one you kept circling back to and kept her in the background."

"So, what are you trying to say?"

"I said it."

"I'm ready to settle down. I'm getting too old to be running through females."

"It'll happen."

"So, what about you? When I'm with someone, are you going to give me away?"

"I'm chilling. I love being myself. Why do you want me to give you away? Why not Gabrielle?"

"Oh, I forgot the summer is rolling back around. You want to be hot in the ass. Some shit never changes. Why not you? You're the only one that had my heart and played with it. I loved Gabrielle, but I was never in love with her. I couldn't force myself to love her."

"Tariq, I'm not about to do this with you. That's why I changed my number. You were slanging good dick for days, but you weren't thinking about me. Some shit ain't meant to be and I'm okay with that. When you meet the right one of course I'll give you away because I want you to be happy. You deserve it. You're a good man and someone special deserves to experience that."

"I'm good enough for someone else, but not you?"

"I didn't say that, don't put words in mouth."

"It was always you Kaniya. I almost died twice and the only thing that I was holding on to was you. I've told you that more than once. I'm glad your marriage didn't work out. I never respected it anyway. Lucky tried me more than once, and you know I'm not a pussy ass nigga. I played shit safe because of you and I was on parole.

Lucky couldn't take a loss, he knew I was marrying you. He did so much to get you, but he still ended up fucking up. You gave this nigga chance after chance, but you've ran out of chances with me huh?"

"Tariq, I don't want to do this with you tonight. How many times do I have to say I'm sorry? Do you know how I fucking feel? Loyalty, it's a gift and curse. If I could turn back the hands of time I would but I can't. I can only right my wrongs and I've done that. What more do you want from me?"

"What's the code to the gate, I'm outside?" She got quiet. "You heard what I said, that's what I want. Can I see you for a minute?" Kaniya hung up on me. I'm not leaving until she lets me in. It's been months since I saw her, almost a year. I thought about her always.

Chapter-18

Kaniya

"**A**re you going to let me in or do I have to sit out here all night. I'll jump the gate if have too."

"It's late Tariq."

"I won't put your legs over your head if you don't want me too." He chuckled.

"If you're thinking about that, you definitely need to go home."

"Kaniya, I'm grown, and you're grown. Let me in and stop beating around the bush." Ugh I shouldn't answer the phone when he called. Why is he here? Who gave him my phone number? How did he know where I lived? I hit the code to the gate and watched him pull in. I opened the garage, so he could park inside.

I didn't need for Lucky to ride by and see him here. I met him in the garage and we just looked at each other. He got out the car and I walked back inside of the house. He ran up behind me and picked me up. He grabbed my waist and started kissing me on my neck. I didn't stop him. I always loved Tariq and I probably will never stop. He'll never know that. It's crazy I never stop loving him.

"Stop Tariq, we shouldn't be doing this. What do you want anyways?" I moaned. His touch alone did something to me. I couldn't be around him. He turned me around and made me look at him. He licked his lips, damn he was fine. He gained some weight in all the right places. His dreads were freshly twisted, and he had them pulled up in man bun. I hated the way he looked at me. Most of all I hated the way his dick looked in those gray sweatpants. I just wanted to grab that big motherfucka.

"You. Don't tell me to stop. You're divorced now I can get at you like I want too, and nobody can stop me, not even you."

"I'm seeing someone." I laughed.

"What the fuck does that have to do with me? Fuck him."

"Tariq be nice."

"Why do you keep fighting us? You can only fight this shit for so long. Look at this shit here?" He took off his shirt and pointed at all his bullets wounds. Tears flooded my eyes. I couldn't take it. Even though he had the tattoos to cover it. I never wanted that to happen to him.

"Put your shirt back on." I cried

"No because even though you put this shit here. I still want you. Come here." I couldn't stop crying. He picked me up and, sat down on the sofa and laid me on his chest." He made me face him as I laid on his chest. This shit was never supposed to happen.

"I'm sorry Tariq, I swear to God I am." He wiped my tears with his thumbs.

"I know Kaniya, but I didn't come over here to make you cry shawty. I forgive you and I just want to forget about this shit and move on. How you been?"

"I'm okay. How are you?"

"I'm cool." Tariq looked me up and down. I couldn't read him, so I raised up to get off him. He wrapped his arms around upper back, so I wouldn't move.

"What, why are you looking at me like this?"

"I can't look at you, who is he?"

"Does it matter? You don't know him, and he doesn't know you."

"I'm tired of competing with these niggas. When I was young my OG use to always say if it's meant to be eventually it'll come back. When I think about us, it's crazy because somehow, we always find our way back to each other. I think it's meant for us, but you keep fighting this shit."

"We're always going to be friends no matter what. A lot has happened between us. It is what it is."

"You keep fighting this shit Kaniya. I don't want to be your friend. I always wanted to be your man. Shit I wanted to be your husband. I don't even like to speak on him. Hear me out. I know in the past I haven't been a perfect nigga.

I'm grown, and I do grown shit. Shawty when I was with you I wanted to be perfect for you. My nose was wide open, and I didn't care. Long as I had you, you were the only thing that mattered and kept a nigga sane."

"Tariq." He kept cutting me off refusing to let me talk.

"Kaniya, let me finish. Yeah, I cheated with Gabrielle, but she didn't mean anything to me. I only circled back because I knew you were still caught up on him after the Yirah shit. I made permanent decisions on temporary emotions."

"Tariq." He put his hand over my mouth.

"Let me talk I know you have something to say. I ran through a lot of females but they ain't you. I keep coming back to you. I want you. I could be anywhere right now, but I want to be with you. Damn what a nigga got to do to be with you?"

Khalid

Let me Introduce myself my name is Khalid Mulsane. You can call me Khalid. I stood about 6'2, weigh about 260 pounds solid, and I'm Panamanian decent. Born and Raised in Kingston, Jamaica. I've been in the city for a minute. I had to handle some business with Mulsane Construction. Tonight, was my last night in the city.

I've been trying to reach Kaniya for the past two hours. Whenever I call she always answers. Something was up. She hadn't responded to any calls or text, everything went unanswered. I hit my partner Dro up and asked him to ask Giselle had she heard from her. Giselle stated that she spoke with her earlier.

I'm feeling the fuck out of Kaniya I can't lie but her mouth is slick as shit and she's used to running niggas. I'm a different breed and she needed a nigga like me to tame the wild shit she does. I should go to my room, but I had to check up on my lil baby and see what the deal is. I hit her line one more time before I decided to pull up and she didn't answer.

Any female that I invest my time into I needed to know what's up because I'm grown ass man and I be damn if she has me out here looking crazy. Kaniya's house was about forty-five minutes away from here. She thought her shit was secure and I couldn't get in. I got rank. My clout and my reach are long. I called up my partner Joe and he answered on the first ring.

"Mulsane, what can I do for you it's late?"

"I need access to a gate code."

"Mulsane what you on, you're a long way from home?"

"Joe, it's my business and not yours. Can you help me out or do I have to jump the gate and take penitentiary chances?"

"Send me the address when you pull up and the make and model of the gate system." I had a feeling Kaniya was on some funny shit. We've been talking for about six months and I can't think of one time she hasn't answered for me. Tonight, was different. For her sake and not mine she better be sleep. I cut my music up because I didn't want to think negative. I'll fuck around and hurt Kaniya.

I made it to Kaniya's and it was a little after 12:00 a.m. I pulled up to the gate and sent Joe a text with everything he needed, and he sent me a master code. I hit the code on the gate and the doors open. I called Kaniya again, she didn't answer. Something was up. I threw my car in park. Fuck knocking on the door, I kicked that bitch open. I knew she was up to some shit. She's laid up on the couch with this nigga.

"Khalid, what are you doing here?"

"I'm asking the fucking questions. I called you numerous of times and you didn't answer. What the fuck is this?" The nigga who she was laid up under was grilling me when he raised up.

"Khalid, we were just chilling, my phone is in my room."

"Grab your shit and let's go because I didn't give you permission to chill with any nigga. It's me and you. Not you and him."

"Kaniya, your single right. Last I checked you were divorced? Which means you're up for grabs."

"Kaniya get your shit and don't answer no fucking questions. I didn't get a name from you son. I'm Khalid and when you see Kaniya that's me. I'mma need you move around and clear this motherfucka." He was grilling me. Kaniya was about to make me catch a case in the states because she wanted to be friendly with a nigga.

"I'm Tariq and it's been me and Kaniya for years. She's single again and I'm getting in where I fit in. All of this she's mine and shit, if a ring ain't on it, it means nothing to me. I'll clear it for now. Kaniya I'll see you tomorrow get your shit together because I'm coming for you and I'm not about to let nobody stop me." He went through the garage and grilled me as he walked out.

"Aye Tariq may the best man win. This time around it ain't no circling back. Don't get your hopes up." I swear she wants a nigga to kill her ass. I walked upstairs to her room. She sat on her bed playing with her phone. She looked up at me. She knows I caught her ass.

"What's Up Khalid?"

"Grab your shit and let's go." She grabbed a few things and started huffing and puffing and sucking Her teeth.

"I need less attitude from you, beat your feet and grab some more shit. Call your mother and tell her to keep the kids for a few days because I got an issue with you."

"Okay." That sad shit doesn't work with a nigga like me. I went downstairs to fix Kaniya's door. I'll have somebody from my construction company to fix her door tomorrow. She finally brought her ass downstairs.

"You Ready let's go." She walked behind me. I opened the door for her and slammed it shut. I pulled off doing 80 mph. No words were spoken between us. She knew I was pissed.

"Khalid." She sighed.

"Kaniya, what the fuck was that back there? Don't fucking play with me or lie to me?"

"He stopped by Khalid, I don't know how he knew where I laid my head."

"Bullshit. Why were you laid up with this nigga and you and I are fucking around? He was too close for my liking. Does he have hope?"

"No, he doesn't have hope. He gave me a hug that's it."

"Kaniya don't lie to me, I know what the fuck I saw. I don't play games lil baby. I'm a grown ass man and I'm not beat or pressed for the shit that comes with you. If you fuck with me then you fuck with me. The worst thing you can do is play games with me. I'll fuck around and hurt you and that nigga. Call him and tell him don't show his face no more. I'm not like Lucky, if I touch a nigga he gone see Lucifer first then God. If you care that much about him, make sure he stays the FUCK up out your face. Tonight, was a warning that's all you get." I cut the music up...

Chapter-19

Lucky

From time to time, when I'm in my zone. I'll ride pass my house that Kaniya and I shared. I battle with going in and trying to work shit out with my wife. I was in my zone tonight. Yirah was nagging the fuck out of me.

My mother was scared to stay at the house because she thought Kaniya was coming back through. I hit the corner and saw a dunk at the gate. It's only one nigga in the city with a Candy red dunk sitting on 28's and that's Tariq.

What the Fuck is he doing at my house? He sat outside of the gate for a minute and that bitch finally let up. He pulled in the garage. I saw Kaniya standing in the garage looking like she was ready to get fucked. It took everything in me not to run up in my house and kill him and her. I sat across the street for a while. I wanted to see how long that nigga was going to be in there because I was going in. I rolled two blunts.

I sent Kaniya a text and told her I don't want that pussy ass nigga around my kids. No response. Two hours later a Bentley Truck pulled up to the gate and pressed the code to the gate. How in the fuck do these niggas got all this access to where my kids lay their heads? I refuse to let any man raise my kids. It's not happening.

To make matters worse this nigga didn't even knock. He kicked my fucking door open. To think I was trying to work shit out. She was trying to be hoe. My momma always said you can't turn a hoe into a house wife. I sat across the street watching 30 minutes later Tariq pulled off and ole boy was fixing my door. I watched Kaniya and the guy get in the car and he slammed the door. I sent her text.

Wife-We need to talk

She didn't respond she just read it. Kaniya got the game wrong I don't give a fuck what she does, but she ain't doing shit with Tariq or where my kids lay their head. She can't move around freely and do shit while she's still carrying my last name. Since she wants to be sloppy with the shit I'll contest the divorce and file for full custody and put her ass back on child support.

Kaniya

Oh my God. Khalid caught me. My heart dropped. I know better than that. I'm way fuckin' smarter than my actions. I was weak for Tariq. Knowing damn well I'm enjoying this thing that Khalid and I have going on. Khalid means so much to me. I grabbed my phone out of my purse to call my mother to see if she could watch the kids a few extra days. She answered on the first ring. She probably thinks something wrong because I'm calling her this late. I could hear her sucking her teeth in the back ground.

"What Kaniya Nicole Miller? I have your children so what could you possibly want?" She sassed.

"Ma, can you watch Jamel, Jamia and Jeremiah for a few extra days?" I sighed and pouted.

"For what, what's wrong with you Kaniya. I'm not raising your kids because nobody raised mine." She laughed. I swear sometimes I can't stand her. It had to be important if I'm calling this time of night. Now isn't the time for her to be playing games with me. Khalid snatched the phone for me.

"Mrs. Miller I'm sorry to bother you because it's late. Your daughter was trying to play me with Tariq. I got a problem with that. We have a few issues that need to be addressed. Send me an invoice and I'll pay you for your services." He stated.

"Mr. Mulsane this one is on the house. Be careful with my daughter. Kaniya Nicole Miller stop playing with him. I taught you better than that. Keep your ass way from Tariq. I'll see you in a few days," she argued and sassed. Why was Khalid putting my mother in our business? Khalid snatched my phone away from me.

"You heard what your mother said? You should try listening," He argued. I wasn't about to argue with Khalid. I was tired. He was mad at me and it's our first disagreement. My heart can't take it. I could care about Khalid a lot. I don't know where we're going. I'm scared to ask because he's driving like a maniac. "Khalid where are we going?" I asked.

"I'm asking the questions sit back and ride. You'll find out when we get there. You were booed up earlier, did you think about me when you were laid up in that niggas arms?"

"I always think about you Khalid Mulsane." He didn't even say anything back. Who told him to come to my house? Crazy ass kicked my damn door open. I fucked up. I shouldn't have done that. I should've shot that shit down. I can only be mad at myself. I closed my eyes trying so hard to forget everything that just happened. It seems like we were driving forever. I dozed off. Khalid yelled in my ear.

"Let's go, you should've gone to sleep instead of laying on that nigga." He opened my door and left it open. I wiped the little sleep I had in my eyes away. I stepped out of the car and we were at an air strip. It was a jet waiting for us. Khalid walked way ahead of me. I was behind him. I finally approached the jet. The flight attendant was standing there waiting on me.

"You must be Ms. Kaniya Miller," she asked. She had a thick Caribbean accent.

"I am." I smiled and shook her hand.

"It's nice to finally meet you. I've heard good things, so far. Mr. Mulsane is pissed. I'm guessing you're the reason?" she asked.

"Yeah." I whispered.

"Kiss and make up, please." She laughed.

"I'll try." I finally made it to the plane. Khalid was in his seat with his it reclined all the way back. He was looking through my phone. I didn't care about him going through it. I don't have anything to hide. It's a whole lot of conversations about him. I took a seat right beside him. We made eye contact with each other and he turned his head quick. He continued to play with my phone.

"Khalid, can we talk about it or you're going to stay mad at me? I'm tired of you ignoring me." He didn't answer me. Thank God this jet hasn't pulled off. I can take my ass back home. "Don't say nothing. I'm leaving I'm not about to do this with you. I'm sorry Khalid I fucked up. I was wrong I'll admit that." I walked away. Khalid was right on my heels too. He grabbed my hands. I turned around to look at him. I wanted to see what he had to say.

"Kaniya bring your ass back here. I'm only telling you once. I'm not even trying to handle you like this Kaniya, but you tried me. You didn't do anything, but you still gave that nigga hope. He shouldn't have even been that close to you. Why would he even be at your house at that time of night? It's disrespectful as fuck. It's your fault. You can't even recognize when a nigga preying on you. You always accepted whatever they were offering. Don't ever settle for less, you don't have too. Know your worth," he argued. Khalid was speaking facts. "Go take a shower, while you're standing up. Put those clothes in the trash and throw on a wife beater and a pair of my basketball shorts. Our flight doesn't land for three hours." Khalid was still mad at me. I knew better. I walked to the bathroom and took a long hot shower. I soaked in everything Khalid was saying. I handled my hygiene. I felt the plane take off. I took a seat and sat beside Khalid. He looked up at me and pulled me into his lap. He wrapped his arms around me and started biting my neck. I knew my neck was covered in teeth marks.

"You know you're mine, right? You need to act like," he stated.

"I know Khalid, I'm sorry."

"I believe you, but action speak louder than words." He stated. I wrapped my arms around his neck. He bit my bottom lip and gave me a big bear hug. I needed it. We talked for a little while until sleep finally consumed us. I haven't had this much sleep in a long time. Maybe it was because I was with him?

———

"Wake up Kaniya," he whispered in my ear. He gave me a face towel, so I could wash my face.

"I'm tired Khalid," I yawned. I wasn't ready to get up yet.

"I know, I am too. I'm trying to get you home, so we can get some rest but you're prolonging it. I want to feed you and put you back to sleep."

"Okay. I yawned and pouted. He grabbed my hand and we walked off the plane together. It was beautiful, hot, and very humid. We were on an island and palm trees were surrounding the air strip. Sand was everywhere. I could see the ocean and hear the sea gully's chirp.

"Where are we?"

"Mulsane Island." He smiled. I swear he keeps some shit up his sleeve. He said he lived in the Islands, he never said he owned one.

"Mulsane Island, Khalid?" I blushed and shook my head. Mr. Mulsane had to have some long bread, if he owns an Island? Maybe it's best that I didn't know. I probably wouldn't have given him a chance, if I knew he was eating like this. He's so humble. I knew he had some money, I just didn't know how much. I didn't care because I had my own bag. My mother always told me to get your own regardless. It's one of the reasons why I hustle like I'm broke. I swear he never seems to amaze.

"I wanted to surprise you, that's why I didn't say anything," he laughed. "I just want to see you smile lil baby." God sent me an angel. I prayed for this many late nights. The moment I met Khalid I've been smiling and living my life. We pulled up to Khalid's castle. This motherfucka didn't have a house. I had to act like I was used to shit. It was big and luxurious. The lawn was well manicured and palm trees cascaded it. It had to have at least thirteen bedrooms. The foundation was the prettiest shade of brown brick I ever saw.

The inside was amazing. He had two pools and a private beach. I could get use to this. He introduced me to his mother and his son. They were both very welcoming.

"What do you want to do lil baby?" He asked.

"Swim and tan of course. I need a swim suit."

"Cool we can go get you a few. I need you to get those lucky charms tattoos covered up." He stated.

"I plan on it Khalid."

Khali

Ali in love. It's been a minute since those words slipped out of my mouth. I knew Kaniya was special to him the moment he told me about her. I can't think of the last time he told me about a female with me, since Joy. My grandson's mother, she's deceased. May she rest in peace. Khalid is a lot like his father, that's a good thing. He didn't bed a lot of women. He's a hard worker, when he's passionate about something. He goes all in. I haven't had the chance to sit down with Kaniya, but I wanted too before she went back to the states. Every day she had something planned for all four of us to do. I like that she included my grandson and I in their plans. I could see why he was attracted to her.

The way the two of them look at each other, you could tell they were destined to be together. He's so attentive to her, it's crazy. She cooked dinner for us last night and it was amazing. She made a Caribbean dish that Khalid gave her the recipe too. She moved around his kitchen like she owned it. I sat far off in the corner and watched him watch her. Every time she would look up and catch him, she would have the biggest smile on her face.

She could feel him looking at her too. She makes him sweat too.

KJ loves her. She baked him some brownies and cookies. They played NBA2k19 all night. Khalid was jealous he made KJ go to sleep, so he could get some alone time with Kaniya. Khalid and Kj went out to get Kaniya something so it was, just the two of us. She was in Khalid's office working. I knocked on the door.

"Come in," she yelled.

"Good morning Kaniya, are you busy?"

"No, not at all. Is everything okay Mrs. Khali?"

"I wanted to talk to you about my son and my grandson." Kaniya's whole face changed. Her nosed flared up and she had an evil look on her face. "Don't do that Kaniya. Real women do real things. I would never make you feel uncomfortable.

I like your spirit. I love how you love my son. I love how you interact with my grandson. I love that about you. I love how Khalid loves you.

I'm going to ask you what are your intentions with my son? Let me speak before you answer. Khalid loves hard. I don't know if he told you or not, but he killed Joy? Kj's mother, she was playing games with him. I don't want that for you."

"Excuse my language. Oh, HELL no, If KHALID MULSANE, brought me over here to this island, to KILL ME. I guarantee you that motherfucka IS coming with me. I'm not going out like that Mrs. Khalid." She argued. I wanted to bust out laughing but I couldn't. Kaniya was dead serious too, this is the other side that Khalid was talking about. I saw the fire in her eyes. I could tell she was a force to be reckoned with.

"Calm down Kaniya. I didn't mean to get your blood to pumping. I was just playing with you."

"Mrs. Khali you play too much. You were never supposed to see that side of me," she laughed.

"I prefer the real you."

"Mrs. Khali, I'm going to be honest with you. I love Khalid Mulsane. Shhh, don't tell him I told you. My intentions are good. My life isn't perfect, but I'm working every day to be a better me. I have anger issues. I go from zero to a hundred quick. I'm scared because I've been hurt more times than I can count. I'm strong but I have feelings too. I don't look like what I've been through. We're taking things one day at a time. I wouldn't play with Khalid because he doesn't deserve that. I didn't know what a real man was until I met him. It's no comparison. He stimulates my mind and soul. He's different and I'm falling in love with how different he is."

"Great answer. If the two of you decided to get serious. Would you consider moving here or would you want him to move to the states?" Kaniya was blushing, she was too cute which means she's been thinking about it.

"I want to be wherever he is. I wouldn't mind living here. I'm open and adapted to change."

"Kaniya, I wish you and Khalid nothing but the best. Never put a time limit on love. Your life was already written. Live your life to the fullest and always stay true to yourself. All I ask is love Khalid as much as he loves you. Everything else will fall into place and work itself out."

"Thank you, Mrs. Khali. I appreciate you more than you'll ever know. Thank you for your warm welcome. I've came across a few mother's before but none of them can compare to you and I'm not just saying this. It's the truth."

"Thank you." Khalid told me what she did to her mother in law. Looking at Kaniya. I wouldn't think she was capable of that. I wouldn't mind having her as a daughter in law. Khalid needed him a rider. She was the definition of that. Kaniya and I finished talking. Khalid and Kj walked in and he looked at my face trying to read my facial expression.

"Ma, I hope you're not bothering Kaniya?" He asked. He was so protective of her.

"Khalid Mulsane, I got this. I raised you."

"Don't do that Khalid. Your mother and I were having a serious conversation, she's good."

Khalid

Kaniya and I have been together for five days now. We needed this time alone. I hate when tomorrow comes and she's leaving me. I can't wait to see what the future holds for us. We've been patient with each other. I'm ready to get serious with Kaniya but I'll have to make sure that's she all in. The little run in with Tariq pissed me off but that shit wasn't about nothing. She's perfect. My mother adores her. My son, he loves her too even though he just met her. I can't have anybody around my son. I haven't met her children yet. Yesterday morning I wanted to take Kaniya for a walk on the beach while the sun was rising. KJ beat me too it. I really enjoyed the time we've been spending together. I'm feeling lil baby for real. Kaniya was laying on my back, braiding my hair. I had a lot of things on my mind, even though she was here in the flesh, she consumed all my thoughts.

"What's wrong Khalid, why are you so quiet? What are you thinking about?" she asked. Kaniya could read me as well as I could read her.

"Are you sure you want to know?" I asked. Kaniya popped me in head.

"Yes Khalid," she pouted. She's always calling me by my government name. I flipped Kaniya over on her back side. I hovered over her body. Her eyes were piercing through mine. I stole a few kisses. Her breath always smells good. Fresh, like berries. "Are you going to tell me or what?"

"I'm thinking about you Ms. Miller and how much I'm going to miss you when you're gone. I like this shit we have going on. I want the real thing one day." I sighed. We'll have to make some changes real soon.

"Ugh I swear I wasn't ready to think about leaving here, until I actually step foot on the jet. I love Mulsane Island. Give me a reason to come back Mr. Mulsane," she smiled and bit her bottom lip. Kaniya was in heat too. Every time I laid on top her. I could feel the heat coming from between her legs. I'll put it out soon. She was tugging at my shorts. Every time she did that shit, my dick went crazy.

"I'm trying to give you plenty of reasons to come back to Mulsane Island. Keep playing your cards right. You better keep them hands to yourself before you get yourself in a lot of trouble," I chuckled. I was serious too. Kaniya was hardheaded, she kept doing that shit. "You feel him, run your hands down it. I promise you ain't ready for that lil baby. When we get there, I'm going to take you down through there." I meant that shit too. Kaniya moaned and bit her bottom lip, she ran her tongue across her teeth. I've been real patient. More than I would like too. I'm waiting for my moment.

"You know trouble doesn't have a hard time finding me. You know that's my middle name," she pouted and moaned. "Have you ever been raped before," she laughed. I swear this motherfucka is wild. "Khalid, if you keep making me wait, I'll fuck around and take it." She moaned. She kept playing with my dick. I raised up off Kaniya and she freed my dick from my pants. I swear she wanted me to bend her thick ass over so bad. I swear she don't want me to take her down through there.

"I heard but I'm trying to help you change that. I don't want trouble finding you."

"I know I've been staying out the way." Kaniya and I laid up in the bay window and listened to the rain. It was a bad storm coming through.

"Lil baby, Kj and I got you something while we were out earlier."

"I didn't need anything else Ali. You've given me much already."

"Yeah but I only got you one of these," I stated. I pulled the ring out of my pocket, opened it up, and placed it on her ring finger.

"Ali I can't accept this," she stated.

"You can, and you will. It's a promise ring. I want you to promise me, that you'll always stay true to me? Promise me that I'll never catch you in the arms of another man?"

"I promise Khalid."

Chapter-20

Yirah

"Yirah, you live in the mall. Do you need anything else? Jamila and Jamal have everything, what more could they possibly need? We've been at the mall, every day this week. You finally snagged you a boss," My best friend Chelsea laughed. We slapped hands with each other. Chelsea and I have been best friends since the third grade. She knew everything about Lucky and me. She's Jamal and Jamila's God mother. I love her to death. If I had a bag she had one too. Me and Chelsea ball together. Lucky gave me his black card months ago and I swipe that motherfucka every day. My children deserve everything. If their father had it, we had it. I blow through at least $7,000.00 a day. If I spend more than that, he gets a call. I always brought her something whenever we went out.

"I know Chelsea, I'm an impulse shopper. I wanted a girl so bad and I finally got one. Girls have the cutest stuff. They're always sending me these coupons to get more shit. I always end up buying extra shit. I can't wait to meet my princess. After I have Jamila, I'm done having babies for Lucky. I want the ring. I already have the house. Life is good right now." I'm happy. I'll be happier when Lucky gets his divorce. I'm being patient because we're not hiding our relationship. Kaniya knows about us and that we're expecting thanks to Cynthia.

"I can't wait meet my little diva. Yirah is that Kaniya over there?" she asked. Chelsea damn beat my back in. So, what if that's her. I squinted my eyes and she pointed in the men's section. I damn near broke my neck. That was her. I haven't seen Kaniya in forever.

"Cynthia said, she was fat after she had Jeremiah. Bitch where?" Who was that she was with though? I didn't want to stare too hard but damn I couldn't help myself. He was fine and handsome. He was built nice too. I had to walk a little closer. He had a nice full beard and lips, and mysterious eyes. His skin was the color of fresh bottle of Georgia pure honey.

"Damn Yirah take a fuckin' picture," she laughed.

"I'm about to do more than that." I've thought about it for months. What would I do if I saw her, since Lucky and I are official. I wanted her to see me pregnant and glowing by her husband with his black card. Yes, bitch I'm in your bag. Yes, bitch I fucked your husband on a numerous occasion. Kaniya thought nobody could have Lucky. Bitch I got him.

"Chelsea follow me." I sassed. Chelsea was right on my heels too. I approached the men's section. Kaniya and the guy she was with was trying on a blazer. She was picking out him a button down and a tie. "I need to get my husband some underwear too." Kaniya never looked up at me. The guy she was with walked up behind her and wrapped his arms around her waist. He was whispering sweet nothings in her ear and she was blushing like a school girl. She looked up and our eyes locked with each other. She rolled her eyes and bit her bottom lip. He grabbed a handful of her ass.

"Bitch you didn't tell me, she had somebody?" She asked. Lucky never said anything about her moving on. I follow her on social media. She never posted a picture of him. Lucky's MCM all day every day.

"Bitch I didn't know." I hope she keeps him because I'm keeping her husband. "I fuck on ya husband lil bitch. I'm your kid's step mother too, hoe. I'm in your husband's bag." I laughed. Chelsea busted out laughing too, Kaniya doesn't want any problems with us. Chelsea wouldn't hesitate to fight. We would tag team that bitch the same way she tagged me a year ago at Sonya's house. The guy Kaniya was with looked in our direction and gave me a menacing stare. I wasn't talking to him. Kaniya knew I was talking to her.

Kaniya

Yirah is the silliest bitch I know. Whose thinking about you? Clearly, I'm not. Who the fuck are you? The same way you gain them is how you lose them. She couldn't wait to fuck Lucky knowing we were together. It's a bitch waiting in the cut right now to fuck him. The sad thing about it, he's going to do it. More of the reason why he can get the fuck on. She's really in Nordstrom's acting stupid behind Lucky. I got what I want and it's not Lucky. You got him, kudos to you. Tell that nigga to sign the divorce papers so I can fuck on Khalid Mulsane. I can't wait to bust it open on a real nigga whose worthy of this pussy.

She wanted to throw her little slick shots. I'm not with any talking period. Don't let this cute face fool you. She already knows how I give it up. I know you're pregnant, but I will stomp the fuck out of your face. I have a lot of anger built up inside too. Trust me, she doesn't want me to unleash on her ass. She better be glad Khalid is with me because if he wasn't, I would show my ass right along with her. Then drag her through this fuckin' store. I wouldn't embarrass Khalid like that. He grabbed my hand

and we walked out of Nordstrom's. Khalid looked at me and I could tell he was about to say something.

"Do you know them? I'm glad you're classy and know how to act in public." He stated. My man was laughing at her silly ass. Big facts. I got me real one with all this faithfulness right here.

"Thank you. I only know the one with the mouth. That's his other baby momma." I laughed. Khalid looked at me as if I were lying. "Yep that's Yirah, my REPLACEMENT," I laughed

"Oh okay. Good thing she put you back on the market. She's mad at my lil baby with her fine ass?" Yep, I guess I can look at it like that. I would've never ran across Khalid if Lucky wouldn't have been cheating.

"Come on, are you ready to go?" he asked."

"Yeah but I want a cinnamon bun or a cookie? Khalid and I walked to the food court and ordered us two cinnamon buns and a frozen lemonade.

I found us a seat in the corner ducked off. He finally made his way over to me. He placed our cinnamon buns in front us. I fed Khalid a piece of my cinnamon buns and he got cinnamon on the side of his face being greedy. I grabbed a wet wipe from purse and wiped his mouth.

"Greedy ass," I mumbled. Khalid bit his bottom lip.

"Her breath even smells good," he chuckled. I can't stand him. I swear I can't. "Ugh, Kaniya I wanted to invite you to Lucky and I's baby shower, since you're my children's step mother," she laughed. Khalid and I looked at each other.

"Excuse me Khalid." I stood up to address this bitch, since she wanted me to acknowledge her. Khalid wrapped his hands around my waist to stop me from getting at Yirah. He whispered in my ear, "Calm down lil baby, she ain't worth it. Let me speak with her."

"Ms. LADY I need you to fall the fuck back. You're REACHING for no reason. You're going out your way for HER to see you. I ain't never FUCKED you nor do I plan too. We don't see you. I'm trying to enjoy my lil baby without these lil slick disses," he argued. Khalid checked Yirah and her little friend. She walked off mumbling under breath.

"Thank you. I was about to go to jail. I swear I didn't want to embarrass you in this mall, but she was asking for it. I told you they be provoking me. I can only take so much." I sighed.

"I know. Your chest was heaving up and down. I knew you were about to show my ass. I couldn't have you doing that out her. I got you though."

———

I was tired, we had a long day. Lucky picked up the kids for the weekend. Tonight, was Khalid's last night in the states until next month. I wanted as much alone time with him as I could get. I be having withdrawals and shit. I don't think I could do this long-distance thing with him for too much longer because I miss him so much. Khalid and I were laid back on the sofa watching a movie. He was massaging back and thighs. It felt so good that soft moans escaped my lips.

"My lil baby getting thick." He slurred. We both had two shots of Don Julio and an edible. We were feeling lovely. I couldn't even pay attention to the TV because his hands felt so good.

"What are you trying to say?" I asked. I turned around to face him. I glared in his eyes. I didn't think Khalid noticed I put on a few pounds.

"You heard what I said Kaniya. I like meals, I don't eat snacks." I politely turned around and started looking back at the TV. Khalid pulled my hair back and I gazed up at him. He stole a kiss from me. My phone alerted me that I had a text. I grabbed my phone and it was an Instagram Alert from a name that I didn't know. I logged on immediately and it was a video of Jamia and Yirah. Yirah grabbing Jamia's cheeks talking about step momma's the best. I instantly jumped off the couch and put my shit on. Khalid raised up behind me.

"What's wrong, where are you going KANIYA?" he yelled.

"Khalid I'm going to jail today." I threw my phone at him, so he could look at the video." He grabbed me and sat me down on his lap. "Let me get up Khalid, I got to go. Fucking with me is one thing, but fuckin' with my children that's a no, no."

"Calm down lil baby, you know I can't let you leave up out here? She mad baby. They're fans. I know how you feel about your babies but cool out. Chill with your man, Lucky maybe a lot of things but he wouldn't let anyone hurt your kids." True, but Yirah wanted a reaction out of me and for that reason alone I'm going to beat her ass tomorrow, when Khalid is long gone. A bitch can't keep trying me.

Chapter-21

Kaniya

Sleep didn't want to find me tonight. The devil has been dancing around all in my head and sitting on my back. My mind was his playground and I for damn sure was his victim. I've thought of a million ways to kill Lucky and Yirah. I thought I would be over it by now but I'm not. Before Khalid and I went to bed we prayed. It's a difference when a man prays for you instead of preying on you. Lucky was preying on me. He knows how I give it up. He used my kids to fuck with my mental. He knows I would die and go to hell for them. He wanted a reaction from me and he's failed miserably getting it. Lucky tried my whole fuckin' life when he let Yirah post pictures of my daughter on her social media. Don't grab my fuckin' daughter's cheeks.

Khalid stopped me from going over there earlier but night has fell and he's asleep. That shit is still heavy on my mind. I'm a night crawler. It's time for a bitch to feel me. Touching Lucky's momma wasn't enough. A bitch won't be satisfied until I snatch their fuckin' soul. Khalid should've prayed for Yirah because she was my fuckin' prey. I don't have anything against Yirah or her relationship with Lucky but the worst thing you can do is get besides yourself and fuck with me. Yirah has tried me one too many fuckin' times. She thinks because she pregnant I won't touch her. That's a lie. Her face ain't pregnant. I can't let this BITCH this slide, can't no BITCH get a pass with me. I kept her alive so Lucky could be happy with her. She's so dumb. She's going to fuck around and make me kill her stupid ass and she won't even be able to enjoy his trifling ass.

I don't want his ass, she can have him. I tapped that ass one time, but I guess that wasn't enough. I wanted to beat her ass senseless. I'm so fuckin' tired and over all this bullshit. Khalid stopped me a few weeks ago we were at the mall. She was fuckin' with me and he saved that ass. What I'm about to do could make or break what Khalid and I have going on. A bitch can't send for me without any repercussions. I'm coming the worse way every fuckin' time. I was content with being by myself. I tried to go to bed several times, but I've been tossing and turning all night.

I should be taking advantage of lying in Khalid's arm's, but I couldn't even enjoy it. Sleep would only find me when I touch a bitch. I wanted to be a better person, but I don't think now was the time for me to change. I heard everything Khalid was saying, but I wasn't trying to hear that at all. I swear I'm trying to grow up and move with caution because of my kids.

Lucky doesn't want to see me happy at all. I like Khalid a whole lot, shit I love his ass to be truthful. I can't turn the other cheek like he wants me too. I'm not that bitch. I couldn't take it anymore. A bitch had to feel me. I politely got up out the bed kissed and Khalid on his lips. I had to handle my business. He started stirring around in his sleep.

"Kaniya, where the fuck are you going?" He asked and yawned. I jumped, I could've sworn he was asleep. Khalid was so fine, I swear God sculpted him to perfection. He stood to his feet and wiped the sleep out the corners of his eyes. He pulled me in for a hug, and I wrapped my arms around his neck.

"I can't sleep Khalid." I sighed and pouted. His hands roamed my body. I hate he has me so wide open. He can read me as if I was book he wrote. I could tell he was about to say some shit I didn't like.

"You kissed me as if you were about to leave and it was our last time. I'm asking you again where the fuck is you going, and you're fully dressed? Stop fuckin' playing with me. Let me guess you're going to run down on Lucky? You're willing to risk what the fuck we have going on just to play your get back games with him? I already told you I'm not the guy for it Kaniya. A real man doesn't want you to chase him. He wants to chase you.

You're smart. Its game and he want you to keep playing with him. Trust me he's waiting on your arrival. If you leave out this door to go fuck with him, don't come back. I'm not leaving the door open for you to come back. Think about that on your way out." He argued. So much for sneaking out the bed. Khalid removed me from his embrace.

"I'm not running up behind Lucky, Khalid. It's not about Lucky. It's about me and my fuckin' respect. I've been over Lucky, but I don't have to clarify shit for nobody. I'm leaving and I'm going to handle my business regardless of the consequences. It's okay for everybody to fuck with me but as soon as I defend myself it's a fuckin' problem.

I can't turn the other cheek Khalid, not on this one. I never start anything. I'm always on the receiving end. Maybe it's not meant for us. You always see your way and not mine, and I'm okay with that. We can agree to disagree. I'll be honest with you with you Khalid, if you were in my shoes and a man kept coming at you sideways. I'll tell you to get at that nigga fuck that. I appreciate you more than you'll ever know." I explained. I wasn't saying good bye.

"Look don't use me as an example. Maybe it's not meant for us? Really Kaniya, is that how you feel? Maybe you need to let your husband go and the bullshit that comes with him. It's a crime for me to tell you to stand down? Every reaction doesn't need a reaction. Yirah knows she's reaching. What do I know? No matter what, the two of you share Lucky because of your kid. All the extra shit, you need to move past it for the sake of your kids and hers.

You can leave Kaniya and chase your baby daddy and his new baby momma. I know you would rather be somewhere else than here. I need me a woman that's willing to listen. I'm not trying to keep you if you don't want me too. I play for keeps Kaniya but only for the right one. I'm guessing that's not you. I'll see you around." He explained. I wasn't about to go back and forth with Khalid about what I'm doing and why.

"Khalid, no matter what you think, I love you." I cried. I ran out the door and I didn't even give him time to respond. My Uber driver was already downstairs waiting on me. It wasn't about Lucky or Yirah. It was about me and my feelings. If I was willing to walk out on Khalid and lose the small glimpse of peace I have. I'm not the one that'll be missing out on something, trust me. I grabbed my phone out of my pocket to call my mother and she didn't answer. I refuse to call my dad because I didn't want to hear his mouth. I'm not calling Killany. Let me call Mook, I know he should be up. Thank God he answered on the first ring.

"What's wrong?" He yelled. He knew something was wrong because I never call him this late.

"Aye Mook. Everything, but I'm not calling about that I'm about to go to jail. I tried to call momma, she's not answering the phone. I got my bond money on me. Tell her to get my kids from that PUSSY ASS NIGGA. If I don't call back within two hours meet me on Rice Street."

"Let that shit go Kaniya. Where the fuck you at, let me handle this shit." He argued.

"No, Mook I got this one; it's on me. I'm tired of motherfuckas coming at me. Let momma know what's up."

"I swear to God Lucky want me to touch his ass for real. I try so hard to stay out of your shit, but that nigga kept reaching. Do you want me to touch him? Where the fuck is Khalid," he asked.

"I'll tell you about Khalid another day." I finished chopping it up with Mook.

———

Yeah nigga, this shit real out here Running through the red light

Looking through your rear-view Nigga might just sneak up on the car and try to spray you. We're playing for keeps, down here in the A

Future's Red Light was blaring through my speakers. I finally made it to Lucky's house. I knew he was asleep. It wasn't a single light on. I hope he's sleeping well because I couldn't get any sleep. A few months ago, when Lucky came by the house, he had his keys lying around. I ran to the store while he was sleep and made copies. Something told me they would come in handy one day. I'm going out the same way I came in, harder than a motherfucka.

I unlocked the front door. It's been over a year since I've been to this house. Lucky tells so many lies he couldn't even keep up with them. He swore he sold this house when we got married. I knew he was lying, but he wanted me to sell all my property. I stopped at Jamia and Jamel's room and kissed them on their cheeks. Jeremiah was in his crib stretched out. He was stirring around in his sleep. He probably was dreaming, or he smelled me. He was used to sleeping underneath me. I gave him a big kiss too. Jamal looked just like Lucky's no-good ass the older he got. I knew he was his all alone I just didn't want to believe it.

I wanted to believe he wasn't his, but he was. I couldn't believe Lucky would do that to me. It's all good though, it is what it is. I approached Lucky's bedroom. Yirah was lying on the right side of the bed and Lucky on the other side.

God is good, he must have known they deserve everything that's coming to them. It was perfect. Yirah was sleeping so peacefully. It's a shame the devil is on my back right now and she's my fuckin' prey.

I approached the right side of the bed where Yirah was lying. I grabbed her cheeks with so much force you could see her teeth. I pinched the fuck out of her ass. She opened her eyes, looked at me, and she tried to raise up. She was staring down the barrel of my AK47. I knelt, I wanted to be eye level with her. Fucking with me, it's consequences. I hold bitches accountable for their actions. I whispered in her ear.

"You fucked up playing with a bitch a like me. I don't have a heart. The nigga that's lying next to you, he took that shit from me years ago. I don't give a fuck about you being pregnant. Jamia, she's my daughter, not yours. I don't fuck with you and you know that. Never post a picture of my daughter on your social media and tag me in the shit on some petty shit. For that reason alone, I got to touch you. I don't give a fuck about you and him, BITCH you can have him. In my twenty-eight years of living I ain't never came for NANN bitch, behind that nigga. They always came for me.

You sent for me, so I'm here in the flesh to handle mine. It ain't no fuckin' fun when I got the gun and you're my fuckin target. You better ask that nigga about me, straight fuckin' head shots. If you don't know anything about me, know this, you gone respect me PERIOD. I'll stay at a bitch neck about my respect. I'm at your neck Yirah. I've put a few bitches and niggas on a RIP T-shirt. All the little petty shit you've been doing, I think your face deserves to be on a t-shirt too. Give me one reason WHY I shouldn't make that shit happen? Bitch I ain't got one."

"I'm sorry Kaniya. I got kids to live for," she cried and whispered.

"On some real shit, that's not good enough for me. You should've thought about your kids when you decided to fuck with me. You're only sorry because I got this AK in your face and you know I'll let this bitch rip. You see this hundred round drum in your face. I'm in love with Khalid Mulsane. I risked our future to come here and handle my business. All my life I've taken losses and I've bounced back every time.

I've lost something special to me, because I couldn't let a bitch slide. You feel me? I hope you're willing to lose something too. I smacked duct tape on Yirah's mouth. I still had the AK trained on her face. Tears were running down her face, but that shit didn't move me. I don't give a fuck.

"Watch me work." I stripped naked in front of her. I walked over to Lucky. I pulled the covers back. Her eyes were still trained on me. He started stirring in his sleep. I mounted him and pulled the covers over our body. I looked over at Yirah and smirked. Lucky's hands roamed my body, she could see it through the sheets. She was sick to her stomach. I always hit a bitch where it hurts. I was way thicker than Yirah. Lucky knew that. He knew my body. It didn't stop his hands from roaming, nor did he open his eyes. I sat on his face and start riding him. I grabbed my AK from the middle of the bed, she closed her eyes.

I tapped her head with the butt of the gun twice. I forced her to look at me. I tried to tell her this isn't what she wants; she'll lose every time. I rode his face like my life depended on it. I came at least three times. Lucky grabbed my breasts. I knew he felt my nipple rings. I kept riding him. I nutted all on his face. I turned around and rode his face from the back. He was eating my ass and sucking my pussy. He finally opened his eyes and looked at me, and he was confused. He tried to raise up. I grabbed the AK and pointed in his face. I pushed him back down. I released the safety.

"Kaniya, what the fuck is this? What are you doing here and where's Yirah," he asked. I busted out laughing.

"Lucky, I'm asking the motherfucka fuckin' questions not you. Listen to me while I'm fuckin' talking. I'm tired of you and this bitch fuckin' with me. You know when I'm fed up, ain't nobody fuckin' safe, not even the BITCH that's lying next to you. You pushed me so I'm pushing you. The difference between me and her is, a bitch gone feel me. I'm touching motherfuckas. Y'all two got some shit to lose. She should've learned from your fuckin' MAMMY.

I don't play with hoes especially behind a nigga like you. I want my divorce finalized today. I want full custody of my fuckin' kids. I need you to make that happen TODAY my nigga. You FEEL ME or I'm going to touch your MAMMY and this BITCH in the worst way." I argued.

I raised up off Lucky. He jumped up and tried to back me in the corner. I pressed my finger on the trigger. This nigga got one time to touch me and I'mma let this bitch rip, not giving a fuck my kids are two doors down the hall. "TRY and DIE." I spat. That's what the fuck I thought, he knows it ain't no bitch in me.

"You better tread lightly. Go check on your bitch that's lying over there in tears. Make me shoot your pussy ass. Yirah you see what type of nigga you are running up behind. I'm his muscle. I got that come back pussy. He always comes back. This time around it ain't no coming back. He had no problem eating this pussy. The only thing he can do for me is eat my pussy and my ass, that's it. He'll never be able to feel me again." I laughed. I politely put my clothes on. Lucky rushed to Yirah's side. She had blood covering her hands and she was holding her stomach.

"Lucky, I need to go to the hospital," she cried.

"Kaniya, if she losses my baby. I swear to God I'm going to kill you. I put that shit on my momma," he argued and snarled his face. Lucky didn't scare me at all. I cocked my head to the side. I pointed the AK in his face.

"Come on Lucky, let's shoot this shit out once and for all. I'm sick of you. You know I don't give a fuck about raising my kids by myself." I argued. He turned his back. I shoved the back of the AK in the back of his head. I didn't ease up until I saw fuckin' blood. I blacked out. I don't give a fuck about hurting him. Lucky fell to the floor. Yirah was screaming.

"Stop you've done enough," she cried. I looked over my shoulders.

"Bitch who the fuck are you talking too?" I asked. I know she wasn't talking to me. I shoved the butt of the gun in Yirah's face two times. I walked out and headed to Jamia and Jamel's room. I woke them both up and I grabbed Jeremiah. As soon as I stepped outside on the porch Atlanta Police Department was waiting on me, this bitch called the police.

"Excuse me we received a phone call for trespassing and assault. We have to take you in, do you have someone that could get your children?" The officer asked. Police bitch ass, for that reason alone she deserved everything she got tonight.

"I do apologize officer, but this is my house. I'm Mrs. Jamel Williams LEGALLY. I caught my husband and his SIDE BITCH having an affair in my home, while my children were asleep. The only person going to jail is the SIDE BITCH that called you. She's trespassing, this is my house. All the utilities are in my name. Run my tags my vehicle is registered here.

My name is on the DEED. If you excuse me, I need to find my kids and I a place to lay our heads tonight." I argued. The police escorted me and my kids to the car.

I fastened them all in safely. I pulled off. I wasn't going to jail. I was going home to rest. Sleep finally was ready to consume me. No, my name wasn't on the deed or the house, they didn't need to know that. Legally I'm Mrs. Jamel Williams until he signs those papers. Lucky and Yirah better learn to stop fuckin' with me. I come with straight heat and they'll get burned every fuckin' time. My babies were asleep. I knew Khalid was still up, if I wake up in the middle of the night. I wouldn't have a problem with calling him and he'll answer. I called him blocked. I put the phone on mute.

"Hello," he yelled. I was too scared to say anything. We just sat there and held the phone. He was waiting for me to say something. I couldn't get the words to come out. Tears were blaring my vision. I had to pay attention to make sure I got my kids home safely. I did all that and I still feel like shit because I'M missing HIM. I just wanted to be WITH HIM.

"If you called just to hear my voice Kaniya, why the fuck did you leave? I heard what you said lil baby. I love you too, but love wouldn't have let you walk out of that door." He explained. He disconnected the call.

Chapter-22

Lucky

Kaniya knows she took shit too fuckin' far. I swear to God I'm going to fuckin' hurt her ass. Yirah lost our fuckin' daughter, she had a miscarriage because her blood pressure was through the roof, and she was stressed out. I got this big ass gash in the back of my head along with eleven stitches fuckin' with her. The police refused to press charges since Kaniya was still my wife and it was a love triangle. Yirah was livid she lost our daughter. My mother was all up in my ear and Yirah's mother too. I told Yirah to stop fuckin' with Kaniya a few weeks ago but she wouldn't listen.

"Lucky, you need to divorce Kaniya. You lost your fuckin' daughter because of her. I'm sick of that BITCH, do you hear me? Do you see my fuckin' lips Lucky? No matter how much skin I get applied each month, my lips will never look the same anymore. Let that BITCH go, she's crazy. I don't want to have anything to do with her or her kids. Their MAMMY ruined it for them," my mother argued. Everybody had an opinion but didn't want to hear the facts.

"Momma, for once shut the fuck up. Own up to your shit. I should've listened to KODAK when he was trying to tell me about you. I hate what happened to you, but you asked for it. Kaniya ain't never came at you wrong. It was always you, coming for her. Yirah own up to your shit, you've been fucking with Kaniya for as long as I can remember. I told you to stop but you wouldn't fuckin' listen and now our daughter is dead. Stop fuckin' with somebody that's not fuckin' with you. Be prepared for the consequences. Roll with the fuckin' punches that you're putting out there."

"Lucky are you," I cut my mother off.

"Momma you heard what the fuck I said. Listen when I'm fuckin' talking." I'm not trying to hear any of that shit. Yirah's momma was looking at me like I was crazy, but I was dead serious.

Yirah

I can't believe she did all that shit too me. I lost my fuckin' daughter. I had a miscarriage. When the paramedics came my blood, pressure was 240. I almost had a heart attack. "I lost my baby" I cried. To make matters worse. I watched Lucky eat her pussy and ass, while she shoved her gun at the temple of my head. He knew that wasn't me. "I lost my daughter because of you Lucky." I cried. I couldn't stop the tears from falling.

"No, you lost our daughter because you couldn't stop fucking with Kaniya. If you want to blame anybody blame yourself. I told you about that shit, but you wouldn't stop. You ain't got shit to prove Yirah. We all know what it is," he argued. I know he didn't try to flip this shit on me. He got me fucked up.

"It's my fault you cheated on your wife with me multiple times? We created two children together while you were with me and married to her? You won't even sign the divorce papers, why Lucky?" I cried. He doesn't get it. I hate that I'm in love with him. I did all this crazy shit because of him. I lost my princess. The tears wouldn't stop. Lucky climbed in the bed with me and held me. He whispered in my ear, "I'm sorry Yirah, you know I didn't want this to happen. I'm fucked up about it too. We can try again. I want to try again." My body tensed up hearing him say that.

"I don't want to have another child with you, if you're still married. Losing our daughter was a wake-up call. I'm leaving. I can't do this anymore. I won't do this anymore." Lucky eyes turned dark. My hairs raised up of the back of my neck. He wrapped his hands around my throat. His face was tight and snarled up.

"Where the fuck do you think you're going? You wanted all this. You wanted to fuck me knowing I had a wife. You wanted me to lose my wife. I've lost my wife. Everything you wanted to happen, happened. You just got touched in the process. As for you, you're not going anywhere. I need a bitch that's gone listen and ride. I need a bitch that can stand in the paint and take all the heat she created. I need you to be that bitch you claim to be. You had no problem letting Kaniya know every time you fucked me, when and where. Suck up your fuckin' tears you're living to see another day."

"I need a nigga that's single. I need a nigga that doesn't have a wife. I don't care about riding for you. Why won't you divorce her? Lucky if she wants a divorce grant her one. How is that fair to me? When are you going to give a fuck about me? I love you Lucky, but I don't think you love me. You like this? She's unhappy and so am I." Something has to give.

"You're worried about the wrong shit."

Chapter-23

Kaniya

Giselle and I have been on the phone for over an hour talking about everything up under the sun. We don't get to wrap like we use too, because we've both been busy. Khalid has been in the city for a few weeks and that's not like him. Mrs. Khali said I was stressing him out, clearly that's not the case. I know he's been around the shop, because my employees said they've seen him all week. Pretending like he was making sure the renovations were working properly. I was good on Mr. Mulsane. I don't want Giselle reminding me of how much I fucked up.

"Kaniya I want you to come to the block party with me that Alonzo and Dro are throwing."

"Giselle, I don't know. I'm not trying to run into Khalid at all. I'm not ready for that. If I catch him with another bitch I don't think I could handle that seriously." I missed Khalid something serious. Sometimes when I'm alone I call his phone just to hear his voice. I wonder if he knows it's me.

"Kaniya, you love him, don't you? Why are you fighting it? I don't think Lucky and Yirah were worth walking out on Khalid." She asked. They weren't but she wasn't about to keep fuckin' with me. Giselle and I get along so good because I'm a hot head and she's not. I'm not use to the soft approach.

"Giselle, it's not that simple. You and I agree to disagree all the time. Listen I love Khalid and he knows that. He was willing to walk away from us so easy. I had to handle my business for my sanity. Khalid made it about Lucky, it wasn't. I'm not chasing Khalid. Giselle, if that's what he wants than, it is what it is." Khalid has no understanding. It's all good though.

"Kaniya, I know you're going to handle your business regardless. I think it was more about you leaving him in the middle of the night to handle Yirah and Lucky. You get it, Khalid didn't want you doing that. I didn't want you doing that either, that's why you didn't call me until after you did it, but it's whatever," she laughed.

"First of all, you can't do what I do. Dro's isn't letting you leave the house at 1:00 a.m. to ride shot gun with me to fuck up Lucky. Whatever Giselle, why is it okay for everybody to fuck with me? I can't turn the other cheek.

I can't FUCKIN' do it, no I WON'T fuckin' do it, Giselle."
I argued. A bitch got me fucked up.

"I know but you have too, if you want to get Khalid
back," she laughed. Giselle was up to something. I ain't got
time, bitch don't provoke me.

"What's so funny? Bitch fuck Khalid. I'm not
thinking about his ass." I laughed.

"Bitch you're funny. That's your fuckin' problem,
you need some dick. When was the last time was your cat
blown out? I don't see how you do it, I'm not about to be
crazy behind no man if I haven't sampled the dick. Dro
made me mad as hell when he tried that shit on me. You're
not fooling me Kaniya, you're scared of Khalid. Come to
the block party with me? IF you're not thinking about
HIM." She laughed.

"Look Giselle, stop playing with me. I'll come and
I'm only staying for an hour or so. I have a date anyway.
Fuck you and fuck Khalid. Send me the address and I'll see
you soon."

"Date, with who? Bitch I need details name and
location please?"

"Bye Giselle, send me the address," I laughed. I hung up in Giselle's face. Nosy ass, I don't know why she was playing with me anyway. Khalid told me about this block party months ago. They throw it every year. I guess I'll go. Giselle's always inviting me to things. I'm her plus one so she doesn't have to be bothered with Nikki and Alexis. I needed to get out the house anyway. I didn't want to be in the same space with Khalid, but it is what it is. It's the beginning of fall and it's still 91 degrees. I love the weather and I'm dressing according to it.

Jeremiah put that pound game to me. I was thick as fuck. Thicker than my great grand momma's grits. I feel like showing my ass today and a whole lot of skin. If Khalid was with a bitch, he wouldn't be for long. I'm playing for keeps behind that one. Everything is different and a little bit clearer with that one. I had a little pudge and a lot of stretch marks from that little motherfucka. I had a cute white Balmain baby doll dress, it stopped at the middle of my thighs. If I bend over, it'll show all my ass.

I grabbed a pair of white True Religion shorts out my closet, because I know I'll be bending over. I grabbed my white and silver Nike Airmax 95. Tariq brought me these shoes for my birthday. He was skeptical about buying them because he didn't want me to walk out of his life. I washed my hair earlier. It's too hot to flat iron it. I braided my hair into two French braids. My edges were on fleek. My hair has really grown out long. It's reaches the middle of my back, inches on you bitches. If my hair ends up touching my ass, a bitch ain't gone be able to tell me shit. These hoes can't tell me shit now.

I finished braiding my hair, fuck some make up. It's too damn hot. I painted my lips nude. I lathered my skin with Bath and Body Works Sunshine lotion.

I glanced in the mirror admiring my look. I was popping. I grabbed my clutch and key fob. Game on bitches. I was more than ready to head out. Lucky had the kids.

Yirah knew not to fuck with me after losing her daughter, and Lucky too, he didn't give a fuck if Khalid and Tariq weren't in the picture. He still hasn't signed those divorce papers. I don't know why he was still holding on and dragging me through court. We're not reconciling shit Every blue moon, he'll call me to conversate. Nope talk to your bitch or your mammy, because I don't have any conversation for you. Enough about Lucky let me get to this block party. It was off Fairburn Road near Ben Hill.

I knew this shit was about to be lit. It was popping. The block was flooded on Fairburn Road from Hot Chicks Wings all the way to Ben Hill park. I hit the alley on the little side street and pulled in the back of Giselle's granny house. Thank God Giselle, save me a spot at her granny's house. Her grandmother stayed right down the street from the park. Kassence and Giselle were standing on the back porch. Where was Ryleigh's cute ass. As soon as I killed the engine Kassence little bad ass snatched the door open.

"Auntie KANIYA. I missed you. You look so pretty. Ma, auntie's so cute, wait until Khalid sees her," she cooed and giggled. I looked at Giselle and rolled my eyes hard. She looked at me and shook her head. I told her about talking in front of her. I guess Khalid was here, Kassence confirmed it. I hit the key fob and grabbed my dark Gucci shades out of my armrest. I refuse to lock eyes with him or openly eye fuck him.

"Damn Mrs. Williams, you're showing out today. Ass and legs all that good shit. You know you my bitch. Khalid, he's here with Rose. Alexis cousin that I was telling you about." She stated. I nodded my head acknowledging what she said. Giselle already knew when I pull up. I'm shutting shit down. The fuck she thought.

"Well this is what single looks like," I laughed. I did a little spin, giving Giselle a full view.

"Yeah right! Bitch please, don't start no shit today please. You're too cute for that. Even though your man is out here on some bullshit with his little company. She's not weighing up to you period."

"I'm not bothered Giselle. He's not my man and he's single. If he's dating, that's cool because I'm dating too and accepting applications. Khalid wouldn't provoke me. He knows I'll cut the fuck up. He's not messy at all. He doesn't have any bitch tendencies, at least I didn't get that the time that we shared. I wouldn't do that at Dro's event." I explained. Giselle and I made our way to the park. We walked passed Journee and her crew. Nikki was yelling my name. I threw my hand up at her. I'll make sure I stop by later to say hi. Nikki was cool once you got to know her. Kassence wanted me to take her to swing. I had to spend some time with her. My niece was my priority. Kassence got tired and complained about it being too hot.

We walked over to the Gazebo where Giselle and Dro were posted up. Dro and Alonzo's Gazebo was deep, it was so many motherfuckin' niggas out here. My eyes wouldn't stop wandering. I felt somebody looking at me. I turned around and it was him, Khalid. Even with a bitch sitting on his lap, our eyes connected. He bit his bottom lip. I turned around quick. I took enough of him in. His beard needed to be lined up and his hair needed to be braided. His hair was in a man bun, but he was still sexy. Giselle looked at me and I busted out laughing. Everybody was looking at us, she caught me looking at him. Can't no nigga make or break me, not even Khalid's fine ass. You can put me in the room with a hundred lions and I won't fold. It's too much eye candy out here to be worried about Khalid Mulsanne.

"Giselle I'm about to go mingle with some single motherfuckas okay. I'll see you in a minute." I laughed. The fuck I want to be around all these couples and shit. It was so much tension between Khalid and me. I couldn't be that close to him, while another bitch was next to him. I made this bed and I'll continue to lay by myself in it.

"What's up Kaniya?" He yelled. I looked over my shoulder and it was Alonzo.

"What's up Zo?"

"You good?" He asked. Who was he asking for, himself or Khalid? Khalid and Zo were cousins. Khalid's mother and Zo's father were brothers and sisters.

"Yes, ZO I'm always good." I sassed and laughed. Alexis was looking at me like she was crazy, because Alonzo was speaking. Bitch sit down, before I put another bullet in your jaw. I've been knowing Alonzo way before he decided to fuck you and only you. I'm not Giselle, bitch its hell when I come through.

I couldn't even leave out the Gazebo good without niggas trying to holla at me. Some nigga was stopping me, he was finer than a motherfucka. I tried to keep walking, but he was persistent. His skin was the color of a snicker. His body was covered in tat and he was built nice too. He had dark brown eyes and perfectly shaped irises. He had full lips and a small nose. He had a low haircut, with a few waves. His mouth was slugged out, he was blinding me with all the diamonds and gold. He grabbed my thigh and I popped his hand. He's fine but don't touch me.

"What you are doing girl with all that?"

"Ooh nothing." I laughed.

"What's all that poking from the BACK? Damn queen you're the baddest motherfucka I've seen today coming through these parts. What's your name?"

"Kaniya."

"I'm Jugg. I had to say something to you."

"It's nice to meet you Jugg."

"I'm Single Again, back on the prowl Jugg. It's recruiting season. I'm a free agent looking for some replacements, I'm currently accepting applications." I sassed.

"Aye Alonzo and Vell. Lil momma got some crazy game, Lil momma said that she's a free agent, she's looking to book for some replacements. I like that shit. I got my work cut out for me with this one. Yo Kaniya, can I get an application or something? How can I apply? I need your name and number first?" He yelled and asked. Jugg was off the hook. Alonzo was giving me that look. Fuck Khalid.

"Jugg, if I see you again I'll give you my number. I'm recruiting it's not easy to get in my good graces. I'll see you around." I smiled. I walked off quick. He was crazy as hell. I like his crazy. I needed to stay very far away from him. My phone alerted me I had a text.

Dimples - Bitch you got Khalid Hot. Stay away from Jugg bitch, he is crazy as hell. TRUST ME. He's still talking about you. Khalid mad.

Fuck Khalid he needs to worry about the chick whose sitting on his lap. She's mighty close. He's cuffing her, but you're looking at me. Boy bye.

Rodica and God momma Valerie was sitting up the hill, so I went to say hey to them. I was about to walk back up front were Nikki and Journee were posted up because I was more than ready to go. Tariq was about to pull up, he was right down the street. He would pull up right in front of Dro's Gazebo. How did he get that Donk in here? He hit my phone up and I walked over to his car. He was on his thot shit. He was fine, it wasn't no denying that. He was draped up Gucci everything. His dreads were freshly twisted. His face was lined up to perfection. Every bitch out here was looking at him. He pulled me into his arms and grabbed more than a handful of my ass. He whispered in my ear.

"You got me all the way fucked up. You want a nigga to put the lock and chain on your ass. Let's go I'm ready for my date, where the fuck are you parked at?" He argued. I laughed in Tariq's face he plays too much.

"Whatever thot. I'm about to get up out of here in a minute. All these ladies out here choosing and openly eye fucking you. Do you know them? I want to see you cuff something?" I laughed.

"I'm trying too. I got a date tonight with somebody I'm trying to cuff," he laughed. He pulled me into his arms for another hug,

"Whatever Tariq. I'll see you later."

"Bet, you got two hours." He stated and kissed me on my forehead. Tariq pulled off. I started walking toward my car. I didn't even tell Giselle bye. I was ready for my date that I've been looking forward to all week. Tariq was fine. I don't know why we were teasing each other. We could be together at this point. I was considering it. I don't care what Lucky, or anybody has to say, He accepts me, flaws and all. I couldn't shake him for some reason. Maybe he's not meant for me to shake. To be honest I'm tired of fighting it, our chemistry is amazing and whatever happen, happens.

Khalid

Kaniya got me all the way fucked up. I knew I was here with Rose, but she straight up disrespected me. Jugg needs to fall all the way back. I told her about Tariq months ago and that shit still stands no matter what the fuck I said. She thinks this shit is game and she's used to playing with motherfuckas however she wants too. I don't play games I meant what the fuck I said. Where the fuck is she going anyway?

"Aye Rose. I need you to raise up. I need to make a quick run and handle some business. Alexis or Alonzo will take you home." I argued.

"Are you serious Khalid? I rode with you. I knew that was her. I didn't want to believe it, until that guy and Alonzo both said her name. Your whole vibe changed. I could feel it.

"Yeah Rose that was her, so what. Alexis and Alonzo will take you home. Don't make a fucking scene. Aye Giselle let me holla at you really quick?" I wasn't about to go back and forth with Rose about shit. What's understood doesn't need to be explained.

"Giselle, where the fuck did Kaniya go and where did she park?" I yelled. I don't give a fuck if Rose heard me or not. She needs to mind her business and not mine.

"She's in her Corvette, she's parked at my grandma's house on Daniel Road. It's the Red brick house on the left," she explained.

"Good looking out, I appreciate that." Kaniya had a nigga on feet looking for her ass. I patted my hip and my back pocket. I had to make sure I had that heat on me just in case a nigga wanted to get ignorant. I saw Kaniya walking too, she wasn't too far ahead of me. What had me hot was Jugg was right behind her. Kaniya gone fuck around and get this nigga killed. She doesn't even notice me walking up behind her. She was too busy laughing and smiling up in his face, ain't shit funny. If I spray his ass, she'll fuck around and be mad and say a nigga was over reacting. I walked passed Kaniya and Jugg. They were walking too slow. I bumped her ass hard too. I wanted her to feel me. My issue wasn't with Jugg it was with Kaniya's friendly ass. She got me fucked up. I caught all the shot's she was throwing back there.

"Really? Excuse you." She sassed.

"Really. Your excused." I yelled. We made it on Giselle's grand momma's street and I started walking backwards. I wanted to see what the fuck her and Jugg was up too. I saw her Corvette parked. I posted up right beside it. Jugg was looking at me. If he knew what's best, he wouldn't ask any questions. I'm still that same nigga don't get shit twisted.

"Yeah Jugg I do have a problem. It's not with you though. It's with Kaniya, she knows why I'm here. All that free agent shit and single again shit, don't feed into none of it. It's sounds good but it's not true. She wanted daddy's attention so I'm here. I'll let her say good bye to you." I argued and snarled my nose up. Kaniya said bye to Jugg. She pushed passed me and tried to get in her car. I slammed the door shut and grabbed her shirt, forcing her to look at me. She turned around and looked at me. Her arms were folded across her chest.

"What Khalid, what's up? Why are you fucking with me? You closed the door remember? I'll see you around. It was good seeing you." She sassed and argued. If Kaniya knew she wasn't on any bullshit, she wouldn't have an attitude.

"Why do you have an attitude? You must be in the wrong, where are you going Kaniya?" I argued. I wanted to know where she was in a rush to. If she had plans to meet up with Tariq or Jugg it wasn't happening.

"I have a date Khalid! Could you please leave me alone, and go tend to your little girlfriend, she's watching us? I'm closing my door, Khalid. Good bye." She argued. I looked over my shoulders and Rose and Alexis were walking this way. I moved Kaniya's hands away from her door. She wasn't going on no fuckin' date today or tomorrow.

"I don't give a fuck who's watching us. I don't have a girlfriend, she's cool. Cancel that date before I cancel you and that nigga. I fuckin' mean it too." I argued. Kaniya was rolling her eyes and smacking her teeth. I'm not hearing none of that shit.

"Khalid, I knew it. You're leaving me here stranded out here to run up behind her? That's fucked up. I can't believe you. We just saw two niggas up in her face. I guess you like hoes though," Rose argued? Kaniya tried to come from behind the car. I was blocking her. I pushed her back in. She lives for drama. I don't want that for her at all.

Alexis was right behind Rose with the shit too. Alonzo needs to get his fiancé.

"Khalid let me go. I didn't say shit to you, while the two of y'all were cuffing. I wasn't bothered, because HERE YOU ARE. A BITCH gone put some RESPECT on MY MOTHERFUCKIN' name PERIOD. I'm not Giselle, BITCH I'm KANIYA NICOLE MILLER, it's HELL when I come through. I'm the ANGEL of DEATH that touch bitches, that gets beside themselves. YOU don't know me, but YOU TWO, for damn sure can get introduced. ALEXIS, that nigga put a hole in your face. I'll put a hole in your chest. I don't make threats. I make fuckin' promises. Y'all got a lot of pressure on your chest. I'll be glad to knock that shit off. Cross that MOTHERFUCKIN' GUN LINE if you want too. I can guarantee you it'll be some SMOKE in the fuckin' city. I WISH A BITCH WOULD. Khalid you better check these BITCHES right now, OR else I'm ready to do some checking and some fucking tagging." She argued. Her mouth is deadly.

"Bitch you bleed just like everybody else," Alexis yelled.

"Cross that MOTHERFUCKIN' gun line Alexis if you want too and find out, who's going to be bleeding. I'll make this motherfuckin' GUN clap." She cocked back her Mac 11. "I can catch two bodies right now and get away with MURDER because you bitches are trespassing. I'm licensed to carry, and I'll rock a bitch to sleep quick." She argued. Kaniya grabbed her Mac 11 and place it on the hood. I heard her cock it back really quick." I grabbed Kaniya's gun and put the safety back on. My lil baby too wild man. I swear.

"Chill out baby. I got it. HUSH and get in the car, let me handle it. Alexis mind your fuckin' business and not MINE. You can take Rose home and get the fuck on. Rose you need to watch your fuckin' mouth. Don't disrespect Kaniya because she hasn't disrespected you one fuckin' time. If you're mad at anybody, be mad at me. If I would've known she was going to be here, I wouldn't have brought you here. You know how I feel about you and you know how I feel about Kaniya. I never led you on. I don't entertain hoes period. What I do and who I do with isn't your business. I need you to fall the fuck back." I argued. Alexis and Rose were still popping off at the mouth saying slick, loud enough so I could hear. Kaniya laughing hysterically only made shit worse.

"Good bye Khalid," she sassed.

"Unlock the door. I'm rolling with you. Alonzo is going to drop my car off at your house."

"No, you're not, just because you canceled your dates, doesn't mean I'm canceling mine. Khalid, your little mind games don't work on me. You better ask these NIGGAS about me! You BETTER think before you speak to me. I'll fuck up your mind, MENTALLY and PHYSICALLY."

"I want you to stop FUCKIN' playing with me. You want to fuck up my mind mentally and physically? How can you do that if you don't won't to listen to me? You wanted a reaction out of me, that's why you came out here. You baited me, so I'm here. Listen to me you can't entertain another man period. You won't be satisfied until Tariq is dead for real because of you. Stay away from that nigga. I don't make THREATS, I make fuckin' PROMISES. Any nigga that's a threat to me I DEAD that shit Kaniya. You better think twice before you want to bait and fuck with a nigga like me." I argued. I pointed my finger in Kaniya face, she had me fucked up and she knew that.

"What are you saying Khalid? Tariq doesn't have anything to do with what WE had going on. It's between you and me. I'm not threatening Rose. Tariq accepts me flaws and all; something you wouldn't know nothing about." She argued and sassed.

"You know what the fuck I'm saying. You're a very smart woman. I accept your flaws, and all, never put words in my fuckin' mouth. If you and I are together Kaniya I don't want you doing hot ass shit, that could jeopardize your future. I care about you. You've been dealing with boys. I'm a man. As your man I don't want my woman leaving my bed in the middle of the night to confront another man. I'm not a sucker ass nigga. I heard about how that nigga talks and word got back to me. I'm very disappointed in you. As your man, you would never have to check a woman behind me. It's all about you. You're enough for me and I don't want to cheat on you. I wouldn't have pursued you if that was my intentions. I can't expose you to real if you won't allow me too.

"You have to do shit my way Kaniya. You won't even try. You've been doing it your way for a long time. I swear I'm not out to hurt you, I want to show you some results that comes with listening to me.

I know what you've been through, I'm not trying to take you through nothing else. If you go on your little date, it's a wrap Kaniya. You've tried me twice it won't be a fuckin' third time. You want a man to chase you. I want to chase you to some places you've never been before; but I got to be the only man in the race. So, what's it's going to be Kaniya Nicole Miller? Are you ready to walk out on me again?" I asked. I stroked my beard. I couldn't read Kaniya's facial expression.

"Khalid, I didn't walk out on you. I had to handle my business the best way I know how. You and my children were my peace to this storm that I'm weathering. I couldn't enjoy my peace because that shit was bothering me." She cried. I pulled Kaniya in for a hug. I wiped her tears with my thumbs.

"Stop crying. I hear you. I got you Kaniya and you know that. I wanted to handle that shit for you, but you didn't want me too. I wasn't going to kill him because that's your children's father. I understand you Kaniya more than you'll ever know. Every action doesn't need a reaction. You're a reflection of me and I want my woman to act accordingly. It's my job to handle that. I don't need you to handle my light work. I got me and you. I want your baggage, all of it. You don't have to get your hands dirty anymore. Lucky knows how I give it up. He hasn't run down on me once about you. He knows I want his EX wife and it's nothing that he can do about it.

"I hear you Khalid Mulsanne." She laughed and sniffled.

"Do you hear me Kaniya Miller? I want you to show me and prove it to me."

"I will Mr. Mulsanne."

"Can I take you out on a date Mrs. Williams?

"Of course."

"Take me to my car and follow me to your house."

Kaniya

Rose and Alexis tried my whole fuckin life. They were really coming for me behind my man Khalid Mulsanne. Khalid must have that good dick? I'm scared to sample it, he stimulates my mind already. I know when he stimulates my body I'll really be gone. I know for a fact his mouth is a fool. We haven't crossed that line for more reasons than one. I couldn't complicate things between us until I was for sure this was the real thing. The only thing we've done is kiss. His kisses alone got me weak. His touch alone would make a bitch stop breathing, he's rough but gentle.

If I ever catch Rose and Alexis by their selves I'm knocking their heads off. I put that shit on God, I'll touch them. Damn I guess I got to cut Tariq and I date short because of Khalid. I prayed for Khalid to come back to me. I know God heard my cry's. I wasn't about to risk this, not again. I want to see the results that he was talking about. I hope Tariq can find someone to love just as much as he loves me. I love Tariq but I'm not in love with him. I know I could fall in love with him, if we had a fair chance. It just wasn't in the cards for us. I don't want him getting killed behind me. I love him enough to let him go. His life means a lot to me and I don't want that on my heart anymore. I swear this is one of the hardest things that I ever had to do in my life. I dialed Tariq's number on my phone and the Bluetooth automatically connected. He answered on the second ring.

"What's up baby are you ready for me to come through," he asked.

"Nope. Tariq don't be mad at, but I have to cancel our date. Something came up." I sighed. I felt a lump in my chest. "It hurts saying this, but we have to let this thing we have going on go."

"I figured that Kaniya. I didn't even pull off. I sat of Fairburn Road at the park for a minute to make sure you got to your car safe. My nigga Honcho said that nigga was eyeing me because of our exchange. He had his niggas on standby in case some shit got ignorant. I watched the two of you up until a few minutes ago. Kaniya real men do real things, and it's a lot that separates the real from the fake. I did a lot of shit to you while we were together.

On some real shit Kaniya I love you shorty, but I don't deserve you. I don't want to say it, but it's the truth. I know I haven't been the best man to you and I could've, but a nigga is paying for that shit now. Out of all the things that I ever done to you, no matter what, you were always there, and you didn't have to be. I'm forever grateful for that. My own family wasn't there, but you were there in the clutch willing to risk it all to make sure I bounced back after everybody counted me out. I love you and I'm sorry for all of it. I always wanted to right my wrongs with you. I may never get that chance and I'm okay with that.

I took your love for granted. I love you enough to let you go. One day I'll find me another K though, this I know. I'm willing to walk away and bow out gracefully because I want to see you happy even if it's not with me. I'm on the outside looking in. Khalid, he loves you and I can see that shit. I saw it today. I never got my fair chance because of Lucky. God sits high and he looks low. I know my time is coming. I'm selfish ass nigga I'm not about to block my blessing. I'm going to fall back and let you and Khalid do your thing. Promise me one thing Kaniya, you won't let Lucky ruin your happiness? You deserve somebody that will love you as hard as you love them. If that nigga fucks up, you know I'm in the clutch waiting."

"Tariq why are you making me cry?" I asked crying.

"I just want you to know how I feel Kaniya. I took you for granted more than once. It's hard watching another man love the one you love. I fucked up a few times. I want to see you get it right with someone else and that's real. I want that for you."

Our love is fire and inside and it's gone burn forever. - Kevin Gates

Khalid

Kaniya got a nigga out here going insane and I haven't even sampled the pussy. She knew I was missing her ass like crazy. I was right behind her in traffic too. She keyed in the code to the gate and I pulled in the garage right beside her. She stepped out and I was right behind her on her heels. What the fuck did I tell her about wearing this little as shit. Before she could even get in the door good. I backed her into the door pane, where she couldn't move. Both of our hearts were beating the same tune. I stole a kiss. Kaniya grabbed my hand and led me to her living room. We took a seat on the sofa. I pulled her into my lap and wrapped my hands around her waist. I missed this.

"I'm tired of playing with you lil baby. What are you trying to do this time around Ms. Miller? I'm not with the games and shit?" I asked. Kaniya stood up and decided to face me. She stood between my legs. I grabbed her thighs. "Say what's on your mind, I'm listening."

"Khalid Mulsane, I'm in love with you. It's crazy because at first, I feared loving you and now that's all I want to do. I want this. I want us, but I'M not doing the long-distance thing with you. I can't be away from you for long periods of time. I want to wake up next to you every day." She explained. I nodded my head in agreement with her. We've been dating for months. I was tired of the long-distance thing too. I'm glad she's being honest about how she feels. She's been keeping her feelings to herself for a while.

"What are you trying to say? Do you want me to move here?" I asked. Kaniya cracked a smile. I never thought about living in the states. It's cool, but it's not for me. If she wanted me to move here I would. I'm willing to make that compromise.

"No, I'm coming to Mulsane Island. I'll find my own house, but I'm leaving the states." She sassed and stated. She placed her hands on her thick hips. Kaniya was serious, if she was willing to move, I wanted her with me every day too.

"Ain't no way you're moving to Mulsane Island, and you're not living with me. When are you trying to move Ms. Miller?"

"Immediately."

"Baby we can change the forecast." Kaniya started tugging at my pants. I've been real patient with her. I didn't want to cross that line unless, she was ready." "You're not ready for that Ms. Miller I promise you ain't."

"I been ready, but you've been holding out," she pouted.

"Yep I wasn't about to give you this Grade A pure beef if you were playing games. You might be ready for it; just know it's no turning back once we take it there."

"I'm not trying to turn back, you told me months ago no circling back. It's only me and you in the circle," she laughed.

"Alright where are the kids, let's pick them up and we can change the forecast. We can be in Mulsane Island in three hours.

———

Kaniya and I made it to Mulsane Island, three hours tops. We couldn't keep our hands off each other the whole plane ride here. I told her she better watch herself. We landed about an hour ago. We got the kids situated and now it was time for us to finally get acquainted. Kaniya was in the shower. I had our room setup perfect.

Candles lit low and a bed full of red roses. I stepped in right behind her. She knelt over and started touching her toes. I wanted her face down ass up anyways. I scooted up right behind her to catch all of that. Her ass sat directly on my dick. Kaniya was thick as fuck. She wanted me to take advantage of her since she was teasing me.

"Aight lil baby, keep playing these little games with a nigga. I'm trying to spare you because we're in the shower. I don't want to break you off proper right here. You've been talking a lot of shit lately. I want you to back all that shit up. Hurry up and get the fuck up out of here, so I can bend you over and stretch that pussy wide open and bury my kids. Kaniya turned around, she had nasty little smirk on her face. She backed me in the base of the shower and dropped to her knees and took me in. I could barely keep my balance. I gripped her hair because she was draining the fuck out of me. "Raise up, I'm trying to cum somewhere else," I moaned and grunted. Kaniya wasn't listening to shit I had to say.

"Shut up Khalid, you ain't running shit. I told you was going to rape your ass. You think this shit is game? I'm a bully in the sheets and I'm in heat. It ain't no tapping out. I want you to cum in my mouth. I'll get you back hard again," she laughed. Kaniya thought she was running shit. "It's only one bully in the sheets and that's me." I politely picked Kaniya up and carried her to the bedroom. I tossed her on the bed she that was covered in roses. She pointed her finger at me, telling me to come here.

"Mr. Mulsane I'm trying to fuck up these sheets tonight. I like it rough." she chuckled.

"Ms. Miller, I don't need any instructions on what I want to do you too. I need you to follow my lead. I don't ever want to fuck you. I only want to make love to you.

Shut the fuck up and let me do me." She mumbled something under her breath. I started at the bottom. I sucked each of her toes. I massaged her legs and calves as I worked my way to her pussy. She did my dick dirty in the shower now she was about to regret all that shit. I sucked her pussy real nasty at a fast pace. Our sheets were soaked, and she was moaning and squirming. Her legs were shaking. "Be still and take this shit like a pro." Kaniya was wet as soon as I slid my dick inside of her. She started rotating her hips as I threw her legs over my shoulder. She thought she was in control until, I started nailing her pussy to the wall.

"Khalid, slow down please," she moaned. "It hurts."

"That's what you wanted." I grunted. I wasn't listening to nothing she had to say. I kept beating it up. I flipped her over from her back side with no effort. She tooted her ass up and I slammed my dick inside of her a few times and she tried to run from the dick. I grabbed her hair and pulled her close to me. She looked up at me, and smirked. I went in for the kill.

"I want you to take this dick Kaniya. Big bad Kaniya running from dick. You can't run from him. He couldn't wait to meet you." I moaned.

"I'm trying Khalid," she moaned.

"Get up here and ride your dick, lil baby." Kaniya and I went at it for hours. I wore her ass out.

Chapter-24

Lucky

"You don't miss a good thing Lucky, until it's gone," she argued. Kaniya always had a problem with waving her hands in my face whenever she was mad at me. Never in a million years would I think, I'd be tired of hearing my wife's, long pitched sexy ass voice. It irks me now though. We're here sitting in our attorney's office discussing our divorce. It's nothing standing in between us but a piece a paper waiting on both are signatures. Kaniya has signed already. I wasn't signing the divorce papers. She'll be my wife until the day she dies. It's until death does us apart. I meant that shit. She wanted to divorce me, so she could be with Khalid. She'll be with him in death, not amongst the living.

"Shut the fuck up Kaniya. I didn't come here to hear your fuckin' mouth. I'm here to handle my fuckin' business. Just know I'm not the only motherfucka that's gone miss someone. You walk around here like I'm not shit to you, but deep in your heart you know you fuckin love me. I ain't gone lie, hell yeah, I'm going to miss you. I love you despite my actions. I'll miss the old you, because I don't fuckin' know you. If you really want me to do this. I'll let you go. What the fuck are you trying to do?" I argued. I slammed my fist on the table. She shoved the papers in my face. I snatched her across the table by her shirt. We were eye level with each other. My paralegal passed me the strap. I pointed at Kaniya's head. "This is the only way you're going out."

"Shoot me LUCKY, I'm begging you too, put me out of my misery or let me fuckin' go. I'm SICK of being married to you. Do y'all see this shit? He wants to kill me because I want a divorce. All the cheating and all the babies, but you still don't won't to divorce me? You don't give a fuck about me, you never had. You just didn't want anybody else to be with me. You don't have to cheat no more. It's only fun when a bitch doesn't know you're doing it. A BITCH like me ain't gone tolerate NONE of the shit you're offering. I got that COME BACK PUSSY. You always came back, and I allowed you too. I'm grown and a little wiser now. You CAN'T come back, my pussy no longer CUMS for you. I've closed the door on us for good.

I took the thrill out of it Lucky. You don't have to creep with Yirah anymore behind my back. You can be with her and have as many babies as you want. Make her happy, because these last two years you couldn't give me that. Give her that, since she's always in your corner. Your mother would want that. I was loyal to you, when you didn't even deserve it. Loyalty is priceless to me. A nigga once told me, we all miss good thing sometimes and it's okay. I didn't know what that meant, but now I see. You can love a person so much, but that doesn't mean you have to be with them. No matter what we went through, we'll always have ties because of our three children."

"Kaniya, you know shit can get ugly really quick, if you say the wrong shit again. I ain't these pussy ass niggas you're used to dealing with. I suggest you shut the fuck up talking to me. If the gun is pressed to your head. I'll make this bitch clap. You don't know shit about loyalty. Loyalty wouldn't have let you nurse my enemy back to health. You betrayed me in the worst fuckin' way. Loyalty wouldn't have let you be a drop off spot for another man, while you were married to me. Loyalty wouldn't have let you touch my mother. You've crossed the line plenty of times."

"We both have Lucky, more of the reason why we don't need to be together. It's not healthy. Let's just call it a day and move on please," she begged.

"We can move on, when I'm good and God damn ready. I'm not signing a motherfuckin' thang Kaniya. I know that nigga got big plans for you, but it ain't happening, not in this life time. You'll carry my last name until the day you die. Are you ready to leave this world today? Tell that motherfucka to move on, because he ain't got no chance with you. I'm a selfish ass nigga and you're my wife. You'll never be his. Keep my kids away from him. Mrs. Williams we're done here." I argued. Kaniya wasn't getting a divorce just so she could go and marry him. I knew she's been staying with him. I always had eyes on her. Kaniya snatched her purse off the table. "I love you to Mrs. Williams." She slammed the door shut. I love Kaniya, but she's has shit confused. If she thinks that we're getting a divorced. Why couldn't we work shit out? I wanted to come back home and start over.

Khalid

Kaniya and Lucky had a divorce hearing with both of their lawyers. Hopefully he signs the papers, so we can move on with our lives. I dropped Kaniya off this morning at 9:00 a.m. at the court house. She sent me text telling me that she was ready. I posted up outside in front of my Bentley waiting on her. Kaniya was strutting hard. I could tell she was mad or upset. It was written all over her face. Lucky was walking behind her talking shit. He yelled, "You're going to be wife until I put you in the dirt. REMEMBER THAT."

"Do WE have a fuckin' problem KANIYA? A motherfucka can't threaten NOTHING I care ABOUT, without any repercussions. If so we can address it now. SHE'S MINE!" I yelled and argued. He heard everything I said, and I meant that shit. He looked over at us. "I'm not TARIQ. When I TOUCH a nigga, he's going to be absent from the body and present with the LORD. You better ask about me and I'm not talking about in these ATL streets." He got me fucked up, the only reason I haven't gotten at him, was because of her. That shit stops today though. He doesn't know me, he needs to get to know me. I'm going to wife his wife rather he likes it or not. I'm going to raise his kids as my own. Kaniya finally approached me. She looked different from when I dropped her off earlier.

"What's WRONG baby? What's that mark on your neck? Come here, don't lie to me Kaniya. Did this nigga touch you?" I asked. She had three deep scratches on her neck that wasn't there when we left this morning. Her shirt was wrinkled too. He has hand problem. He put his hands on her for the last fucking time.

"I'm okay Khalid, we had a scuffle and he didn't sign the papers," she sighed. She's not okay, but I got something for his ass. He'll see me.

"You're not okay, because I'm not okay. He thinks it's cool to put his hands on you? He can't FUCKIN' do that KANIYA. He'll feel me TODAY, if he wants a scuffle. We can do that. When we get home. Give me the divorce papers. I'll get them signed. It's not up for debate. Today will be the last fuckin' day you'll carry his last name or touch you." I argued. He got me all the way fucked up.

Kaniya took her seat in the car as I closed the door. I pulled off and she grabbed my free hand and started massaging it. Lucky's playing with fire, but I'll burn his ass today. I had eyes on Lucky. He hasn't made a move on me, but I know he wanted too. He'll see me later. I need to get my lil baby to the air strip, so she can go back home. We couldn't even celebrate her divorce because of him.

"Kaniya I'm going to handle this shit for you okay? I need for you to go back and home and I'll see you later. Don't wait up on me, I'll wake you up." She turned around in her seat to face me. I knew she wanted to object, but it's for her own good. Our good. I don't need my woman standing in the paint with me.

"Okay Khalid. I trust you."

"Good."

"I got something to tell you. I'm pregnant." She whispered and held her head down.

"Raise your head up Kaniya. I told you about that shy shit. What did you say?"

"I'm PREGNANT." She sighed. I knew she was. I kept staring at her while she was blushing. We've been making love like crazy. It was bound to happen. I had to handle this shit today. Ain't no way around it. He couldn't put his hands on her while she's carrying my seed.

"Oh yeah, you're having my baby, lil baby? I want twins too. Two girls Khali and Khaliah, they better look just like their mother too."

"Don't jinx me, I'll have six kids Khalid, that's a lot." She sighed.

"I'm not going anywhere. I'm taking care of all of them and their mother too." I sent Kaniya back home, to her Island. I had to stay in the states a little bit longer to handle Lucky. Kaniya sent me a text stating that she made it. The only thing that matters was that she's at home safe and sound. I hit up Alonzo and Dro and gave them a run-down of the shit that happened with Lucky earlier. We were parked outside of his club. I had this bitch surrounded. I had a few of my soldiers inside posted up. Killian and Kanan were sitting inside also ducked off in the corner. I entered the club through the front. Lucky was posted up by the bar. I took a seat right beside him.

"Two shots of Don Julio please." I slid the divorce papers right in front of him. He can do shit my way or learn how shit goes the Khalid way. The choice was his.

"I don't drink white liquor. I'll tell you like I told Kaniya, she'll be my wife until I'm ready to divorce her," he argued. I laughed at him because he was funny. He slid the divorce papers back to me.

"Lucky, I don't know you and you don't know me. We've been doing shit your way for months now. I'm sick of it and she is too. Real niggas do real things. I'm a grown ass man. I'm coming at you correct. I know you got niggas posted up in here. I see that red beam on my glass. I got that red beam on you too. If I go, you're going too. I love Kaniya and nobody can change that. I plan on marrying Kaniya Miller real soon. I love your children as if they were mine. I need you to sign these papers, so I can make her happy.

You fucked up. Own up to it and move on. I can't thank you enough for fucking up because I would've never met her. She can get real nasty if she wants too, and not even let you have custody at all. Despite what you're taking her through, she's not trying to do that. She doesn't want anything from you but a divorce. Stop dragging this shit out and sign the fucking papers. I'll bring the kids to the states anytime you want so you can see them." Kanan and Killian walked up behind us. I didn't even know these two niggas were in here.

"Lucky sign the fucking papers," Killian argued. Kanan was posted up behind him.

"Y'all think y'all can come in my club and make me sign papers to divorce my WIFE. Y'all got life fucked and clearly y'all motherfuckas don't know who the fuck I am. Killian you out all people know you did what the fuck I did. Did you divorce KAISHA. Hell motherfuckin NO. I know I fucked up and I don't need a motherfucka reminding me of shit. I live with the shit every day."

"Lucky, stop comparing yourself to me. I had one child on my wife and I learned from that shit. You had two babies on my daughter. The two of you are not meant to be together. Way too much has happened between y'all." Killian argued.

"Correction I had ONE child on her, she killed the other one. So, WE even, this nigga is ready to die behind something that doesn't belong to him. She fuckin' belongs to me no matter what we're going through," he argued. Lucky was ready to die behind Kaniya. This nigga is not trying to give her divorce.

"Lucky, if you love my daughter as much as you claim, you'll let her go. I ain't never got in between y'all and I should've years ago. You should've never left your home. You left the door open for her to close it. Why would you deny her happiness just because she's not with you? Sign these papers, I'm not here to go back and forth with you." Killian explained.

"KILLIAN, I got it from here. I tried to do shit the easy route but it's not working. I got to take a different approach with him, but I'm NOT leaving this motherfucka until he's signed the papers. Lucky this shit ain't up for debate. I'm a business man and I'm not trying make a mess up in your club and kill innocent people, but I will. KANIYA and I are expecting. We're having twins. We live on Mulsane Island. She doesn't have to EVER come back to the states if she doesn't want too. You CAN'T, and you WON'T stop me from MARRYING her.

If you want to hold on to some shit that's dead, you can do it by yourself. I don't ABIDE by the United States law. I'm ABOVE the LAW. Your MARRIAGE means nothing to me in my country. I'm free to MARRY her because she's a resident. Keep playing these little games and you'll never see your fuckin' kids again. They'll call me daddy for real." Lucky snatched the papers out of my hand.

"She's PREGNANT?" I pulled out the ultrasound Kaniya gave to me and showed it to him. "You TELL KANIYA, fuck her and she'll get hers. I WANT to FACETIME MY KIDS EVERY FUCKIN' NIGHT. I WANT MY KIDS EVERY HOLIDAY AND THEIR BIRTHDAY DAYS ALL THREE OF EM. MY KIDS ONLY HAVE ONE FATHER, AND THAT'S ME JAMEL LEE WILLIAMS. THAT'S MY DEMAND IN THE FINAL DIVORCE DECREE." He signed them. I didn't even want to go there, with him but I had too. I knew what he was trying to do. Niggas like Lucky, you'll have to beat them at their own game. I walked up out of his club and couldn't wait to get home to see my baby with her divorced ass. I grabbed my phone out of my back pocket and called her.

"Hello," she yawned through the phone.

"I can't wait to see your DIVORCED ass. I'm on my way home lil baby."

"Baby stop playing with me," she screamed.

'I told you I'll handle it. I can't have my lil baby stressing out while she's carrying my daughters."

"Oh My God, hurry up and get home so I can fax them to my attorney," she screamed.

"I am. I hand delivered them to your attorney, they'll be filed tomorrow in Fulton County Courts. You can get married in 90 days if you want too."

"Hurry up and get home Mr. Mulsane. I'll be at the airstrip waiting on you."

"No, you won't, keep your ass at home. Get some rest and I'll wake you up when I get home."

"Okay, if you say so Khalid," she pouted and whined. I can't wait to get home to my lil baby. We've been away from each-other for almost twenty-four hours and a nigga isn't used to this shit. The jet was ready and waiting for before I pulled up. I hope I can get some sleep.

—

My flight landed and guess who was waiting on me in the car. As soon as I sat in the back seat she was smiling at me. I told her about that shit.

"You're hard headed. I told you not to come here. You knew I was coming straight home to you. I had plans to wake you up when I land. Now a nigga can't wait."

"I missed you Mr. Mulsane. I wanted to see and be with you as soon as you landed. I can't thank you enough. Thank you for everything. I love you so much."

"I love you too. It's nothing in this world that I won't do for you.

Chapter-25

Khalid

I've been on pens and needles all week. I've been throwing hints around all week about marrying Kaniya and she's shut it down every time. I wanted to marry Kaniya before she gives birth to my daughters. She doesn't want to do it because of her weight and stomach. Fuck that my daughters weren't entering the world without, their mother being wife and I meant that. I kicked it to Kaniya that one of my investors wanted us to throw and extravagant party. It's a Royal Affair, I told her it needs to be extravagant.

The only problem is she has too plan it, as if it was her on wedding. She's been planning it for months. She's been really excited about doing it. Today was the actual day and she's been running around acting nervous because she's not sure if they'll like it. I told her long as she did her best, that all that matters. I flew her whole family out here. Dro and Alonzo were my best men. Dro and Alonzo were tripping because they knew Kaniya would cut up once she found out what was going on. I just needed her to say yes that's it.

I haven't proposed to her yet. I told Killian a few months ago that I wanted to marry her, and he gave me his blessing. It had to be perfect because Kaniya has never had a wedding. I wanted to give her all of that. She had no clue that today would be her wedding. Everybody thought I was crazy for not telling her. Shit, I wanted to surprise my baby. She looked beautiful and I hope she doesn't embarrass me and say no.

"I can't believe you're really about to do this," my mother stated. "You know she's going to kill you right," she laughed.

"I'm not worried about that momma, I just want her to say I do. Does she love me enough to say yes?"

"Of course, she does."

Kaniya

Khalid had me plan this extravagant party for one of his investors. I hope they liked it. It's an all-white Royal affair. My whole family and closest friends flew out to attend. It was good seeing everybody. I missed them so much because I don't live in the states anymore. Khalid said the last time they had a Royal Affair on Mulsane Island it was thirty years ago. It had to be a big deal. I planned this to perfection. I was six months pregnant and glad to assist him in any way I could. The twins were wearing me out though. I had to get dressed. The event was scheduled to start in an hour. Giselle colored my hair RED, with a Halo braid, and she left a few tendrils out. It was so cute and pretty. She beat my face to the Gods. I had this gold and diamond head piece that Khalid brought from Dubai. Even though I had a belly I still looked cute. My dress was an all-white Vera Wang. It was fitted and draped in diamonds. Nobody here would look better than me. I finished getting dressed because I hate to be late to anything.

"Kaniya Nicole Miller, you look so beautiful," my mother cried. I turned around to look at her to see why she was crying. I can't think of the last time I ever saw her shed a tear.

"What's wrong with you Ma?" I walked over to her to see what was going on.

"Nothing Kaniya, you're so beautiful, you're fuckin' up my damn make-up. I'm just happy that you're finally happy. I wanted this for you. You and I have always had a conversation about why I never introduced you to your soul mate. Killany, before you say anything. I'm telling you now shut your fuckin' mouth and let me have my moment. You've went through a lot of things just to get to this point. Everything you've went through it was to prepare you for this. I never had to introduce you to your soul mate because you never need any help. I always knew when you find the one everything about you would change. Baby girl you've changed and I'm glad I witnessed that. I'm so proud of you." She cried.

"Thank you, momma." Khalid, Dro, Yung, KC, Mook my father and my uncles. All appeared in the room. Khalid walked over to me. Every time we looked at each other our faces lit up. I swear he was perfect.

"Kaniya, you look so beautiful."

"Thank you."

"Let me massage your feet before, we head out here," he explained. Khalid knelt and started my massaging my feet. I closed my eyes and a few moans escaped my lips. He grabbed my hand and looked at me. "Kaniya Nicole Miller, the moment I first laid eyes on you. I knew I had to have you. The moment you agreed to let me take you out on a date, we took off from there. You complete me in ways that I would never imagine. I love that you love my son as if he were your own. I want to be the best father figure I can to Jamel, Jamia and Jeremiah if you would allow me. I told you months ago that I want to be a part of the picture. I'm ready to make us official Kaniya Nicole Miller, will you marry me RIGHT NOW?" He asked. I know this didn't just happen. Khalid brought me a ring so fuckin' big it gave light to the entire room.

"Oh my God Khalid Mulsane, are you serious?" I placed my hands over my mouth. He nodded his head yes. "Yes, I will marry you." Everybody was screaming.

"Come on baby the preacher is waiting on us, it's our wedding day. I'm ready to make you Mrs. Mulsane." He explained.

"Khalid Mulsane, REALLY you had me do all this, and it's my wedding day?" I pouted.

"Yes, I just want to see you smile lil baby, that's it. You planned the wedding of your dreams. I want to be the only man to give it to you. Come on, I'm ready to say I do." I swear when God created him, he was made for me.

I can't believe Khalid Mulsane pulled all this off. I planned my own wedding without me even knowing it. I can't with him and his surprises. He knew that I didn't want to marry him while I was pregnant. I wanted to get married afterwards. He wasn't taking no for an answer. I love that about him. How could he put me in the spotlight like this? I had to think of something perfect to say to him. His proposal was everything. I looked back at My mother, Giselle, Killany, Ketta, Barbie, Raven and Tianna, none of these motherfuckas told me shit. They were all smiling at me.

"If it makes you feel any better Kaniya he threatened us not to say shit," my mother laughed.

"I don't like being in the blind like this. I almost had a heart attack." I laughed.

"Oh, we know, but your face was priceless."

"I should've known something was up, when you started crying. Come on Ma we're better than that. Mrs. Khali why didn't you say anything?"

"He wanted to surprise you. Hell no, I wasn't going to say anything," she laughed.

"Who gets proposed to and married on the same day. I haven't written my vows to him yet." I pouted.

"Just speak from your heart Kaniya." Mrs. Khali stated. My dad came in and advised that it's time to get started. I swear me, and my father have come a long way from a year ago. I grabbed his hand and he escorted me out.

"Kaniya Nicole Miller, you look so beautiful. I love you baby girl, it's pleasure for me to do this. Thank you for allowing me back in your life. You're the happiest I've seen you in years. I wish you and Khalid nothing but the best. We've had plenty of talks about the two of you. I'm happy to give you away to him." My father explained.

"Thank you, daddy, you're about to make me cry." My daddy grabbed a piece of Kleenex and dabbed my eyes. Khalid III, Jamel and Jamia looked so pretty. As I walked down the aisle, Khalid had his eyes locked on me. I finally made it to Khalid and he grabbed my hands and we looked at each other and embraced.

"We are gathered here today to celebrate the union of Khalid Mulsane and Kaniya Miller. I've known Khalid Mulsane since he was child himself. I married Khali and Khalid Mulsane Sr. on the same day thirty years ago. I saw Khalid and Kaniya out on the Island a few months ago in passing. Khalid stopped me and introduced me to his future wife. I sat back in the far corner and watched the two of them. They lit up the room. Khalid contacted me a few months ago and was telling me about Ms. Miller. I knew then she was someone special to him. I asked him what his intentions with her was. He told me that he wanted to marry her. He'd done enough courting in his life time and she was the real thing.

I called Khali and told her about our conversation. She was surprised because he never mentioned it to her. He came back to me again a few weeks later and told me they were expecting, and he wanted to make an honest woman of her. He wanted her to carry his last name.

I didn't get the pleasure to actually speak with Kaniya, but Khalid told me enough about her. I felt like I knew her. I'm honored to marry the two of them. Khalid

Mulsane, do you have anything you want to say to Ms. Miller before I proceed with the ceremony?"

"I do. Kaniya Nicole Miller. The moment I met you, LIL BABY, you stole my heart. I couldn't shake you. I had to have you. I love you so much, that I don't think I tell you enough. I love everything about you. I'm not a spiritual person, but I feel that God created you just for me. It's nothing in this world that I won't do for you or our children. I want to spend the rest of my life loving you." He explained. I swear Khalid Mulsane is everything. It's a big difference between a boy and man. Khalid Mulsane is a grown ass man.

"Khalid Mulsane. I'm speechless and that's a good thing, because I always have something to say. I don't even think I could put the right words together to express how I feel about you. Never put a time limit on love. Our love has no limit. I've been through so much in my twenty-eight years of living. I've weathered many storms. The moment I met you my life changed for the better. I changed, we changed. You never gave up on me. You should've but you didn't. I love how you love me. I love how we love each other. I love you and I've never been in love or loved how you love me. Thank you, Khalid Mulsane, for loving me."

"Khalid, do you take Kaniya Miller to be your wife?"

"I do."

"Kaniya, do you take Khalid Mulsane to be your husband?"

"I do."

"I now pronounce you husband and wife. You may now kiss the bride." They didn't have to tell us twice. Kaniya Nicole Mulsane. I always loved how that sounded together.

Epilogue

Kaniya

I've been tossing and turning all night. I couldn't sleep. The contractions were coming back to back. I couldn't get comfortable and Ali was lying right next to me. I wanted to scream. I swear these set of twins are wearing me out. The contractions are the worst and I've been on bed rest for three months. I think it was Khalid's orders instead of the doctors. I swear this is the best pregnancy I ever had and my last. I felt a few sharp pains to my side. I couldn't take it anymore; these little girls were killing me. I can't wait until Jamia meets them. I think she'll be the perfect big sister. Lucky had them this week, because Father's Day weekend is next week. I tapped Ali on his shoulder. He wrapped his arms around me and that didn't help with the pain at all. I want his babies out of my body right now

"Khalid, I think it's time." I sighed. He was still asleep and refusing to look at me. We went to the hospital yesterday and it was a false alarm. I think today is the day. I've been in pain all morning.

"Time for what Kaniya and don't say my babies are ready to come?" He argued and yawned. Khalid finally decided to raise up out the bed. I knew he was sick of me, but it was his children. "What the fuck what that Kaniya," he asked. It was a loud pop noise. "Pop." I heard it again. My panties were wet. I know I didn't piss on myself. I stood up and attempted to go to the bathroom. Water trickled down my legs again.

"Kaniya, why are you pissing on the floor, go to the bathroom."

"I'm not pissing on the floor Ali. I think your daughter just broke my water."

"Okay daddy's ready to meet his princess's. I guess they're tired of their mother talking shit about them. Go ahead and take a shower. I'll wake, my mother and KJ up and I'll load the car up. Call your mother and father and tell them to be at the airstrip if they want to be here. Do you need me to help clean you up?" He asked.

"No Khalid just make sure you have all of their stuff." Oh my God I can't believe it. I've been on bed rest for the past few months. I knew the twins were going to come early but not this early. I thought the point of me not moving around, was so that they would arrive on June 19th. I was ready to push these two out of me. I knew these two had attitude problems.

Sometimes when I look at my stomach. I can see two fist pointing at each other, which means they either had a fight that I didn't feel, or they were about to fight. Its June 10th. Khalid and I decided to name them Khali and Khaliah. He wanted to name them after his mother and great grandmother. My mother's petty ass had a mouthful to say about that, so Khali's middle name is Kaisha and Khaliah's middle name is Denise after Kaisha their grandmother Kaisha Denise Miller.

I'm ready to give birth and meet my newest creations who took over and controlled my body. I wanted to be as cute as possible on my delivery. I had a few outfits picked out already. That's why I didn't want Khalid helping me because he would be tripping. My hair was in its natural curly state. I wanted some lemonade braids, but

Khalid's hating ass said, he didn't like running his hands through weave. It didn't feel right.

I jumped in the shower and handled my hygiene. The fluids from my sack was still gushing down my legs. Ugh I've never had this happen before. I can bet you any amount of money it was Khaliah that was the one who broke my sack. We've been going to the doctor every week and she's been the more dominate one. Her butt was always showing. I knew she was going to be my worst nightmare. She was already telling us to kiss her ass. She pushes little Ms. Khali to the back. My mom said Killany and I were the same way. Khaliah acts exactly how I acted, and Khali was Killany.

Khalid thought that was the funniest shit. I didn't find that funny at all because she was going to be a replica of me. I wasn't ready for another me running around. Jamia was already my mini me. Jeremiah always gave her the blues. I couldn't wait to meet the two of them. The 3D image didn't do them any justice. I'm ready to see what Mr. Mulsane and I created. I couldn't wait to hold my babies.

"Kaniya what's taking you so long? I have the car packed and KJ and my mother are waiting on us in the car," he yelled.

"I'm coming." I yelled I wasn't in a rush. I was in labor with Jamel and Jamia for five hours. So, I figured the longer I took to get there by the time I make it, I would have to push at least three or four times. Who knows, these set of twins are a different breed? I couldn't compare these twins to Jamel and Jamia because they have a mind of their own. I cut the shower off and stepped out the shower. Khalid was sitting on the toilet with a towel waiting for me. He was so attentive to me it's crazy.

He insisted on drying me off with a towel and I'm capable of doing it myself. He grabbed the Shea butter and rubbed my body down. I placed a little Vaseline in the palm of my hand and applied to my face. It was too hot to wear make-up. Ali hated when I wore make up, he would go ape shit. I grabbed my lipstick, attempting to coat my lips. He snatched it from me.

"Kaniya you don't need all of that shit on and you're about to give birth to my kids. You're putting my kids in danger by taking your time. Deliver my babies and you can get cute later. Who in the fuck are you trying to impress?" He argued.

"I just want to look presentable for my delivery."

"You look presentable. I love your curves, belly and all, you know that." Khalid sure knows how to fuck up shit. I threw my lipstick on the counter in the bathroom. I'll put some lip gloss on in the car. I had my outfit already laid out. It was cream baby doll dress with some cute Gucci sandals too match. Khalid was standing in the corner watching me. I knew he had something smart he wanted to say.

"Kaniya, where do you think you're going with that shit on? You're not wearing that. Here put this Pink jump suit on." I can't stand him. He put the jogging suit on me and carried me to the car. Thank God the jogging suit was pink. As he pulled off into traffic, I pulled my Peach Matte lipstick out of my purse, and it applied to my lips. I could feel Khalid staring at me. I refuse to look at him. I knew he would say some smart shit.

"What why are you looking at me like that Mr. Mulsane?"

"Because you're hard headed Mrs. Mulsane and you're perfect just the way you are. You know I don't want nobody looking at my wife. I'm jealous as fuck when it comes to you. My wife is something to look at. Act like you know. I want my kids to be able to recognize their beautiful mother without the make-up"

"You don't have to be jealous, because this heart only beats for you. I hear you, but what's wrong with your wife wanting to look good for her husband? I don't want nobody else but you Mr. Mulsane."

"Nothing but you always look good for me. I don't want nobody looking at my wife. I just want to make sure that my babies get here safe, you feel me."

"I'm selfish too and I don't want nobody looking at my husband. I caught those nurses looking at you. You better tell them BITCHES, I'm CRAZY as fuck and I won't hesitate to push a bitch shit back behind Khalid Mulsane." I purred like a kitten.

"Calm down Mrs. Mulsane you know I'm not checking for nobody but my wife. You're the only woman I want. You're the only woman I'll ever married. You're the only woman to carry my last name besides my daughters." He laughed.

"I BETTER BE." I laughed. It's funny now, but when I catch bitches still lusting after him, I will fuck a bitch up behind him. Khalid is the perfect husband. I couldn't ask for a better one. He wants to laugh about it. Khalid isn't a cheater. I love him all of him.

"I can't wait to get my wife pregnant again." He laughed. I wasn't even about answer him. We already have six kids together. We don't need any more kids, six is enough. I wasn't pushing out nothing after these two.

"Kaniya do you hear me?" I was ignoring Khalid.

"I do, but I'm not answering you." I'm too fertile. My ass isn't trying to get pregnant again. He can't wait to get me pregnant again. This has been the best pregnancy ever, but I don't want to be pregnant again no time soon. I love Khalid smothering me. I got way too many small ones running around.

———

We finally made it to the hospital and my mother and father were on their way. Hopefully the girls won't come until they arrive. That's why I wasn't in a rush to get here. I wasn't looking forward to staying here for a day. I wanted my babies at home with me. Khalid grabbed my hand and kissed me on my forehead.

"Mrs. Mulsane are you ready?"

"I'm ready Mr. Mulsane." The nurses escorted us to our room, so they could prep us for delivery. Khalid helped me undress. I refuse to wear a hospital gown, so he brought me my own. I pulled the gown over my head and Khalid pulled my panties down and grabbed them and stuffed them in his pants.

He swore somebody was trying to steal my panties. The nurses came in and started hooking the IV's up to me while checking my blood pressure and my iron. The nurse that I caught eye fucking Khalid she was standing in the door staring at him. She had another nurse with her. She was pointing at us. See these bitches don't know how I give it up. I tapped the nurse on her shoulder. She looked at me.

"Excuse me could you tell that nurse to come here." I pointed to her in the hallway she tried to walk off.

"No don't do that. Kaniya, what are you doing?" He asked. He knew I was with the shit. Every time I give birth some shit is always happening.

"I want to know why, she's looking at my husband and pointing and his wife is right here. I hate a disrespectful ass bitch. If they got a problem, I'll be glad to solve it."

"Kaniya, let that shit go and bring my babies into the world. You already know what it is, don't show your ass up in here. I mean that shit." I love it when Khalid, lays down the law. He cupped my face and he started tonguing me down. Our nurse came in to check and see how many centimeters I was.

"Six centimeters Mrs. Mulsane." Music to my ears, the girls would be here in no time. I couldn't wait to meet them. Khalid was stroking the side of my face looking at me.

"You were trying to show your ass, you know I couldn't let you do that." He laughed.

"Whatever. I hate people trying me." Mrs. Khali and Khalid Jr. entered our room. We were waiting on the Mulsane twins to arrive. I couldn't wait to see what we created. Khalid III. Jamel and Jamia couldn't wait to meet Khali and Khaliah.

"Daddy, I'm ready to meet my sisters."

"KJ, you'll meet them in a few, they'll be here in a few hours." I loved KJ, he's the most handsome, sweetest and smartest little boy I knew. I loved having him around every day. He was my son, we've been connected at the hip ever since we met. He's also a great big brother. Our family has really grown. The nurse came in to check to see if I've dilated some more.

"Mrs. Mulsane, you're at nine centimeters. Let's get you prepped for delivery, so you can meet your babies soon." Thank God I couldn't wait to meet my two finally. Khalid looked at me. I was nervous, and I don't know why. He grabbed a cold towel to wipe my face. I was hot.

"Mrs. Mulsane on the count of three push for me. 1, 2, 3." I started to push. The nurse instructed me to push again. I started pushing too early. I prayed I didn't shit while Khalid was here. The nurse yelled, "she sees hair." I had to push one more time. I tried to tell her my kids are a different breed. They weren't ready to come out. I pushed again. My daughter came out screaming. She was six pounds and six ounces. My other daughter came out right behind her screaming as loud as she could too. Two hell raisers. just like their mother. She was seven pounds and six ounces. Khalid cut their umbilical cords.

"Can I see me my babies Mr. Mulsane?"

"Damn Mrs. Mulsane they're my babies too. I'm the reason they're here and identical. Hush and let them clean you up." The nurses finished cleaning me up. Khalid didn't want anybody touching his daughters, not even me. The nurse was finally finished with cleaning me up. Khalid placed my daughters in both of my arms. They look nothing like me, they look exactly like their father. Khalid was grabbing for them and I haven't even held them for five minutes. He couldn't stop looking at the two of them.

"What's wrong with you?" He laughed. He knew why I was pissed.

"Khalid, why do they look exactly like you," I asked and laughed. They're so pretty. They have all his features. Thick fine brown hair, with lose curls on the tips. Small lips and perfect nose. They had his complexion also. I just carried them for him.

"Daddy did all the work." He laughed. I punched him in his arm.

"Yeah right, daddy laid on his back." I laughed.

"Yeah because that's all you wanted to do was ride this dick. I can't wait for you to get back up there and ride it again." He laughed. I swear I can't stand him.

"Whatever." I pouted.

"Mrs. Mulsane thank you for giving birth to my daughters. Even though you're a little salty because they look like me. You carried them for almost nine months. I love you and I'll continue to do anything to make you happy," he stated and kissed me on my forehead.

"I love you too."

The End

Pushing Pen Presents now accepting submissions for the following genres: Urban Fiction, Street Lit, Urban Romance, Women's Fiction, BWWM Romance Please submit your first three chapters in a Word document, synopsis, and include contact information via email @pushingpenpresents@gmail.com, please allow 3 business days for a response after submitting.

CPSIA information can be obtained
at www.ICGtesting.com
Printed in the USA
LVHW041528241118
598141LV00008B/591/P